The Countess of Lowndes Square, And Other Stories

E. F. Benson

The Countess of Lowndes Square, and Other Stories

Copyright © 2021 Bibliotech Press
All rights reserved

ISBN: 978-1-63637-362-1

CONTENTS

Preface iv

BLACKMAILING STORIES

1   The Countess of Lowndes Square   1
2   The Blackmailer of Park Lane 13

GENERAL STORIES

1   The Dance on the Beefsteak 35
2   The Oriolists 43
3   In the Dark 57
4   The False Step 66

SPOOK STORIES

1   The Case of Frank Hampden 74
2   Mrs. Andrews's Control 88
3   The Ape 95
4   "Through" 109

CAT STORIES

1   "Puss-cat" 118
2   There Arose a King 127

CRANK STORIES

1   The Tragedy of Oliver Bowman 136
2   Philip's Safety Razor 147

PREFACE

I have divided the stories that are here collected under one cover into various classes, so that such readers as want to compare their own experiments, let us say, in blackmailing or spiritualistic séances, with those of other students, may find such tales as deal with their own speciality in crime or superstition grouped together in separate sections of this book. They will thus be spared a skipping hunt through pages in which they feel no personal interest.

In the same way, such readers as are in search merely of the lighter (though not more decorative) aspects of life, will be able to avoid like poison so innocent-looking a title as "The Countess of Lowndes Square," for assuredly they would not find therein the fashionable descriptions of high life which they might reasonably anticipate, but would merely cast the book from them in disgust, when they discovered that one who had been the wife of an Earl, and ought therefore to have known ever so much better, belonged to the most contemptible of the criminal classes. The table of contents, in like manner, conducts the crank and the cat-lover to the pastures where he is most likely to find a digestible snack.

The short story is not a lyre on which English writers thrum with the firm delicacy of the French, or with the industry of the American author. If the ten best short stories in the world were proclaimed by popular vote, it is probable that they would all be French stories; while if the million worst stories in the world were similarly brought together into one unspeakable library, they would probably all of them—with the exception, of course, of the fourteen that make up this volume—be found to be written in America. There is something in the precision and economy of the French, something in the opulence and amateurishness of the United States that renders the result of such a plebiscite perfectly appropriate, and we should only, when the result of the poll was known, find in it another instance of the invariable occurrence of the expected.

Most of the ensuing tales have appeared before in the pages of Nash's Weekly, The Windsor Magazine, The Story-Teller, The Century, and The Woman at Home. The rest are now published for the first time.

E. F. Benson

BLACKMAILING STORIES

THE COUNTESS OF LOWNDES SQUARE

Cynthia, Countess of Hampshire, was sitting in an extraordinarily elaborate dressing-gown one innocent morning in June, alternately opening letters and eating spoonfuls of sour milk prepared according to the prescription of Professor Metchnikoff. Every day it made her feel younger and stronger and more irresponsible (which is the root of all joy to natures of a serious disposition), and since (when a fortnight before she began this abominable treatment) she felt very young already, she was now almost afraid that she would start again on measles, croup, hoops, whooping-cough, peppermints, and other childish ailments and passions. But since this treatment not only induced youth, but was discouraging to all microbes but its own, she hoped as regards ailments that she would continue to feel younger and younger without suffering the penalties of childhood.

The sour milk was finished long before her letters were all opened, for there was no one in London who had a larger and more festive post than she. Indeed, it was no wonder that everybody of sense (and most people of none) wanted her to eat their dinners and stay in their houses, for her volcanic enjoyment of life made the dullest of social functions a high orgy, and since nothing is nearly so infectious as enjoyment, it followed that she was much in request.

Even in her fiftieth year she retained with her youthful zest for life much of the extreme plainness of her girlhood, but time was gradually lightening the heaviness of feature that had once formed so remarkable an ugliness, and in a few years more, no doubt, she would become as nice looking as everybody else of her age.

Her father, the notorious (probably infamous) Baron Kakao, of mixed and uncertain origin, had at one time compiled by hook or crook (chiefly, it is to be feared, by crook) an immense fortune; but long after that was spent, and debts of an equally substantial nature been substituted for it, he continued to live in London in a blaze of splendour so Oriental, that he was still believed to be possessed of fabulous wealth, and had without the least difficulty married the plain but fascinating Cynthia to an elderly Earl of Hampshire, and had continued to allow her £10,000 a year, which he borrowed at a staggering rate of usury from optimistic Hebrews. They thought that Lord Hampshire would probably see to his father-in-law's debts; while, rather humorously, Lord Hampshire was post-obiting himself with others who trusted that Baron Kakao would come to the rescue of his son-in-law.

Consequently, when he and Cynthia's disgusting husband expired within a few hours of each other, the widowed and orphaned Countess was left without a penny in the world, and in Rama was there a voice heard, lamentation and great mourning! Father and husband were both sad rogues, and in death, in more than a chronological sense, it is highly probable that they were not divided.

It will therefore be easily imagined that her childhood and marriage had been a sound and liberal education to Lady Hampshire; for they had taught her that the world in general is very easily imposed upon, and that if you are intending to be a villain, the path of villainy is made much smoother to the pilgrim if he smiles. Shakespeare perhaps had given her the germ of that invaluable truth; but, as in countless other instances, her brilliant brain brought to full flower what was only an immature bud of knowledge. In any case, the villain, so she shrewdly reasoned, must keep his frown to himself, and however dreadful the machinations on which he is employed, must cultivate a dewy bonhomie in public, and pretend to be innocently engrossed in the pleasures and palaces of this delightful world. Lady Hampshire went farther than this (especially since she had taken to sour milk), and actually was engrossed in them for a large majority of the hours of those entrancing summer days. But, like all game fish, she had a close time, which occurred every morning over her post. For to let the reader into her terrible and unsuspected secret, she was an earnest and adroit blackmailer.

It is easy to find excuses (if excuses are needed) to account for her adoption of so vivid and thrilling a life, for indeed it is difficult to see how she could have existed at all without some such source of income as this, and still less could she have kept up her delightful house in Lowndes Square, her cottage in the Cotswolds, her luxurious and rapid motor-car, her box at the opera, her wonderful toilettes at Sandown and Epsom, and Newmarket and Aix and Marienbad.

All these simple pleasures were really a necessity of life to her, while in addition to that she rightly regarded them as an indispensable part of her "makeup" as a blackmailer, a mask behind which she could securely grin. Had she, with her historic name, gone to live in Whitechapel or Bayswater, people would have inevitably concluded that she was hard up, and in the charitable manner characteristic of the world, have wondered how she managed to live at all except by some course of secret and remunerative crime. Whereas the genial and affluent Countess who gave her box at the opera, not to her friend (for she was too clever for that), but to her possible enemies, whenever she did not want it (which was six nights in the week, since she detested music as much as she detested detectives), was a woman who need not laugh at suspicion, simply because there were no suspicions to laugh at. Nobody bothered himself or herself as to how she got her money, just because she always spent it so delightfully. If she had not spent it thus, or if there had been none to spend, there would have been excellent cause for the world to wonder where it came (or did not come) from.

A word is necessary for the sake of those few who may possibly be ignorant of how such things are pleasantly managed, as to her methods when in pursuit of her profession. From an amateur standpoint, and to the world at large, she was, as has been said, Cynthia, Countess of Hampshire; but in her business capacity and to the scarcely less numerous world of her trembling clients she was Agatha Ainslie (Miss). Here she differed from Shakespeare, for she held that there was a great deal in a name, and (apart from the obvious objections to trading as Cynthia Hampshire) there was in the sound of "Agatha Ainslie" much which would inspire a misplaced confidence. Agatha Ainslie, to anyone entering into business relations with her for the first time, would seem to be a not unkindly blackmailer; she might suitably have lived in a cathedral close, with her sister. There was something wistful and pathetic about the title: it was in no way sharkish. She sounded gentle, though her immediate mission might appear diabolical; she was a pleasant dentist who might be supposed to treat you to nasty jabs and vivid extractions for your permanent good.

In Lady Hampshire's life, passed as it was in country-houses and restaurants and Continental spas, it was no wonder that she found many clients. There was scarcely a scandal in London that did not reach her sympathetic ear before it became public, and there were certainly many scandals that reached that eager orifice which never became public at all. She had a memory which bordered on the Gladstonian for retentiveness, and a terrifying and menacing pen, and a few words dropped secretly into her ear came out of Agatha's stylograph with blistering effect.

But with the innate kindliness of her nature, she never allowed Agatha to blackmail any who could not afford to pay, and she had several times deferred the exaction of her little fines until it was certain that her client would not be seriously embarrassed and possibly driven to the desperate course of denouncing her. Never had she had reason to blame herself for a suicide, and she had Sir Andrew Clarke's authority for believing that no one ever died of sleeplessness. She only milked the fat, sleek cows, and twisted the tails of the bulky bulls. Indeed, as she quaintly said to herself, she looked upon the payments they made as a sort of insurance against indiscretions on their part in the future. She protected them against their own lower instincts.

Her arrangements for Agatha were thoughtful in the extreme. Years ago her father had owned a small house in Whitstaple Street, of the kind described in auctioneering circles as "bijou," which backed on to her own less jewel-sized mansion in Lowndes Square. This house in Whitstaple Street had providentially escaped the notice of his creditors when his affairs—if an entire absence of assets can be considered affairs—were wound up, and in order to give Miss Ainslie a discreet and convenient home, it had only been necessary to cut a door through the back of a big closet in her bedroom in Lowndes Square. The rates and taxes of the bijou were punctually paid by Agatha, who had, of course, a separate banking-account and a curious sloping hand, while a secret and terrible old woman called Magsby, whom Lady Hampshire could ruin on the spot for forging a valueless cheque of her father's, opened the door to the clients, and made gruesome haddocky meals for herself in the kitchen.

Upstairs Lady Hampshire kept her Agatha-clothes, in which she looked like some unnatural cross between a hospital nurse and the sort of person who gets more stared at than talked to, and when she had found a home for the guileless young carpenter who fashioned her means of communication between Lowndes Square and Whitstaple Street in a remote though salubrious district of Western Australia, it really seemed as if she might laugh at the idea of detectives. She had but to lock herself into her bedroom, and in five minutes Agatha, with her spectacles and rouge and terrible wig, would be firmly conversing with clients in Whitstaple Street. Then, when a pleasant conclusion had been come to, five minutes more would be sufficient, and Lady Hampshire would emerge from her bedroom refreshed by her rest, and ready to immerse herself in a perfect spate of fashionable diversions.

Such to Lady Hampshire's effusive and optimistic mind was her career as it should have been. But occasionally the hard sordid facts of existence "put spokes" in the wheel that should have whirled so merrily. And as she sat this morning in her elaborate dressing-gown, she found a spoke of the most obstructive kind.

Agatha's letters had, as usual, been placed outside the door of communication by the terrible Magsby, and Lady Hampshire, on the principle of business first, pleasure afterwards, had answered all the letters sent to herself which dealt with the social pleasures of town before she opened the far more exciting packet of Agatha's correspondence. The very first of them made her feel as if she had several lowering diseases in the pit of the stomach. It ran thus:

"To Miss Agatha Ainslie.

"Dear Madam,—I have learned your terrible secret, and know the means whereby you acquire your great and ill-gotten wealth. Believe me, my heart bleeds for you that in your position you should ever have had to descend to the crime of blackmailing, which, you are well aware, is regarded in a very serious and perhaps even brutal light by the otherwise humane code of English law.

"Now I make no threats; I studiously avoid them. But if you can help a deserving and struggling individual already past the prime of life, I assure you, on my sacred word of honour, that you will not sleep the less soundly for it. A pittance of £1,000 a year paid quarterly, and in advance, would be considered perfectly satisfactory. My messenger shall call on you this afternoon at a quarter-past three, and I earnestly suggest that the first payment should then and there be given him.—Faithfully yours,

"M. S."

"P.S.—Motives of delicacy prevent my mentioning my name. A cheque therefore would be less welcome than bank-notes or gold."

Cynthia Hampshire shuddered as she read. Often and often she had wondered with kindly amazement at the hare-like timidity of her clients, who so willingly paid their little mites to the upkeep of her establishment, when a moment's courage would have taken them hot-foot to the smiling and hospitable portals of Scotland Yard. But as she perused this perfectly sickening communication, she found herself, in the true sense of the word, sympathizing with them—that is to say, suffering with them. It really was most uncomfortable being blackmailed for something of an illegal nature which you actually had done, and she no longer wondered at the lamb-like acquiescence with which her clients fell in with the not unreasonable terms that she offered them.

The thought of calling at Scotland Yard with this outrageous letter occurred to her, but at the idea of appealing for protection her soul cried out like a child in the dark, and her courage oozed from her like drippings from a squeezed sponge. Furthermore, so spirited a proceeding was rendered even less feasible by the fact that it was not Lady Hampshire who was being blackmailed, but her Agatha. She doubted very much if she would be allowed by the odious meticulosity of English law to prosecute on behalf of poor Miss Ainslie, who must suddenly have gone abroad, while the idea of going to the house of vengeance in the disguise and habiliments of that injured spinster was outside the limits of her sober imagination. And who could M. S. be, with his veiled threats and nauseating denial of them? She ran rapidly through the list of her clients, but found none whom she could reasonably suspect of so treacherous a feat.

Very reluctantly she was forced to the conclusion that she would have to pay the first quarter anyhow of this cruel levy. Luckily Agatha had been doing very well lately, for London had been amusing itself with no end of questionable antics, and there was a prospect of a good season to come. But £250 per quarter would assuredly take a considerable portion of gilt off poor Miss Ainslie's gingerbread, and it was at once clear to Lady Hampshire that she must raise Agatha's rates.

She was lunching that day with Colonel Ascot, an old and valued friend. Though still only a year or two past fifty, he had made three large fortunes, of which he had lost two. But the third, which he had rapidly scooped out of the rubber boom, had sent him bounding upwards again, and she had more than once wondered if she could get him on to Agatha's list. More than once also, in answer to his repeated proposals, she had thought of marrying him, but she did not think it right to accept his devotion without telling him about Agatha, and it seemed scarcely likely that he would wish his wife to have such an alter ego. For as Agatha she led such a thrilling and tremendous existence that it would be a great wrench to annihilate that exciting spinster in the noose of matrimony. On the other hand, if Agatha's business was to be threatened by these bolts from the blue, in the shape of demands from M. S., the pain of parting with her would be appreciably less severe. The matter required fresh and careful consideration.

Lady Hampshire had several other clients to write to, and it was time (when she had finished this correspondence, and put it through the secret door at the back of her bedroom closet to be collected and posted by grim Magsby) to exchange her dressing-gown for the habiliments of lunch and civilization. A new costume had come for her from Paquin's that morning, and as she was to go to two charity bazaars, a matinée, and as many tea-parties as there was time for between the end of the matinée and the early dinner which was to precede another theatre and a couple of balls, she decided to wear this sumptuous creation.

Anything new, provided the point of it was not to be old, put this mercurial lady into excellent humour, and she set out for lunch, which was only just across the square, not more than half an hour late, looking, as the representative of a fashion-paper who was standing at the corner on the chance of seeing her told her readers the following Saturday, "very smart and well-gowned." She knew she was certain to meet friends, since that always happened; and by the time she took her seat next her host, finding lunch already half-over, she had quite dismissed from her mind the trouble of poor Miss Ainslie.

"But how delicious to see food again," she said as she sat down. "I was so afraid lunch-time was never coming that I didn't recognize it when it came."

"And we were afraid that you were never coming, dear Cynthia," said the Duchess of Camber.

"I know; I am late. But as I always am late, it is the same as if I was punctual. The really unpunctual people are those who sometimes are late and sometimes not. Colonel Ascot has the other punctuality; he is always in time."

Cynthia looked round the table. There were but half a dozen guests, but all these were old friends, and by a not uncommon coincidence half of them were clients of Agatha, while the Duchess of Camber, so Lady Hampshire knew, was quite likely to become one, for she had lately taken to doing her shopping at Mason's Stores, and spent a long time over it.

Colonel Ascot glanced, apparently with purpose, at the Louis XVI. clock that stood on the mantelpiece.

"One wastes a lot of time if one is punctual," he said. "But, after all, one has all the time there is."

"But there isn't enough, though one has it all!" said Lady Hampshire. "To-day, for instance, would have to be doubled, as one doubles at bridge, if I was to do all I have promised to."

"But you won't, dear, so it doesn't matter," said the Duchess. "In any case, there is always time for what one wants to do, and one can omit the rest. I always thought my time was completely taken up, but I find I can do my own shopping at Mason's as well. I buy soap and candles and sealing-wax, and take them home in the motor."

"But not every morning?" asked Lady Hampshire, beginning to attend violently.

"Practically every afternoon. I always find I have forgotten something I meant to buy the day before. Also, it is a sort of retreat. One never meets there anybody one knows, which is such a rest. I don't have to grin and talk."

Lunch was soon over, and instead of having coffee and cigarettes served at the table, Colonel Ascot got up.

"I do hope, Lady Hampshire," he said, "that you and the others will not hurry away, and that you will excuse me, as I have a most important engagement at a quarter-past three, which I cannot miss. It is very annoying, and the worst of it is that I made the appointment myself, quite forgetting that I was to have the pleasure of seeing you at lunch."

"Am I to take your place as hostess?" she asked, as she sat down with him for a moment in a corner of the drawing-room.

"If you will, both now and always," said he.

She laughed; he had proposed to her so often that a repetition was not in the least embarrassing. But somehow, to-day, he looked unusually attractive and handsome, and she was more serious with him than was her wont. Also the thought of doing business for Agatha was in her mind.

"Ah, my dear friend," she said, "I should have to know so much more about you first. For instance, that appointment of your own making seems to me to need inquiry. Now be truthful, Colonel Ascot, and tell me if it is not a woman you are going to see?"

"Well, it is."

"I knew it," she said.

"But you must let me tell you more," said he. "She is an old governess of my sister's, whom I—I want to be kind to. Such a good old soul. The sort of helpless old lady with whom one couldn't break an appointment that one had made."

Lady Hampshire laughed again.

"Your details are admirable," she said. "And detail is of such prime importance in any artistic production."

"Artistic production?" said he. "Surely you don't suspect me of——"

"I suspect everybody of everything," she interrupted lightly, "owing to my extensive knowledge of myself. But go on; I want more details. What is the name and address of this helpless old governess?"

"Miss Agatha Ainslie," said he. "She lives in Whitstaple Street, just off the Square."

Lady Hampshire had nerves of steel. If they had been of any other material they must have snapped like the strings of the lyre of Hope in Mr. Watts's picture. Only in this case there would not have been a single one left. Colonel Ascot going to see Agatha at a quarter-past three.... How on earth did he know of Agatha's existence? What was Agatha to him, or he to Agatha? And surely it was at a quarter-past three that the messenger of the ruthless M. S. was going to call at Whitstaple Street, where he would find the packet of bank-notes for £250 that Lady Hampshire had made ready before she came out to lunch. Would they meet on the doorstep? What did it all mean?

Her head whirled, but she managed to command her voice.

"What a delightful name!" she said. "I'm sure Miss Ainslie must be a delightful old lady with ringlets and a vinaigrette and a mourning-brooch."

"I haven't seen her for years," said Colonel Ascot. "I will tell you about her when we meet again. Do let it be soon!"

"Perhaps you would drop in for tea to-day?" she suggested, expunging from her mind several other engagements. "I shall be alone."

"That will make up for my curtailed luncheon-party," said he.

He made his excuses to his guests, and after allowing him a liberal time in which he could leave the house, Lady Hampshire rose also.

"You are not going yet, dear Cynthia?" asked the Duchess. "I wanted to talk to you about the advantage of doing your shopping at Mason's. And the danger of it," she added, catching Lady Hampshire's kind understanding eye.

Lady Hampshire felt torn between conflicting interests. Here, she unerringly conjectured, there was fish to fry for Agatha, and yet other fish, so to speak, who perhaps wanted to fry. Agatha demanded a more immediate attention.

The duchess's complication must wait: she was dining with her to-morrow. Colonel Ascot was going to see Agatha: nothing must prevent Lady Hampshire from hearing what his business was.

She went across the Square, and let herself into her own house. There were half a dozen telegrams lying on the hall table, but without dreaming of opening any, she went straight to her bedroom and locked the door. Someone—probably the second footman—was being funny at the servants' dinner, for shrieks of laughter ascended from the basement. As a rule, she loved to know that her household was enjoying itself, but to-day that merriment left her cold, and next moment she was in Agatha's house and pursing her lips into the shrill whistle with which she always summoned Magsby.

"I left a note addressed to M. S.," she said; "I want it."

The words were yet in her mouth, when the bell of Agatha's front door rang in an imperious manner, and Lady Hampshire peeped cautiously out through the yellow muslin blinds. On the doorstep was standing an old, old man with a long white beard. He leaned heavily on a stick, and wore a frayed overcoat.

She tip-toed back from the window.

"Give me the note," she said, "and wait till I get upstairs. Then answer the door, and tell Methuselah that Miss Ainslie will be down in a moment."

Lady Hampshire stole up to Agatha's room, and hastily assumed her grey wig, her spectacles, her rouge, her large elastic-sided boots, her lip-salve, her creaking alpaca gown, and with the envelope containing bank-notes for £250, addressed in Agatha's dramatic sloping handwriting to the messenger of M. S., descended again to her sitting-room. Methuselah rose as she entered, and she made him her ordinary prim Agatha bow, and spoke in Miss Ainslie's husky treble voice.

"The messenger of M. S.," she observed. "Quite so."

"That is my name for the present," said the old man in a fruity tenor.

"I received your master's note, sir," said Agatha, "and you cannot be expected to know what pain and surprise it caused me. But what does he suppose he is going to get by it?"

Lady Hampshire was not used to spectacles, and they dimmed her natural acuteness of vision, besides making her eyes ache. Before her was a sordid old ruin of humanity, red-eyed, white-bearded, a prey, it would seem, to lumbago, nasal catarrh, and other senile ailments. Probably in a few minutes—for it was scarcely a quarter past three yet—Colonel Ascot would arrive; and again her head whirled at the thought of the possible nightmares that Providence still had in store for her.

Methuselah blew his nose.

"I fancy my master rather expected to get £250 in notes or gold," he said. "He knows a good deal about Miss Ainslie, he does. He is quite willing to share his knowledge with others, he is."

Lady Hampshire raised her head proudly, so that she could get a glimpse of this old ruffian under her spectacles. The ways of genius are past finding out, and she could never give a firm reason for what she said next. A brilliant unconscious intuition led her to say it.

"There is nothing the world may not know," she said; "in England it is no crime to be poor, and though I have been in a humble position all my life, my life has been an honest one. There is no disgrace inherent in the profession of a governess. For many years I was governess to Colonel Ascot's sister."

"Good God!" said Methuselah.

That was sufficient for Lady Hampshire. She took off her spectacles altogether and closely scrutinized that astonished rheumy face. And then her kindly soul was all aflame with indignation at this dastardly attempt to blackmail poor Agatha.

"In fact, now I look at you," she said, "I recognize you. No wonder you blaspheme. I remember the bright boy who used to come in and sit in the schoolroom while my pupil and I were at our lessons. You have aged very much, Colonel Ascot."

In that moment of recognition, she made up her mind. She could never marry him; she could never even lunch with him again. He was atrocious.

Methuselah rose.

"You are labouring under some strange mistake," he said; "I will call again."

"There is no mistake at all," said Lady Hampshire quickly, forgetting, in her perfectly natural indignation, to employ the husky treble tones which were characteristic of Miss Ainslie, "except the mistake you have made in thinking that you could with impunity blackmail a defenceless old governess like me. Where is Scotland Yard? I shall drive there immediately, and you shall come with me. I shall ring the bell."

She got up quickly, and then sat down again exactly where she had been, and Methuselah looked at her very carefully. Then he suddenly burst into peals of bass laughter.

"But you have aged very much, too, Lady Hampshire," he said.

"Good God!" said Agatha Ainslie.

Magsby, waiting in the passage outside, felt uncertain as to what her duty was. She heard her mistress's voice and the voice of another, shrieking with laughter, which seemed to gather volume and enjoyment the longer it went on. Eventually she thought best to retreat to the basement and prepare haddocks for dinner.

"But, my dear, let us be serious," said Lady Hampshire at length. "Tell me, before I begin to laugh again, how on earth you ever heard of my poor Agatha!"

"A mutual client," said Colonel Ascot, fanning himself with his long white beard. "Poor Jimmy Dennison. He told me, in a fit of

11

natural exasperation, when I was reminding him about what happened at Brighton last September, that he could not afford to pay for the same thing twice over, once to me, and once to Agatha Ainslie. The poor boy showed me the counterfoils of his cheque-book. It was Agatha Ainslie and Martin Sampson all the way. It was but natural, since he could not pay, that I should turn to Agatha and see if she could."

"But are you really one of us?" said Lady Hampshire.

"Apparently. Are you?"

There was a fresh relapse of laughter, and then Lady Hampshire pulled herself together.

"I will go halves in Jimmy Dennison," she said, "whatever we may get. You may say you have squared Agatha. He ought to give you something for your trouble. Or I will say I have squared Sampson."

"It makes no difference," said Colonel Ascot. "But I am afraid our interests conflict in many quarters. For instance, the poor Duchess of Camber."

"Shopping at Mason's," interrupted Lady Hampshire. "My dear friend, she is mine. She was going to tell me all about it this afternoon, only I had to come over here to see about Agatha."

Again Colonel Ascot exploded with laughter.

"But she told me about it yesterday," he said, "and I had already drafted a short letter to her from Martin Sampson."

Lady Hampshire was annoyed at this, since the Duchess was so very rich and so very silly.

"I don't know what we can do," she said; "we can't appoint an arbitrator, can we? No arbitrator of really high character would undertake to settle the differences of two blackmailers. It is very important that an arbitrator should be beyond suspicion."

"We had really better make it one firm, Cynthia," said he.

She had often considered his proposal before, but never so favourably. Agatha need not be annihilated now; Agatha would probably grow even more tumultuously alive.

"Yes, perhaps we had," she said. "Oh, yes, most decidedly!"

So they lived happily and wealthily and amazingly for another twenty-four years—there is much yet that might be said about them.

THE BLACKMAILER OF PARK LANE

Arthur Whately had known very well what it was like to be desperately poor, and in consequence, when he became so desperately rich that money ceased to mean anything to him, his pity for the penurious was not hysterical or exaggerated. He could recall very vividly what it felt like to have neither tea, dinner nor supper, and to wake in the morning, stiff and cold as armour, on a bench on the Embankment and see the ridiculous needle of Cleopatra stonily pointing heavenwards against the sky, in which the stars were beginning to burn dim at the chilly approach of day. He had known how icy the feet become when they have been close clasped all night long in the frayed embraces of gaping leather, but he had known also how sweet and surprising it is to eat when food is imperiously demanded by the cravings of long-continued abstinence, and how ineffably luxurious to get warm when limbs have ached themselves numb. He would have been willing to confess that unveneered destitution had its inconveniences, but it was false sentiment to deny that it had its compensations also.

It was when he was just sixteen that Luck, the great veiled goddess whom all the world so wisely worships, had paid him her first visit. He had been hanging about at the covered portico of the Lyceum Theatre one night watching the well-fed world being lumpily deposited at the doors, when a silly old pink gentleman, in paying his cabman, dropped a promising pocket-book in the roadway. For one half-second the boy deliberated, wondering instinctively (though he had never heard of the proverb) if honesty was the best policy, in other words, how much the pocket-book contained, and how much the foolish old gentleman would give him if he picked it up and returned it. A couple of pence, perhaps, for he looked a coppery gent.

But the debate lasted scarcely longer than it took the pocket-book to fall; in a moment his wise decision was made, he had picked it up (recognizing in that delightful incident the smile of the great goddess), had dived under the Roman nose of the cab horse, and fled into the street where a chill, unpleasant rain was falling. Luck still smiled on him, for the night was foggy, and as soon as he had crossed the street he dropped into the habitual shuffling pace of the homeless, and returned to the portico which he had so lately quitted, since it was theoretically impossible that the thief should do anything so foolish.

The silly old pink gentleman had not yet ceased to gesticulate and jibber in the direction in which he himself had just vanished, and an obsequious policeman was apparently taking down all the bad words he used in a neat notebook. Arthur wondered if he would arrest the old man for indulging in language redolent of faint praise in a public place.

Meantime, he had thrust the pocket-book—that incarnate smile of the beneficent goddess—into his shirt, and it slid comfortably down against his skin, till it was brought to anchor by the string which he had so strictly tied round his braceless trousers, since pressure in those regions minimised the abhorrence of vacuum. Then he slouched back to the Embankment, and with head bowed over his knees as if in sleep, he counted the tale of his treasure, taking out each item separately, and screening them from the parental scrutiny of policemen in the cavern of his hand.

There were two pieces of the fabulous crinkly paper, there were three sovereigns, and, what was immensely important for immediate purposes, a couple of shillings, translatable without suspicion into rich fried fish. One of his trouser pockets was a secure harbourage, and into this he piloted the golden ship. Then, with a stroke of high wisdom, he thrust the pocket-book through the interstices of the bench instead of keeping about him so incriminating a piece of merchandise, and slouched away, saying good-bye to roofless bedchambers by the sweet Thames-side for ever.

To-night, as he sat in the great dining-room of his house in Park Lane, the memory of that divine evening was vividly brought to his mind. Three friends had dined with him, and as the night proved foggy, they had abandoned the idea of seeing the most incompletely-clad dancer that the London County Council had at present licensed, and had decided to stay at home and play bridge.

"A cold, foggy night, sir," had been the pronouncement that followed the butler's news that the motors were round, and the simple words had conjured up that wonderful night of his boyhood with the vividness of hallucination. Bates, too, had a Roman nose, just like the cab horse, and Bates, by a strange coincidence, had just laid by his plate a couple of bank-notes and some change, since he had found himself completely destitute of coin. Had he ever enjoyed himself so much in all these fat years as on that cold, lean, foggy evening so long ago? Honestly (or dishonestly) he could not believe that he had. For there had been about it the one and only and original spice; then for the first time he had heard the clear call of the great golden goddess. She had called often since; indeed for years she had never ceased calling, and it was not too much to say

14

that for years she had been madly and unreasonably in love with him. He received her with yawns now, like some poor discarded mistress, but the chilly reception never deterred her. She never noticed that he was bored, and his indifference seemed but to inflame her ardour.

Solid, monotonous good luck had followed him all the days of his life. Ever since the night when he was sixteen and so happily stole the pocket-book, all he had touched turned to gold, all he had desired had been granted him, all his ideals (such as they were) had frozen into cold suetty facts. Half of the thirteen pounds which were the result of his original theft had been expended in reach-me-down clothes and ready-made boots (which, in those happy years, could be purchased by others than millionaires), for it was symptomatic of him never to grudge money when it was probably a good investment, and between his natural smartness of face and carriage and the acquired smartness of his new clothes, he had at once got a place as hall-boy in an hotel.

He learned to swim in the Chelsea Baths, and August was scarcely begun when this recreation was turned to solid account, for, being at Margate on bank holiday, a pleasure-boat conveniently capsized near him, and he easily rescued the only daughter of a prosperous bookmaker. That gentleman seemed not to resent the unexpected survival of a rat-faced child, had given him fifty pounds in cash, and, subsequently, several racing tips by way of a gilt-edged security for the fifty pounds. These proved not to be gilt-edged only, but completely covered with pure gold.

Then came the news of possibilities in South Africa, and, gambler as he was in every drop of blood in his body, he had gone for these with a thousand pounds to his credit. He threw his thousand pounds at the Rand, and, as if he had given it a little emetic pill, the Rand belched gold at him. In ten years (though he had enjoyed those years quite enormously) the savour of money-making grew stale, and with a brilliant excursion into American rails, which returned him his fortune more than doubled, he quitted the speculative arena, and for the last decade and a half had looked with eyes of incredulous wonder at the extraordinary gentlemen who continued to go to offices in the city all day long and industriously accumulate what they did not want.

There was one such here to-night, a great, round, dark man with yellow hair, the colour of a London fog. He took a grudged month's holiday in the year, but otherwise sat in an office with his ear to a telephone and his mouth to a speaking-tube. Perhaps it amused him, for certainly there was always in his eye a remote twinkle, as if he had constant grounds for private mirth, and Arthur

15

Whately had often suspected him of being a secret humourist. Yet in the ordinary commerce of social life none was so heavy or so commonplace. He and his wife were social climbers of pathetic industry, who gave parties that tried to be smart and only succeeded in being garish. Yet there was that secret twinkle in his eye....

The same good luck had dogged Arthur Whately in affairs more intimate to his happiness than gold. He had married the woman whom he adored, and just when his adoration had cooled and she was beginning to bore him to extinction, she had run away with somebody else. He had wanted the particular house in which he now sat, and the owner had died just when his demise was most convenient, leaving his affairs in unutterable confusion, and his executors were delighted to sell everything. He had, again, in artistic spheres, conceived a violent passion for the pictures of Giovanni Bollini, and an impecunious peer, foreseeing that income taxes and death duties were swelling like inflated footballs, had sold him his priceless collection, which now hung round the walls of his dining-room. Finally, on this particular evening, when he felt very much disinclined to go out, Providence had sent a fog to serve as an excuse for stopping in. And yet bridge was rather a stale affair. There was a certain intellectual pleasure in thwarting other people, but it was not much fun being clever when the rest were, comparatively speaking, such fools.

His private band had been assembled in the gallery of the ballroom, in case music was required, but they had been dismissed, since the four went straight from the dining-room into the fan-room, where a card-table was laid out. These fans were famous, and had once been the property of Marie Antoinette and other ladies, whose goods had been disposed of after their death by their executors or executioners, and Arthur Whately had acquired them at immense expense during the year of his married life to please his wife.

Shortly after he divorced her, an attempt had been made by a burglar to steal them, but an ingenious device, invented by himself after his wife's departure, had impeded the idea, for anyone entering the fan-room after the apparatus had been set caused merry peals of electric bells to break out in the rooms of the butler, footmen, odd man and other able-bodied persons, and the intended burglar had been caught fan-handed. But his confession that the late Mrs. Whately had commissioned him to attempt this job so interested Arthur Whately that he took no proceedings with regard to him, except to give him supper. His wife, simultaneously, rose considerably in his estimation; he had not known she had so much blood in her.

16

The fan-room overlooked the Park, and regardless of possible interpretations Arthur Whately had straw permanently put down in the roadway to deaden the noise of traffic. There had been a ruffle with the vestry on the subject of this straw. Men with pitchforks came and took it up. But as often as they took it up he had it renewed, and by now it had become as much a feature of Park Lane as the omnibuses. Occasionally a policeman, new to the beat and fired by professional enthusiasm, would question the straw-strewers, but the mystic whisper, "A friend of Mr. Whately's," had the forcefulness and wit of brevity about it.

The game was tepid; not even his opponent's remarkable and reiterated revoke in no-trumps really warmed it, and Arthur Whately was glad when his guests departed, for, unaccustomed as he was to brooding over imaginary troubles or dulling his very acute brain with the narcotic poisoning of self-analysis, he was a little anxious about himself to-night, and was glad of a quiet hour before going to bed to examine the cause of his disquietude. It was still early when they left, for there was a dance somewhere to which the two ladies with the irrepressible enthusiasm of advanced middle-age were going on, while the financier was going home. On the doorstep he confided to his host that his name was to appear next morning among the peerages given in honour of the King's Birthday, and Arthur Whately supposed he was going to seek the privacy of his own study to practise writing his new name, which was to be Peebles, in memory of pleasure.

He adjusted the bell-pealing apparatus in the fan-room, and retired to his own sitting-room, which adjoined his bedroom. Half a dozen exquisite Watteaus decorated the walls, and the bureau which stood opposite the door was from the effects of the unfortunate Queen of France. Often and often he had thrilled at the thought that she had sat there and written those little ill-spelled notes in her sprawling hand, but to-night he would not have cared if he had found her sitting there in person.

Tædium vitæ, the weariness, the boredom of success, which poisons the lives of emperors and scratch golfers, had laid its heavy hand on him. He had poached the world like an egg. But he could find no salt....

So it was that which ailed him. Often of late he had found he had little zest for this pursuit or that, but it had not struck him till this moment that the whole affair was flat. And yet it was not himself, so he felt, that was to blame. He was still but a year or two past fifty, handsome and healthy, and his powers of enjoyment he knew were undimmed, provided only he could find something to exercise them on. In himself he was eager, alert, longing for excitement, but to do the same thing over and over again did not excite him; the early years of hunger and struggle and achievement had accustomed him to a high level of emotion. He wanted to burn, not to smoulder quietly away, as most people were content to do.

Indeed, he had done everything he could think of. He had loved and married, and been bored, and had no intention of tempting the ennui of domesticity again. Nor had he any tastes for the more irregular pleasures of the senses; they were all poached and saltless. Material possessions, of course, had ceased to interest him, since he was completely surrounded with all that he thought most exquisite in the world of art, and to accumulate for the mere sake of accumulation seemed to him an exhibition of pig-trough greed. And it was so easy; he could buy anything that was for sale. Perhaps if Mr. Morgan or some insatiable hoarder owned a desirable piece or picture and would not part with it at any price, he might find a secret rapture in attempting to steal it, just as his wife had done with the fans, but otherwise the act of acquisition had become too easy to be any longer agreeable.

Everything wanted salt, but that was the fault of the objective world. He, subjectively, had as good an appetite as on the entranced and canonized evening when he stole the pocket-book of the silly pink man, that unconscious founder of his fortunes, who, vastly sillier than ever, had dined with him only last week, and had had a fatal apoplectic seizure immediately afterwards.

To-night he almost cursed his memory for his foolishness thirty-five years ago, for it was that theft which had led to this weariness. If only the poor pink departed had caught him and given him a taste of gaol, Arthur Whately felt that he might now be rapturously pursuing the thrilling hazardous paths of the hardened criminal, to whom every house is a possible crib to be cracked, every jewel in a woman's necklace a week of delirium and drunken debauch. But where is the fun of stealing if you already own more than you can possibly want?

In his mind he swiftly ran through the ten commandments, and found, as he had feared, that it would not give him the slightest pleasure to break any of them. There might be a little excitement about bearing false witness against your neighbour, but then that would entail appearing in a law court and listening to the pitiful humour of some fussy judge. As for the rest of the commandments, they suggested nothing amusing. There was nothing to be done with the fifth, because his father and mother had been dead for years; the sixth implied blood and violence, and violence was foreign to his nature. But for a moment he lingered over the picture of strangling Lord Peebles and burying him in the straw in Park Lane. There was something grotesquely attractive in the notion, but probably the coroner's jury would give their verdict that he had been strangled by natural causes, and that death had been accelerated by the immediate prospect of a peerage.

He himself had thrice been offered a peerage, once by the Liberals, once by the Conservatives, and once prospectively by the Labour Party. His invariable answer had been that previous engagements prevented him accepting their kind invitation. That had amused him at the time; now it seemed deplorably witless. But could he not devise something for Lord Peebles that should spoil his pleasure? Why should Lord Peebles have that secret twinkle in his eye? Why should he, at his age, be still enjoying life? Whately felt a murderous impulse towards his friend's mirth.

But he could think of nothing, and with a sigh he took up a copy of that unique journal which is so justly famed for chronicling that which has not occurred and prophesying that which will not possibly happen, and scarcely glancing at the leader, probably inspired by Ananias, and the fashionable intelligence, certainly gleaned by Sapphira, he turned to the more reliable records of the police courts. There had been a brutal murder—apparently the transgression of the sixth commandment was not wholly unattractive to people less tiresomely fastidious than himself—and a certain blameless archdeacon whom he knew slightly had, after the receipt of a series of threatening letters, to which answers were requested to be sent (accompanied by stout remittances) to A. M., Martin's Library, Wardour Street, reluctantly taken proceedings against the blackmailer, who had been rewarded with five years of enforced seclusion.

Arthur Whately wondered whether he himself would have the courage to prosecute a blackmailer. Probably not; with his wealth it would be easier to satisfy the most rapacious. It was brave of the archdeacon; no doubt his artificially fostered sense of duty sustained him.

His thoughts wandered on as he stared at the newspaper. Would he himself ever have the courage to blackmail anyone else? It must be the most exciting game, and to play it successfully would demand an extraordinary amount of intuition and knowledge of human nature. All depended on the character of your proposed victim. It would be as hopeless to try to extract money with threats out of some men, however scarlet the secrets of which you had possessed yourself, as, singlehanded, to extract a lion's teeth. Others, no doubt, would equally certainly yield at once to the most veiled menace....

Suddenly the paper which he held began to rustle with the

19

involuntary tremor of the hand that held it, and an eager excitement shot up like the light of a petroleum-soaked beacon in his dulled eye. He need no longer seek for agitation. He had found, when he least expected it, the answer to his fruitless appeals to the universe to supply him with interest. In the excitement of the moment he poured a liberal dose of whisky into a tumbler, but next minute poured it back. He had to keep his head cool; artificial stimulant only led to subsequent reaction and torpidity of thought. But through the prison bars his spirit grasped hands with the archdeacon's victim. He would certainly blackmail somebody.

There were two questions to settle. Whom should he blackmail, and what had his victim done? A moment's incisive thought told him that the second question, as to what the supposed crime had been, was alien and superfluous. The poor man need not have done anything. He need only be told that the events which occurred between, say, August 2 and August 10 of the year before last were known to his persecutor. All else depended on the selection of a suitable victim. If an unsuitable subject was chosen, one whose life (could such be found) was of virtue so monstrously Spartan, that he would not mind the events of August 2 to 10, or those of any other date, being known, it was clearly impossible to proceed. On the other hand, if his life was so voluminous a catalogue of crime that there were terrible affairs in every week of it, a notified period like this would create no particular impression.

Yes, it was the character of the victim that must be studied if the æsthetic blackmailer was to have any fun, for, of course, in the case of Arthur Whately, the mere extraction of two or three hundred pounds (thousands, perhaps, if his prey was wealthy) meant nothing at all. And the largest ingredient in the fun would be the uncertainty as to how the victim would behave, whether he would take proceedings or pay. He must therefore be cast in no iron mould; there would be little sport in writing just one letter and then being sent to join the poor worm so grindingly crushed by the heel of the valiant archdeacon, nor, on the other hand, would there be any zest in the punctual receipts of cheques whenever demanded. He had to think of somebody not too good and not too bad, not too brave and yet not pigeon-livered. For a while his mind hovered, singing like a skylark in the exultation of this absorbing preoccupation, then suddenly it dropped to earth again. There was none so fit as Lord Peebles.

His hand trembled for the pen that was mightier than the sword, and after a few moments' concentrated thought, he dashed off these cold, cruel lines, which would serve as the basis for attack:

My Lord,—While congratulating your lordship on the well-deserved honour which the King has paid you, I feel it my duty to let your lordship know that the events which took place between August 2 and August 10 of the year before last are completely in the possession of the undersigned, and are supported by documentary evidence of such sort that nobody who saw it could ever doubt its authenticity. I am prepared to give up to you all such papers as are in my possession for the sum of £2,000.

I am a poor man, and a desperate one, but am strictly honourable in all business matters such as this, and on receipt of that sum in gold I will strictly carry out my obligations. Should your lordship take no notice of this communication or refuse to comply with my request, the whole affair will be made public.

I am well aware that I put myself within reach of the law in thus addressing you, but I would ask your lordship carefully to consider the results to yourself if you prosecute me. The circumstances of which I am possessed will then all come out, and while it matters very little to me whether I pass the next few years in prison or not, I think that the consequences to you will not be so lightly regarded by self and family. You have a great deal to lose; I have nothing.

Kindly communicate with me at Martin's Library, Wardour Street, by to-day week at latest. Having no club or settled address at present, I call there daily for letters and occasional parcels.—Faithfully yours,

George Loring.

In obedience to the business-like qualities which had raised him to the position of multi-millionaire his mind instantly went into committee over details. It was but very rarely that he employed his own hand in writing, for his correspondence was entirely dealt with by secretaries and typewriters, but it would be well to disguise his ordinary caligraphy. Or, stop—there was a safer way, and the next minute the Remington typewriter which stood in the corner of the room was opened and gleamed with bared keys. He was no adept at this clattering finger-exercise, but after a few abortive trials he made a clumsy transcript of the letter, and directed an envelope by the same mechanical device.

Already the cautious instincts of the habitual criminal had awoke in him, and after replacing the cover on the typewriter he carefully burned both his manuscript draft and the insane gibberish of his first typed attempts, and opening his window let the

21

blackened ashes float down into the straw-covered roadway. It would never do, again, to let the incriminating document lie among the other letters for post, and he hid it below the shirts in a wardrobe drawer in his bedroom in order to post it himself at some central letter-box next morning after verifying the existence of Martin's Library. Then, since it was already very late, he went to bed with eager anticipation for the morrow and many morrows.

The next week was full of delightful interests; it passed in a spasm of absorbing moments, and he was astonished and disgusted at himself for not having entered sooner on a course of blackmail. True artist that he was, he did not pay constant visits to Martin's Library, as soon as it was possible that there might be an answer to his letter, and ask if there was anything for George Loring, but with a higher æstheticism, preferred to taste the delights of suspense, and determined not to make any inquiries till the notified week had elapsed. But he could not avoid haunting Wardour Street, picturing to himself with artistic gusto his official visit to the library. Once only was the flesh too strong, and, though the week of grace had not yet expired, he could not resist the temptation of entering the library.

The shop was empty, and, somewhat to his disappointment, showed no lines of filled and fitted shelves, as he had hoped. He had imagined the smell of leather bindings, bookcases full of venerable volumes of the fathers, a dignified and courtly librarian. Instead, he found a small deal counter, on which were displayed the more odious of penny publications, and a stout old woman of comfortable appearance looked up from her knitting as he entered. But behind her—and his heart beat quicker at the sight—were rows of capacious pigeon-holes, each initialled with a letter of the alphabet. But, even as she asked him in a hoarse, fruity voice what she could do for him, he called on his finer instincts again, and instead of asking if there happened to be anything for George Loring, contented himself with buying "Society Pars" and "Frivol and Fashion." With these prints in his hand, he left the shop without even looking at letter L.

But after all, perhaps, the commonplace sordidness of the establishment was of greater artistic value than his preconceived idea of it; it was a grimmer affair like this; it was more piquant, more trenchant that white-faced men, trembling and unmanned by the possibility of dreadful disclosures coming to light, should bring their forfeits to this ordinary little establishment, that their unseen and terrible persecutor should ask for letters from a comfortable old lady over a dingy deal counter.

Hardly had he emerged when there drove by a motor in which, of all people, Lord Peebles was sitting, who waved an absent welcome to him. He saw at once how dangerous had been his visit. Supposing he had asked for letters for George Loring and had staggered out of the shop with a scarcely manageable parcel of gold, to encounter such a meeting, it was distinctly within the bounds of possibility that that nobleman would connect him with George Loring. His blood ran cold at the thought, and yet it was a pleasing shiver which at once suggested a further precaution, delightful in the devising. A disguise was imperatively necessary.

He hailed a taxicab and spent an enraptured afternoon. George Loring had probably done this sort of thing before, and it might be supposed that though poor and desperate, he retained from the fruits of his last crime clothes of a flashy and ill-fitting description. Such as he would certainly wear a gaudy check suit and cheap patent leather boots. His tie, of the Brussels carpet type, would assuredly be pinned with something too magnificent to be possibly valuable; detachable cuffs and dicky, a hat with a furrow in it would complete his detestable array. Arthur Whately himself was clean shaven and solidly English in face; a moustache and imperial, therefore, suggesting a Polish conjurer were indicated. These must be of convincing make, incapable of detection; and a visit to an expensive perruquier's, with a brilliant tale of a fancy-dress ball, made the last visit of a thrilling afternoon. And that night, when the great house in Park Lane was silent, and the electrical apparatus in the fan-room adjusted, a figure, appalling to contemplate, strutted and pirouetted before the big looking-glass in his locked bedroom.

All this, so exquisite to his pleasure-jaded palate, was but the material aspect of his adventure. Far sweeter and more recondite was the psychical honey of it. For, two days after George Loring had sent his letter, Lord Peebles telephoned to know whether Arthur Whately would play golf with him, and though he detested and despised the game, he gave an enthusiastic affirmative, and drove down with him to the Mid-Surrey links at Richmond. Certainly Lord Peebles looked worried and anxious, and the grey streak above his ears seemed to the vigilant eye of his friend to have assumed greater prominence.

"It's so good of you to ask me to play," said Whately as they started. "I am a wretched performer, and I know your prowess."

"Oh, I expect we shall have a very even match, a very even match," said the other. "And I needed a day off, though it is not Saturday. But there has been some worrying business lately, and I wanted to get into the country and forget all about it. Very worrying business."

Whately's eye gleamed secretly; these worries fed his soul.

"Indeed, I am sorry to hear that," he said.

"Thank you, thank you. A purely private affair. Don't let us talk of it. Pretty the country looks. What's that river we are crossing?"

"The River Thames," said Whately almost tremulously.

"Perhaps," said Lord Peebles.

He cleared his throat. "The Thames," he began, and then changed the subject to something amazingly foreign to that topic.

"It is strange how one's memory plays tricks with one," he said. "A couple of days ago I was trying—quite idly—to recollect where I spent the early days of August the summer before last, and was totally unable to recall what I had been doing. My wife remembers that we went to Scotland on the 11th, but she, too, has quite forgotten what we did just before. She inclines to think that I was paying some visits without her. Curious!"

Arthur Whately laughed in a sprightly, rallying manner.

"Ah, ah," he said, "she is probably right, eh? Trust a wife's memory, my dear fellow, on that sort of point."

"No doubt she is right," returned the other, "but it is strange that we can neither of us recollect where I went."

"Perhaps you never told her," said Whately gaily. "But come, dismiss those evasive topics. Let the past bury its dead. It is only the present that is truly ours."

They had arrived at the club-house, and Whately stepped out, followed by the heavier-footed peer. It was almost too good to be true, that by sheer accident he had lighted on days that seemed hard to account for, and, treading on air, he hurried into the dressing-room, where, in momentary privacy, he was forced to indulge in a few toe-pointing capers of delight. And, after all, though the emotions with which he had supplied his friend were of anxious and ominous description, still, emotions after all, of whatever sort, are the salt of life, and here was a new one for him, something with a strong flavour about it. But he could afford to be generous, since he himself was being so richly entertained, and he did not grudge him one pang of the worry and anxiety inseparable from his position.

Arthur Whately's golf was generally of the most wayward description; he cut balls savagely to point and topped them ventre à terre into cavernous bunkers, while Lord Peebles played a dreadfully steady game, that, as a rule, walked arm-in-arm with bogey round the links. But to-day a strange upset of form took place, for while Lord Peebles seemed unable to hit any ball in the requisite direction or with the requisite force, Arthur Whately, by virtue of the inscrutable laws that govern golf, performed with incredible excellence, and not unnaturally concluded that blackmailing is very good for the eye. Not for years had he felt so keenly the zest and ecstasy of living, and while watching his unfortunate opponent digging his ball out of tussocks of rank grass and eviscerating bunkers, he planned many similar adventures for the future. He felt as if he had awoke at last to his true nature; by accident he was a millionaire and the architect of his own colossal fortune, but by instinct and birth he seemed to be an æsthetic criminal. And the discovery had come upon him, though late, yet not too late. There might be many ecstatic years in store for him yet.

The days of that enchanted week passed slowly, and each moment that brought him nearer Friday morning, when he would don his atrocious disguise and visit Martin's Library, brought him no nearer any firm conjectures as to what he should find there. It so happened that he met his victim several times in the course of the week, and if, as on the occasion of their golf match, his mental and physical aspect seemed to indicate that he would assuredly lack the courage of the archdeacon and obediently pay his fine, on other occasions he showed a calmness and control that was consistent with more aggressive proceedings. To Whately's knowledge he transacted during that week a very difficult and intricate financial undertaking that caused certain bankers in Berlin to curse his acumen, and later he won the Mid-Surrey monthly medal, which looked as if his aberration had been only temporary. And the uncertainty and suspense thrilled and fascinated his persecutor.

It was about twelve o'clock on the Friday morning that a dejected four-wheeler stopped opposite Martin's Library, and the ambulatory population of Wardour Street, accustomed to all manner of eccentricities, looked with wonder at the garish figure that emerged. Two hours before, Arthur Whately had set off from Park Lane with a small portmanteau and had driven to the Charing Cross Hotel, having adjusted moustache and imperial with the aid of a small looking-glass in the cab, and had taken a room for a widower of the name of George Loring, paying for one night's habitation. There he had effected his change of clothes and left the valise containing the outer garments of Arthur Whately, at present in a state of suspended existence.

He entered the library with a strutting martial air, and, as once before, the comfortable old lady looked up from her knitting and asked how she could serve him.

"I have called for letters and parcels for Mr. George Loring," said Whately in a falsetto voice, which was the result of diligent practice. But a glance at pigeon-hole L showed him that it was empty....

"Yes, parcel and letter for Mr. George Loring," said the old dame, "but the parcel was too big to put in the pigeon-hole, let alone

25

lifting it. So I put them together somewhere. Deary me, now, where was it?"

"This is a strange way to conduct a public library," said Whately, forgetting all about the assumed falsetto, "that the librarian should not know where she has deposited the property of her subscribers. Mr. Martin would be far from pleased. I am pressed for time, madam. Business in the city——"

The old lady turned slowly round and beamed on him.

"And if I wasn't sitting on it all the time," she said, "just for safety, as you may say. There, young man, you'll find it heavy, and there's sixpence to pay."

"A most reasonable charge, madam," said Whately. "And—and can you tell me who left the parcel—what he looked like?"

She nodded at him.

"Such a fur coat I never see," she said, "and his motor fair stopped the traffic. I didn't take much account of his face, though I would swear to a beard."

"A shrewd observer!" said Whately in his most genial tones, and staggering out of the shop with his parcel, deposited it on his own toe as he stepped into the cab. The pain was severe, and for the moment damped his ecstasy and caused him a loss of self-control.

"Charing Cross Hotel, you old idiot!" was his unjustifiable direction to his cabman.

As he drove there he tore open the note. It ran as follows:

> "Dear Sir,—You have me completely in your power, and I send the money you demand. Kindly forward me at once the documentary evidence you speak of.
>
> Faithfully yours,
> Peebles."

Again he felt vaguely disappointed. The fish had given him less play than he hoped; he had but towed its sulking carcass to land. But, then, he did not know that there followed him, threading the intricacies of traffic close behind him, a taxicab in which was sitting a quiet-looking gentleman with pince-nez. Its destination also appeared to be Charing Cross Hotel.

The hall porter opened the door of his cab, and Whately indicated his parcel.

"Move that into the bureau, if you will be so kind," he said. "It contains a—a model, a metal model, and is heavy. I am going upstairs to change my clothes, and will be down again in ten minutes."

Less time than that was sufficient for him to resume the habiliments of Arthur Whately, and stow the apparel of the vanished George Loring in his bag. His imperial and moustache he still wore, for it was his intention to use depilatory measures in the cab which took him back to Park Lane lest the complete transformation might prove too staggering for the hall porter. This time he himself took the parcel, a wooden box, clearly, wrapped up in brown paper, to his cab, put it, not on his own foot, but on the seat opposite, and genially told the driver to take him to Park Lane. Close behind him followed the taxicab containing the gentleman with pince-nez, modest, secluded, and unobserved. And from a few doors off he saw Mr. Arthur Whately, burdened with the parcel he had brought from Wardour Street, stagger into his own house. His business seemed to be not yet finished, for having seen him home he drove back to an office in the City, and was at once taken in to see the head of the firm. His interview lasted about half an hour, and he left behind him when he went a very much astonished gentleman, over whose mobile face a succession of queer secret smiles chased one another like gleams of sunshine on a cloudy day. Excellent business man though he was, he gave for the rest of the day but a tepid attention to his work.

Arthur Whately meantime was closeted with his gold. With the aid of a pair of nail-scissors (for prudence counselled secrecy) he succeeded in raising the lid of the box, and found it packed inside with smooth, discreet little sausages of white paper. A couple of these he unfolded, and from each flowed out a stream of clinking sovereigns. In each were a round hundred, and the little sausages were twenty in number. He put a liberal handful of gold in his pocket; he locked the rest into the safe that stood in the bedroom. And those two thousand pounds were somehow sweeter to him than his whole unnumbered fortune: they seemed to him the reward of a cleverness that was more peculiarly his own than that which had amassed so huge a harvest in South African mines and American options. They were doubly sweet, for they were both the fruit of secret criminal processes and had been wrung by terror out of his friend.

He lunched out that day. His soul basked in the heaven of high animal spirits which had so long been lost to him, and in the stimulus which the last week had brought to him he felt like a peri who had regained Paradise. Perhaps reaction would come, but for the present it held aloof, and in case it did he could always, as he phrased it to himself as he walked lightly down Bond Street, apply the squeezers again to poor Peebles. The vocabulary as well as the spirits of a schoolboy had come back to him; long-forgotten slang tripped off his tongue, and he examined shop-windows with eager enthusiasm. There was a beautiful Charles II. rat-tail spoon in a shop of old silver, and he entered and bought it, paying for it on the spot with fifteen of his newly acquired sovereigns. The purchase gave him more pleasure than any he had made for years: it was the fruit of his splendid stroke of blackmail.

At another shop he bought for five pounds a charming figure of a seagull in Copenhagen china. Lord Peebles had a collection of this pale fabric, and his friend felt it would be a privilege to add to it. That also was paid for in gold, and after he had left each shop a quiet man entered and conferred privately with the proprietor, leaving a companion outside, who strolled after the millionaire.

Returning home, he sent out a number of invitations for a dinner party in ten days' time. A royal princess had intimated that she would like to dine with him that night, and he included in his invitations Lord and Lady Peebles, both of whom were snobs of "purest ray serene." Later on he would ask them again to some similar function, for he felt that two such invitations would make full compensation for the anxiety he had caused. He did not regard the bagatelle of gold; that meant nothing to either of them. Then after an hour with his beautiful collection of Greek coins he dressed and went out to dinner.

Lord Peebles was of the party, and the two cut into a table of bridge afterwards, and played for a couple of hours, with luck distinctly against the newly created peer. Generally his losses caused him exquisite agony: being very rich, he could not bear to be ever so little poorer. But to-night he laid down a couple of ten-pound notes with a smile.

"I pay you, my dear Whately," he said, "fourteen pounds, is it not? I wonder if you can give me six."

Whately could and did.

"You have had the worst of luck," he observed genially, "but it's only a game. By the way, I hope I shall see you and your wife to dinner on the 23rd. I sent you an invitation this evening."

Lord Peebles took up his change and looked rather carefully at each sovereign in turn, as if to question its genuineness.

"Curious thing," he said, "each of these sovereigns is marked. There is a small capital 'P' scratched on the field in front of St. George."

He passed one over to Whately, who felt as if some warning whistle had sounded remotely in his ears. But he contrived to speak in his natural voice, and got up.

"I see," he said; "I wonder what that means. Bates gave me them just before I came out."

"Indeed," said Lord Peebles negligently. "Yes, the 23rd would be delightful. Are you going?"

"Yes, I think I shall be off," said Whately.

He drove back to Park Lane, and without setting the pleasant peal of electric bells in the fan-room, went straight to his bedchamber and got out the box which had thrilled him with such exquisite pangs of pleasure that morning. He stripped the paper off sausage after sausage of gold, until his bed was piled with the precious metal. And on each shining disc the same ominous discovery met his eye: just in front of St. George's head on every one that he took up was scratched a small capital "P."

He slept far from well that night, for his mind, spinning madly like a whirling top, came into collision with a series of hard angles of uncomfortable circumstances. He told himself that it was inconceivable that his friend should have suspected him of the odious crime of blackmailing, but his friend evidently when paying the ransom had taken steps to trace its destination, with a view to the apprehension of the criminal. By a most strange coincidence it was he, Arthur Whately, who had supplied him with a clue, though he had had the presence of mind to say that Bates had given him these six pieces of evidence.... Then with a pang of alarm that made him sit bolt upright in bed, he remembered that there were four more of them in the shop where they sold china cats and seagulls, fifteen more in the silversmith's, where he had bought the Charles II. spoon, and two others in the hair-cutting establishment in St. James's Street, where he had so lightly purchased a safety-razor and a small indiarubber sponge. At all costs he must repossess himself of these, and how was that to be done? In this short summer night there was scarcely time, even if he had had the tools, to make a series of single-handed burglaries, yet if he did not get those accursed sovereigns back, he was letting the tap of evidence drip and drip and drip. What, again, was the use of those nineteen hundred and odd sovereigns on his bed if he could not put them in circulation without multiplying the evidence already in existence? The suspense of the last week, it is true, had been thrilling and delicious, but it appeared now that there were at least two sorts of suspense, and the other, though quite as thrilling, was not so pleasant. Sinking into an uneasy slumber, he dreamed of skilly.

Haggard and unshaven (in spite of the new safety-razor), he was in Bond Street next morning early, with cheque-book and bank-notes in his pocket. The shop that dealt in old silver was only just open, and he went hurriedly in.

"I am Mr. Whately," he said, "Mr. Whately, of Park Lane. Dear me, that is a very pretty tankard. A hundred pounds only! Please send it round to me to No. 93. The fact is, a rather curious thing has happened. I bought a Charles II. spoon here yesterday afternoon and paid for it in sovereigns. For certain curious, I may say family, reasons, I very much want those sovereigns back again. There are sentimental associations with them, you understand. Could you kindly let me have them back and take my cheque or bank-notes in exchange?"

The shopman laughed.

"Well, sir, a very curious thing happened here too," he said brightly. "You had hardly left the shop when a gentleman came in and asked if I could let him have any change for some bank-notes. There were your sovereigns lying in the till, and I gave him them all. I offered him five more as well, but after examining those he said he did not want more than fifteen."

Arthur Whately couldn't suppress a slight groan.

"That was very precipitate of you," he said. "What was the gentleman like? Was it—a stout, dark-faced gentleman with yellowish hair and—and probably a fur coat?"

"No, sir, a clean-shaven gentleman with a sharp sort of face."

"Not Peebles," said Whately to himself, as he skimmed out of the shop. "It may still only be a coincidence."

The shop of Danish china was open, and again he told his lame and unconvincing tale. Here again the fever for gold had run riot yesterday afternoon, and a gentleman with a big moustache had taken five sovereigns and left a bank-note. And his scuttling footsteps took him to the aseptic hairdresser's.

"I am fighting single-handed against a positive gang of these wretches," was his bitter comment.

But the aseptic hairdresser's was still shut, and after ringing several wrong bells belonging to different floors, he gave up in despair and went home to the mocking splendour of No. 93. A fresh-faced stable-boy was just laying down the straw in the street, whistling as he plied his nimble pitchfork. Whately wondered whether he would ever whistle again.

For an hour he sat there lost in a scorching desert of barren thought. Visions of oakum and broad arrows flitted through his disordered mind, and every now and then he came to himself as some fresh circumstance of dawning significance rapped on his brain.

Once he hurried upstairs, remembering that the awful attire of George Loring still lurked in a locked cupboard of his bedroom, and he took the criminal's coat and stuffed it in the fire in his sitting-room, with the intention of burning all that costume which had seemed so exquisitely humorous. But the coat seemed

30

impervious to flames, and it was not till a quarter of an hour later that he came downstairs again with roasted face. Even then there were trousers and shirt and patent leather boots to get rid of, and trouser buttons and the base metal of his gorgeous tie-pin would be found amid the ashes. And even when it was all done, he would only have destroyed one thread of evidence, leaving a network of imperishable circumstance unimpaired.

Truly there was a dark side to the game on which he had so lightly embarked, which the callous world could not ever so faintly appreciate, or would probably but imperfectly sympathize with even if it did.

But for the sake of saving his sanity he had to occupy himself with something, and after vainly attempting to follow the meaning of a leader in the Times, he began reading, purely as a "sad narcotic exercise," the Agony column. And then he fairly bounded from his seat, as the following met his eye:

"To George Loring. A packet of marked sovereigns, twenty-eight in number, will be forwarded to the above-named at any address or given to a messenger who hands to Mr. Arthur Armstrong (resident for this day only at the Charing Cross Hotel) the sum of £4,000 (four thousand) in bank-notes or bullion."

He groaned aloud.

"It spells beggary," he said to himself, "but I must have those sovereigns. But let me see first whether twenty-eight is the full tale of them," and he snatched up a piece of paper and wrote:

$$
\begin{array}{lr}
\text{To Lord Peebles} & 6 \\
\text{Silver Shop} & 15 \\
\text{Copenhagen China} & 5 \\
\text{Haircutting place} & \underline{2} \\
& 28
\end{array}
$$

and at that, in spite of the ruinous expense, his heart bounded high within him. It was wiser not to appear himself (he had, so it struck him, appeared rather too frequently already), and sending for his secretary he scrawled a cheque for £4,000, and bade him have it changed into bank-notes and take it at once to the Charing Cross Hotel. There he would ask for a certain Mr. Arthur Armstrong, who would give him a packet containing twenty-eight marked sovereigns.

"It concerns a widowed aunt of mine," he added, "and I cannot tell you more. Speed and secrecy are essential to save her from ruin."

The zealous secretary was back within an hour, and with a sob of relief Whately, when he was alone, opened the packet he brought. Next moment with a hollow groan he spilled the contents all over the table. The sovereigns were marked indeed, but each of them had neatly incised on it, not a "P" but an interrogation mark. Back went the zealous secretary again to explain that these were not the right ones, and, if necessary, to implore Mr. Arthur Armstrong, for the sake of his mother, to give up the others. He was soon home again with the news that Mr. Arthur Armstrong had already quitted the hotel, leaving no address.

Later on that abject day there arrived a note from Lord Peebles, saying that it was doubtful whether he could come to dinner on the 23rd. Events, at present private, might render it impossible. But he would like a game of golf at Richmond next day if Whately was at liberty.

Again this proposal of a recreation detestable in itself and intolerable to one with shaking hand and trembling knees! Yet if Peebles had proposed a game of leap-frog Whately could not be so imprudent as to refuse, for at all costs he must keep up friendly relations. He had half a mind (but not the other half) to tell his friend that it was indeed he who had attempted to blackmail him, for a joke, and that the retaliation was getting beyond one. But it was not certain as yet that a confession was necessary; there was nothing to show that Lord Peebles had identified him with George Loring. It looked like it; it looked uncommonly like it, but what proof had he? Whately, it is true, had given him half a dozen of his own marked sovereigns, and no doubt Peebles knew that he had expended others on Copenhagen china, Charles II. silver and American articles of toilet, but that was all. It certainly was a good deal——

There is no need to dwell on his further anguish. The game of golf was a cruel parody of sport, and Peebles was in his most pompous mood, speaking of the House of Lords as "we." At other times he spoke with strange persistence of the horrors of English prisons, and mentioned that he had been appointed visitor to Wormwood Scrubs. Whately did not know with any accuracy where that was, but Peebles described exactly how you could get to it. Long-sentence men stayed there.

Another day he would see or think he saw a stranger watching his house. Sometimes a second would join him, and if one was clean-shaven and the other had a moustache, Whately's heart would leap to his throat and creakingly pulsate there. His appetite failed him; his brushes were full of shed hair; dew suddenly broke out on his forehead. And seven dreadful days passed.

Then the end came.

Lord Peebles telephoned to him asking if he could see him on important business, and of course a welcoming affirmative was given.

"You appear far from well, my dear Whately," he said, looking anxiously at him, "far from well. A little dieting, do you think, a little regular work, a little abstention from alcohol?"

Whately gave a haggard glance out of the window. It was a foggy morning, and in the roadway he could but faintly distinguish a large black van which had approached noiselessly over the straw and now stood there. At that sight there was no longer any doubt in his mind that Peebles had adopted the ruthless archidiaconal attitude towards blackmailers, and was going to have him arrested. But harassed and unnerved as he was by a succession of sleepless nights and nightmare days, he still despised and refused to parley with the conventional narrowness of his accuser. Yet Lord Peebles still wore his pleased and secret smile, and it was not good manners to look like that in the act of committing a friend to a convict prison. Whately drew himself up and spoke with wonderful steadiness and dignity.

"I see it's all up!" he said, "and that I shall soon get all the things you so feelingly recommend. But after all I had a perfectly amazing week when I waited for your answer. I don't deny that you have given me an awful week, too, or that there are many rather cheerless weeks in front of me. It's no use my attempting to explain; you would never understand. Your soul doesn't rise above sovereigns."

Lord Peebles came a step nearer him, looking vexed.

"For those remarks," he said, "you deserve to be treated as—as you deserve. You don't seem to realize that I have had a week of the most thrilling enjoyment. You think that nobody has a sense of humour except yourself. That attitude of yours has often annoyed me, for I have a remarkably keen one, and for pure æsthetic pleasure I have just had the week of my life. The fact that it was sugared with revenge hardly enhanced it at all, nor did the fact that whereas you got two thousand pounds out of me, I got four thousand out of you. You have been like a monkey dancing on a hot plate. I have been the hot plate."

Whately was scarcely listening; with chattering teeth he looked at the huge ominous van in the street, and Lord Peebles followed his gaze.

"You deserve that that van should be Black Maria," he went on in injured tones, "to take you to Wormwood Scrubs, where I am visitor."

"Is—isn't it?" asked Whately.

Lord Peebles peered into the fog.

"The harmless, necessary pantechnicon," he said.

Then he subsided into a chair and his great bulk began to shake with spasms of ungovernable laughter. And gradually the colour came back to Whately's face, and shortly after an uncertain smile hovered on his mouth.

"And is it all over?" he asked.

Lord Peebles took a small sausage of sovereigns out of his pocket.

"I brought these along with me," he said, "please count them; they are all marked, and there are twenty-eight of them. I will exchange them with those you possess marked with an interrogation point."

"You shall!" said Whately. "God bless you!"

"I was not certain, when I came here," continued Lord Peebles, disregarding this interruption, "whether I should put you out of your suspense or not, but your haggard and emaciated appearance, my dear fellow, decided me. Besides, I am two thousand pounds to the good, or nearly so, for I owe some small sum to detectives. If I did not have mercy on you, you would probably be too unwell to give your party for the princess on the 23rd, and I should be sorry to miss that. Otherwise I might have let you have a week or so more of excitement. I had several other little notions, little tunes for you to dance to."

"You shall sit next her," said Whately with quivering lips.

GENERAL STORIES

THE DANCE ON THE BEEFSTEAK

This Midsummer day, the early hours of which were bathed in so serene a sunshine, has ended in storm and hurly-burly. Only this morning the general outlook was as unclouded as is now the velvet blue of the star-scattered Italian sky, but this evening our very souls are driven like dead leaves before a shrivelling blast. Nature, unsympathetic, indifferent, still holds on her great unruffled courses; the stars wheel, the north wind blows lightly from across the gulf; the little ripples shed themselves in lines of phosphorescent flame; Naples lies a necklace of light on the edge of the sea, the loveliness of the Southern night is undiminished. But Mrs. Mackellar has danced on the beefsteak, and she has dismissed Seraphina.

To the dweller in cities or other light-minded and populous places this may appear but the most farcical of tragedies, worthy of no more than the scoffing laugh of a passer-by. But such do not know Mrs. Mackellar, nor Seraphina, nor life in Alatri. For in Alatri as a rule nothing happens—certainly nothing unpleasant—our lives are as smooth as the halcyon summer seas, and it will, I am afraid, be impossible to give to any but the most imaginative reader an adequate idea of the devastating nature of the catastrophe.... It will be necessary in any case to recount in brief the events of the last twenty-four hours.

Yesterday afternoon we were all en fête; Mrs. Mackellar gave a party for two reasons, either of which was amply justifiable. The first was that the engagement of Seraphina her cook to Antonio her man-servant was definitely sanctioned by her, and so made food for public rejoicing; the second that Seraphina had been with her as cook for an entire year. Now in Alatri servants do not, as a rule, stop with Mrs. Mackellar more than a few weeks. Then they leave. There is no dissatisfaction expressed and no public quarrel. They just lose their nerve and go away. But the days had added themselves into weeks, and the weeks into months, and before any of us knew where

35

we were, Seraphina had been a year with Mrs. Mackellar. Hence the party.

There were in fact two parties, for Seraphina and Antonio entertained their friends in the kitchen, while Mrs. Mackellar received on the house-roof. She is an immense Scotchwoman, broad in bosom and in accent, and feels the heat acutely. Consequently when I received an invitation for four o'clock on an afternoon in the middle of June, it was clear that she must have a real desire to celebrate the event.

The Duchess of Alatri—to her more intimate friends, Bianca— came with me by special invitation. Her Grace is a huge white Campagna sheep-dog, so tall that she can, when sitting down, put her chin on an ordinary dining-room table and eat your bread when you are not looking. At rest she resembles a large rug (and as such is not infrequently trodden on), and when in motion she resembles nothing that I have ever seen. Her sole method of progression is a trot; she never walks, and she cannot gallop, but the trot varies from a pace so surprisingly slow that she appears only to be marking time, to that of the passage of an express train. The other day she was investigating interesting smells in the piazza, when out for a walk with me, and so got left behind. I did not miss her till I was some half-mile away, and looking round saw a distant white speck where the road leaves the town. I whistled shrilly on my fingers, and without appreciable interval she was with me. She belongs not, alas, to me, but to an American, who has left the enchanted island for the summer (unless perhaps it is more just to say that he belongs to her), and committed Her Grace to my care. Her passions are being combed, cheese and dancing.

This latter I discovered by a happy accident. For the first afternoon that she was with me she was very sorrowful, and though I ran up the Stars and Stripes on the flagstaff, instead of the Union Jack, wondering if this would give her the thrill of home, she remained dispirited. But shortly before going to bed, hoping in some vague way to cheer her, and being myself futile, I danced round her, snapping my fingers. The effect was magical. The rug shuffled swiftly to its feet, and began gambolling. She jumped in the air, she turned briskly round and round, she took little leaps with her head down like a bucking pony, she upset a small table on which was standing an open tin of biscuits, and scarcely pausing to sweep up the greater part with her tongue she lurched heavily into an oleander-tub on the veranda, snapping the shrub off short. And when, about ten minutes later, I sank into a chair breathless and exhausted, the Duchess was herself again. Only once when passing her old home did she show any desire to remain there, and even then I had but to execute two fantastic steps down the path, when she gave a sort of choking cry, her apology for a bark, and came after me behaving like a rocking-horse.

So Bianca and I went up the steep path to Mrs. Mackellar's shortly after four yesterday afternoon. She lives in a stucco castle with battlements. There was already a tarantella going on in the kitchen—Seraphina is a notable dancer—and Bianca brightened up. She said, "This is the place for me," and brushing rudely by me trotted down the back-stairs and I saw her no more. So I went alone to the house-roof.

"All Alatri" was there, perspiring under an Oriental awning, which Mrs. Mackellar had put up for the shelter of her guests. It seemed calculated to concentrate the heat of the sun, and to exclude all air. The German doctor, who has not left the island, even to go to Naples, for nine years, was talking the native dialect to a Swedish painter; the mysterious Russian widow who plays picquet every evening with her man cook was chattering voluble French to a circle of mixed nationality; and Mrs. Mackellar, resplendent in tartan, was treating bewildered listeners to the Peebles speech. The ices had transformed themselves into a delicious fruit-cream, and the sugar was melting like tallow off the cakes. We indulged in the usual topics, the impossibility of leaving Alatri that summer, the promise of a fine vintage, the apocryphal shark three metres long, whose dorsal fin had appeared only a few yards from the shore of the Bagno, the iniquity of servants in general, and the conspicuous virtue of Seraphina.

Mrs. Mackellar, in the democratic spirit that helps to make Alatri so wildly interesting, had added that when the feasting in the kitchen was over, and when no one wanted to eat more ice-cream on the house-top, the party from below should join the party up above, so that we all should be one on this happy occasion.

Accordingly, after a while she leaned over the battlements of her castle, gave a loud war-cry, and up came Seraphina's party. She led the way with her promesso, in a state of high hilarity, and all the servants of all Mrs. Mackellar's guests brought up the rear. There was no blushing possible, for everybody was scarlet with heat already, and we split off into domestic groups. Francesco sat by me, and began to tell me why nobody went to mass on this name day of St. John the Baptist. This was interesting, but on the other side of me was Seraphina discussing trousseau with her mistress, and the loud arresting Italian of Mrs. Mackellar only permitted me to give half an ear to the story of San Giovanni. However, Francesco could tell me about it again to-morrow, in less distracted conditions, and when the discussion about the trousseau was over (I had gathered several plums, un tartano di Edinborgo being a fine one) I left.

Next morning I had a crisis of affairs. In Alatri, if one has anything whatever that must be done, it, like the grasshopper, becomes a burden. But I had several things that must be done, and I was nearly crushed by the prospect. In the first place breakfast was ready before I was out of bed and I therefore had to postpone shaving till afterwards. This alone would have made a troublesome morning, but this was far from all. On coming down I found two letters that had to be answered, one (and I was sorry for my sins) containing an uncorrected proof, and while I was still prostrate from the blow Francesco came in with household accounts. These, for the sake of morality, I make it a rule to check (Francesco's addition is always right, mine always wrong), and thus it stood to reason that I should not be able to start down to the sea to bathe till nearly eleven. However, "no Briton's to be baulked," and I marched manfully across the thirsty desert of affairs.

An hour in the sea and the consciousness of duty done restored equanimity, and when after lunch Francesco brought me coffee on to the veranda and seemed disposed to linger, I remembered the half-heard story of San Giovanni.

"Tell it me again," I said, and Francesco told it.

"The signor must know," he said, "that in Italy there are many unbaptized children, and if San Giovanni came to earth like the other saints on his name-day, he would be furious at such neglect, and burn up the earth with fire. God knows this, and, being unwilling that we should all suffer, he sends San Giovanni to sleep the day before his name-day, so that he sleeps for eight days. Then when he wakes up he says to God, 'Is not my name-day yet?' And God replies, 'O San Giovanni, you have been to sleep and your name-day is over while you slept. It will not come again for another year.' Thus it is that we do not go to mass on the day of San Giovanni, for where is the use if he be asleep? But the priests say— Ah! has not the Signor heard the news?" he broke off suddenly and excitedly.

"News! I have heard no news."

"How can I have forgotten? The Signora Mackellar has danced on her beefsteak, and Seraphina is dismissed. So when will she marry Antonio?"

Now the two things a Southern Italian loves best are telling a story and causing a sensation. And it was with the most exquisite enjoyment that Francesco continued, for both were here combined.

"The market boat came in from Naples this morning," he said, "and on it was a fine beefsteak for the Signora. Salvatore, the

38

carrier, took it up, and it so was that both the Signora and Seraphina were on the house-roof when he came, and the Signora was ordering dinner. And it seems she was angry, so said Salvatore, at the cost of the ice cream yesterday. So he was ordered to bring up the beefsteak, and the Signora smelt it, and said it was not food for dogs. And Salvatore—you know he is a sharp fellow—he replied 'Indeed it is not food for dogs,' meaning thereby——"

"Yes, I understand," I interrupted.

Francesco was getting gesticulative, and he went on with the fire of a prophet.

"Then gave the Signora the beefsteak to Seraphina," he cried, "and said 'Smell it thou also.' And Seraphina, having smelt it, said, 'Signora, it seems to me very good.' At that the Signora turned on her like one goaded and cried—'Thou too art in the plot to cheat me! To-day thou art no more my cook'; and as for the beefsteak—ecco! And she threw it down, and danced upon it with both feet together, so that the roof trembled. Also she said many strange words in her own tongue."

And Francesco, like a true artist, did not linger after making his point, but turned on his heel, resisting even the temptation to talk it all over, and went into the house.

Here was a bolt from the blue! The summer had begun, there would be no fresh visitors to Alatri till the winter, and Seraphina would be out of place all these months. Antonio's wages would not keep them both, if Seraphina was out of place, and had to pay for her board and lodging with some friend, and who knew whether Mrs. Mackellar's wrath would not spread like a devouring flood, and overwhelm Antonio also? Nothing was more likely, for I remembered how on the dismissal of Mrs. Mackellar's last cook, her washing had been withdrawn from its customary manipulator, simply because she was the cook's cousin by marriage. How then should Seraphina's promesso escape? Already the smell of the marriage bake-meats was in the air: they were like to eat them with a sauce of sorrow. To attempt to interfere or to reason with Mrs. Mackellar was out of the question. Her nose would go in the air, and she would say "Hoots!" Those who had heard Mrs. Mackellar say "Hoots" seriously, knew what fear was.

Two days have passed after that terrible dance of death on the house-roof, two days of paralysed inaction. There was of course no other subject in the mouth of the folk, and grave groups formed and reformed in the piazza and at Morgano's, and looked at the question this way and that like impotent conspirators wanting a plan of action. I happened to be sitting at that café before dinner on the second evening, and we were shaking our heads over it all when

Mrs. Mackellar herself came snorting and stamping round the corner. Like children detected in some forbidden ecstasy, we all sank into silence. She did not even sit down to enjoy her vermouth, but sipped it standing, with loud, angry sucking noises, as if it was the life-blood of Seraphina.

We all froze under the contempt of her blue tremendous eye, and then, most unfairly, she singled me out, and pointing the finger of scorn, hissed at me:

"I ken fine what the hale clamjanfry of ye has been talkin' about," she said, or words to that effect, and, without deigning to translate, this tempestuous lady swept on her course. She stepped so high in her indignation that the Duchess of Alatri, lying for coolness' sake on the pavement outside, thought that Mrs. Mackellar was dancing for her, and rising to her feet, Her Grace trod a circular Saracenic measure. Hardly pausing to swing a string-bag containing such comestibles as would be easily rendered palatable without the aid of a cook, Mrs. Mackellar turned to me again, and spoke in English in order that I might understand.

"If I were you," she said, "I should be ashamed to keep a dog that eats as much as six Christians, I'll be bound, be they Presbyterians or Roman Catholics."... Even as she spoke, who should come by but Seraphina herself? Though she had been hounded out of the Casa Mackellar only yesterday, with every circumstance of ignominy and Highland expressions, Seraphina, sunny and incapable of rudeness, gave her late employer a little smile, and a little obeisance, and said, "Buona sera, Signora!" Without the smallest doubt, Mrs. Mackellar returned that smile.

Now in Alatri, I must have you know, we are all great psychologists and students of character, and often talk about each other's actions and the gloomy traits of character exhibited therein, so that if you didn't know the seriousness of our aims, you might think we were gossips. But the true character of Mrs. Mackellar, who she is inside herself, had always puzzled everybody. No one could pull her together into any sort of personage who would pass muster in the wildest work of fiction as being conceivable. Why, for instance, did she who averted her chaste eye from the naked foot of a fisher-boy herself wear a tight silk bathing dress that reached not quite to her knees, and nowhere near her elbows? Was it, as Mrs. Leonards said, to display the atrocity of her own figure and thereby strengthen the rickety morality of the world in general? That could hardly be the case, since on other occasions she laced herself so tight, and wore such a killing hat, and so many Cairngorms and garnets, that she could not be found guiltless of making a public temptation of herself. Why, again, by what possible psychological consistency, did she revel in a game of poker and reserve the hostility of her finest colloquialisms for those who took tickets at a lottery? Why, again—but there is no use in multiplying her contradictions, for she entirely consists of them.

But the salient point on which every psychologist's eye was pensive to-day was why she had dismissed Seraphina after a year's harmonious co-operation for agreeing with Salvatore that a particular beefsteak did not stink. Never had she had such a servant as Seraphina, nor ever would, and well she knew it. Someone suggested that Mrs. Mackellar had determined to be an eater of uncooked foods, and others who remembered her welter of appreciation over an ordinary mutton cutlet, hardly troubled to reply to so inadmissible a conjecture. As we whittled away at her, the point of the discussion grew ever sharper, for why had she so clearly smiled in answer to Seraphina's greeting just now? The idea that the smile was purely sardonic had most supporters: one or two who kindly upheld the view that she was meaning to make it up with Seraphina were hissed down. The most obdurate alone stuck to it, and had the hardihood to bet five liras that this was the true explanation of the smile, and the readiness with which he found takers for that bet, caused him to experience an access of prudence, and to explain that he only meant to bet five liras all told, and not fifty. Alas!

No one was walking in my direction, and some half an hour later I went slowly home. Already I was beginning to regret that I had not taken more of those bets, for the shrewdest analyst of motive and psychology in Alatri had been bound to confess that Mrs. Mackellar's motives, like the path of the comets that should, according to all calculations, periodically destroy the earth, were, when all was said and done, completely unconjecturable. No application of logic, or reason, of the movements of heavy bodies seemed to apply to them, and for that very reason I had rejected the sardonic nature of that smile for Seraphina, and in the spirit of "Credo, quia impossible" had taken it for a smile of reconciliation. But I stood to win five liras, and who would quarrel with so enviable a conclusion, especially since it implied the re-installation of Seraphina? That was not a wholly altruistic consideration, for Leonard had said in so many words that Mrs. Mackellar would probably attempt to seduce Francesco away from my service with the lure of higher wages. That was a horrible thought, and I quickened my steps as I came near to my villa.

I heard bounding footsteps coming down the outside stairs from the front door into the garden, which could only be Francesco's, and I wondered whether he was prancing towards me in order to communicate his wonderful good luck in going as cook to Mrs. Mackellar, at twice the wages he at present received. I believed Mrs. Mackellar, like the prophet Habakkuk, to be "capable de tout," but I didn't really believe this infamy of Francesco. The garden door flew open, and he met me with a face of mourning.

"The Signora Mackellar," he cried, "walked up with Seraphina to her house. Through your telescope, signor, I saw them kissing and kissing on the roof. Dio! Why does a woman want to kiss a woman? There are many strange things in the world, signor. St. Peter, he had a wife, and also his wife had a mother, and one day—"

"Tell me about it after dinner," I said. "And bring up the bottle of English wine, the port wine, which I brought from Rome, I have won five liras, Francesco."

"Sissignor," said Francesco. "But the dinner is not yet quite ready, for I was watching with your telescope. Five liras!... There was once a man who backed five numbers at the Lotto, and behold they all came out even as he had backed them. He won a hundred thousand liras, and an estate in Calabria, and——"

"Dinner," said I, and Francesco ran to the kitchen.

I walked on air. Alone that evening I had had the courage of my opinion, and for once had divined Mrs. Mackellar's mind to the extent of backing my divination for five liras. That is a lot of money here—for a stall at the cinema (front row) only costs one.

THE ORIOLISTS

In spite of the unaccountable absence of a Cabinet Minister who should have sat between our hostess, Mrs. Withers and Miss Agnes Lockett, I felt that this luncheon-party must be considered as perhaps the most epoch-making that had, up to the present date, been enticed beneath that insatiably hospitable roof. Never had the comet-like orbit of our entertainer ascended quite so high towards the zenith.

With the negligible exception of myself, for whose presence there I shall soon amply account, there was not one among us, man, woman or child (for that prodigy on the fiddle, Dickie Sebastian, in his tight colossal sailor-suit, was of the company) whose name was not thrillingly familiar to the great percentage of the readers of those columns in the daily Press which inform us who was in the park on Sunday chatting with friends, or at the first night of the new play looking lovely.

Briefly to tell the number and brightness of these stars, there was a much be-ribanded general from Salonica, a girl just engaged to the heir of one of our most respectable dukedoms, a repatriated prisoner from Ruhleben, a medium possessed of devastating insight, a prominent actress from a révue, a lion hunter (not our amiable hostess, but a swarthy taciturnity from East Africa), and the adorable Agnes Lockett, lately created a Dame in the Order of the British Empire in connexion with Secret Service. She had just been demobilized, and, as she freely admitted, four years of conundrums and traps had undermined the frankness of her disposition. Schemes, plans, intrigues had become—for the moment—a second nature to her, and she was not happy unless she was laying a trap for somebody else, or suspecting (quite erroneously) that somebody was laying a trap for her. She had also become a smooth conversational liar. These things had not, it may be mentioned, affected her charm and her beauty.

Finally, there was myself, who had no claim to distinction of any kind beyond such as is inherent in living next door to Mrs. Withers and being honoured with the friendship of Agnes Lockett.

I had been asked by telephone just at luncheon-time, as I was in the act of sitting down to a tough and mournful omelette alone, and I naturally felt quite certain that I had been bidden to take the place of some guest (not the Cabinet Minister whom she still expected) who had disappointed Mrs. Withers at the last moment.

43

This was confirmed by the fact that she told me in her clearest telephone voice that I had promised to come to-day (which I knew was not the case) and that she was merely reminding me.

Obviously, then, she was in urgent need of somebody, for it was not her custom to "remind" all her expected guests at the very moment when they were due at her house, and my inclusion in this resplendent galaxy was certainly due to the convenient fact that, as I lived next door, I should not keep the rest of her party waiting.... It is, I hope, unnecessary to add that, with the unfortunate exception of myself, everyone present appeared in the informing pages of "Who's Who," so that his work and recreations were known to the reading public and would afford a good start to the medium in case we had a séance afterwards.

As the currents of conversation set this way and that, I was occasionally marooned in a backwater, and could hear what Mrs. Withers was saying to Agnes Lockett. The latter had been to the new play last night, and an allusion to it produced from our hostess a flood of typical monologue delivered in the judicial voice for which she was famous. She was a big lean woman who radiated a stinging vitality that paralysed the timid, and as she spoke, her eyes patrolled the distinguished table with the utmost satisfaction and controlled the service.

"Yes, Roland Somerville is marvellous in the part," she said, "and I told him he had never done a finer piece of work. But I thought Margaret had not quite grasped his conception of it. I went round, of course, to see her afterwards, and as she asked me what I thought I told her just that."

At this moment the telephone bell rang in the room adjoining, and Mrs. Withers, though continuing to analyse the play with her accustomed acumen (it had produced precisely the same effect on her as on the author of the critique in the Daily Herald) was a little distraite in manner till her parlour-maid communicated the message.

"Ah, that accounts for Hugh Chapel's absence, who was to have sat between us," she said to Agnes. "He was sent for to the Palace at a quarter-past one and is lunching there. And I ordered golden plovers especially for him. Hugh was at Priscilla's last night, looking very tired, I thought. You know him, of course, Miss Lockett?"

Agnes was looking a little dazed.

"Not yet," she said. "You asked me here to meet him."

Mrs. Withers made a gesture of impatience at herself. As a matter of fact she had, in asking Agnes Lockett, told her that Mr.

Chapel was coming, and in asking him, had told him that Miss Lockett was coming, thus hoping to kill two lions with one lunch.

"Of course! How stupid of me," she said. "Let us instantly arrange another day when you can both be here. Ah! do come to a little party I have on Thursday night. You will find Lord Marrible here too; he only got back from America ten days ago. Poor Jack! he had a terrible voyage, and he is such a bad sailor."

A look of slight astonishment came over Agnes's face, and remembering that she and Lord Marrible were old and intimate friends, I wondered whether she was surprised at this odd allusion to "poor Jack," for he was known to his intimate circle as John. Personally, I had had the felicity of making him and my hostess known to each other only a few days ago, and I too wondered a little at the speedy ripening of the acquaintanceship. I did not wonder much, for I knew Mrs. Withers's friendly disposition, and her tendency to allude to everybody by his Christian name. But at the moment a too rash act of swallowing on the part of Dickie Sebastian, who sat next me, made it my duty towards my neighbour to thump him on his fat back for fear that we should never hear his violin again, and my attention was distracted. When the fish-bone in question had been safely deposited on the edge of his plate, the telephone had again been ringing, and Mrs. Withers was retailing the reason for the absence of somebody called Humphrey, whose place I conjectured that I was now occupying.

During the discussion of the golden plovers provided for the absent Mr. Chapel, I became aware that Agnes Lockett was being drenched and bewildered with the flood of celebrated names that was playing on her as if from some fire-hose. Actors, authors, politicians, social stars, soldiers and sailors were deluging her, and, without exception, they had all been here, by their Christian names, last week, or at any rate were coming next week. Without exception, too, each of them had told Mrs. Withers in confidence what she repeated now to Agnes, knowing that it would go no farther. George had assured her of this, Arthur had hinted that, Jenny had thought this probable, Maudie had scouted the idea altogether, but however much they had disagreed, it was certain that they would all be here on Thursday evening, and Agnes could talk to them herself.

As I listened and looked, I saw that a species of desperation was seizing Agnes; she was finding the recital absolutely intolerable. Then an idea seemed to strike her, and looking round to catch a friendly eye, she caught mine, and spoke to me across the table.

"Have you seen Robert Oriole lately?" she asked in her delicious husky voice, that was so unlike the canary-tone of Mrs. Withers. But as she asked me this, she gave me a peremptory affirmative nod of which I could not miss the significance. I had never heard of Robert Oriole before, but I was certain that Agnes for some reason of her own insisted that I did know him, and accordingly I answered in that sense.

"We went to a play together last night," I said. At that precise moment, without a pang or a cry, Robert Oriole was born.

The new name, of course, instantly challenged Mrs. Withers's whole attention, as Agnes had designed that it should. Devoted as she was to old and celebrated names, new names that she had never heard of demanded the keenest of inquiries.

"Robert Oriole?" she said. "Who can it have been who was speaking of Robert Oriole the other day?"

Agnes's brilliant smile shot out and sheathed itself again.

"Ah! who isn't talking about Robert Oriole?" she said.

Much as Mrs. Withers liked appearing to know, she liked really knowing better, and surrendered.

"Was it Maudie?" she said. "I can't remember."

Once against a fresh current of conversation claimed my hearing, but rather uneasily, I could catch little enthusiastic phrases in what Agnes was saying to our hostess, and wondered if I should be called upon to invent anything more about this unknown personage. I could not, a moment ago, have done otherwise than I had done, for Agnes unmistakably commanded me to say that I either had or had not seen Robert Oriole lately. I was bound, at any rate, to convey in my answer that I knew him, and so it made no particular difference as to whether I had seen him lately or not, and I had said that we had been to the play together because I had to say something, and it was clearly much more suitable at Mrs. Withers's table to have done that sort of thing.

For all that I knew for certain there might be such a person; but I strongly suspected that there was something "back of" Robert Oriole, as our American friends say. What that was I could not conjecture, but I felt that I was acting under Agnes's direction in some Secret Service. My apprehensions increased as I heard his name figuring largely in her conversation, and were confirmed when, as she passed me on her way out, she said in a Secret Service undertone, not looking my way as she spoke:

"I shall come back with you almost immediately to your house, where we must have a serious conversation. For the present just keep your head, and remember that you know Robert intimately."

Half an hour later, accordingly, we were seated together in my house. The wall between mine and Mrs. Withers's drawing-room was not very thick, and the bountiful roulades of Dickie Sebastian's violin were plainly audible. Agnes, with a flushed face, like a child who had been triumphiantly mischievous, was sipping barley-water, for she felt feverish with imagination.

"So that's that," she said decisively, after a lurid sketch of what had happened, "and it's no use regretting it. We must save all our nervous force to go through with it."

"But what made you invent Robert Oriole at all?" I asked. "And then why have brought me in?"

"I couldn't help inventing him; it may have been demoniacal possession, or more likely it was a defensive measure against my going mad, which I undoubtedly should have done if Mrs. Withers had told me any more at all of what the great ones of the earth said to her in confidence. I should either have gone mad, or taken up a handful of those soft chocolates and rubbed her face with them. So I was obliged to know some glorious creature whom she didn't know. Obliged! She knew all the real ones, so I had to invent one. And does she really call them by their Christian names?"

"At a distance," said I.

"Then she ought to do it right. She called John Marrible, Jack, when nobody else had ever called him anything but John; and she spoke of you as Frank, whereas nobody had ever called you anything but Francis. In a week from now she will be calling my darling Robert Oriole, Bob. But he really is Robbie."

She put down her empty glass.

"That has calmed me," she said, "and so now we will get to business. I must repeat all that I told Mrs. Withers about Robbie. He is thirty-one, and is the most marvellous airman. He has yellow hair and blue eyes, and is like the Hermes at Olympia (she thought I meant Earl's Court). It is perfectly clear to Mrs. Withers's ferreting instincts that I am in love with him; about that you had better say, if she asks you, that we are merely great friends. He flew over to France about a week ago, piloting three Cabinet Ministers. They won't fly with any other pilot——"

"That won't do," said I. "I went to the play with him last night."

"I am not so stupid as to have forgotten that. He came back yesterday, and left for Paris again this morning, carrying a new cypher to the Embassy. He writes the most wonderful poems, which he composes as he is flying."

"She will ask for them at Bickers," said I.

Agnes thought intently for a moment.

"She may ask for them at Bickers," she said, "but she won't get them because they are not published. They are type-written on vellum, and he lets his friends see them. Perhaps we had better write one or two. What is vellum?"

My head whirled.

"But what is it all about?" I cried. "I don't mean his poems, but himself. Why are you making all this up?"

She looked at me as at a rather stupid child.

"Now, try to understand," she said. "I invented him originally to save myself from going mad, and we are making up delicious details about him to save ourselves from detection. We have both of us said that we know Robbie Oriole, and so we must know something about him; the more picturesque the better. We must be able (I have already done so and am telling you about it) to describe his appearance, his career, his tastes. If you told somebody you knew me, and couldn't say anything definite about me, people would think that you didn't know me at all. It's the same with Robert Oriole: we must be able to tell Mrs. Withers about him, and say the same thing. You would be quite despicable if, having said you knew a glorious creature like Robbie, it appeared as if you didn't. What a delicious name, too! It came to me in a flash, and I felt as if I had known him all my life. Fancy poor Mrs. Withers not knowing Robert Oriole! How bitter for her!"

"Ah, that's your real reason," said I. "Now you are serious."

"Not at all; that is the humorous side of it. It is to save ourselves that we have got to build up this solid, splendid presentment of our friend, and that is why I am telling you so carefully all I have said about him to Mrs. Withers. When it comes to your turn, as it undoubtedly will, to describe him further, you must always telephone to me at once what you have said.... Where had we got to? Oh, yes, his poems. Haven't you got some joyous little lyrics in your desk which are his? Or better, some vague morbid little wailings? Yes: that shall be the other side of Robbie, known only to his most intimate friends. To the world, which worships him, he is all sunshine and splendour, but to us, his dear friends, there is another side. His grandmother was a Russian, you must remember. I think I had better write the poems."

Somehow, incredibly to myself, the fascination of creating and building up and furnishing out a wonderful young man like this, who had no existence whatever, began to gain on me. Also, as Agnes had said, there was the instinct of self-preservation to spur on the imaginative faculty. There was also the pleasure of going one better than Mrs. Withers and of pretending to know intimately somebody whom nobody could possibly know.

"He is an orphan," I said. "And may he be an American? That would make him easier to get rid of than if he was English."

She shook her head.

"Orphan—yes," she said. "American—no. I can't bear American poetry, and I am sure I couldn't write it. But his parents lived in India. They are both dead, and he hasn't got any relations whatever, which makes him so romantic and accounts for that salt soul-loneliness in his poems. We will give him a home—just a little remote house by the sea, in Cornwall, near St. Ives, and the Atlantic rolls in on the beach in front of his grey-walled garden. His poems have the beat and rhythm of the sea——"

I sprang from my chair.

"Never, never!" I cried. "Mrs. Withers goes to St. Ives every summer."

"We will give him his home, then, in the Lake District," said Agnes thoughtfully. "There is no beat and rhythm of the sea in his poems, but the eternal melancholy of lakes and mountains. He must have somewhere pretty far off to go to when he is demobilized, as he will be almost immediately. His constant presence in London would lead to detection."

"Then why demobilize him?" I asked. "He can always be in France when it is convenient to us."

She was quite firm about this.

"It would never do," she said. "Mrs. Withers might make inquiries about him from some General in the Flying Corps. Indeed, I am almost sorry he was an airman at all, but that can't be helped now."

"He can go to India to see his parents' graves," said I, "if we want to get him out of the country for a long period."

"Yes, but he can't always be doing that. No one would make constant visits to India to see graves, however beloved were their occupants. Besides, it takes so long to go to India and back. He had much better be in his lovely home in the Lakes, and pay flying visits to London—here to-day and gone to-morrow—just giving us a new poem on vellum. That will be much more fun. Oh, a most important point! He must have some other friends besides us who are worthy of knowing him. John Marrible will be a nice friend for him; John will appreciate him. I will tell a few trustworthy people about Robbie, and you must do the same. We will call ourselves the Oriolists."

Mrs. Withers, of course, telephoned both to Agnes and to me to bring Robert Oriole to her party on Thursday evening; but there were so many new and resplendent friends there that she did not, except for a passing moment, regret the absence of that poetic airman, who was up in Westmorland. We had each of us provided him with two or three nice friends, who were in sympathy with him, but for some days after that he made no particular developments, and I began to think that, having served his purpose in protecting Agnes from insanity at Mrs. Withers's luncheon party, she was losing interest in her benefactor.

Then suddenly he burst out in renewed glory, for it came to Agnes's ears that in allusion to that same luncheon party Mrs. Withers had said to a mutual friend that dear Aggie had told her the most wonderful things about the Secret Service which she could not possibly repeat. This was sufficient to put new life and vigour into Robert Oriole. Agnes—who had never been called "Aggie" before—dragged me from the music-room at an evening party, where Dickie Sebastian was playing all that had ever been written for the violin, and recounted this outrage on the stairs.

"I have seen that woman three times," she said, "once when I was introduced to her, once when I lunched with her on the day Robbie was born, and once when I didn't bring him to her Thursday evening. And now I am 'Aggie,' and told her all about the Secret Service! I was almost inclined to let Robbie fade away again, but now she shall see. Heavens! There she is!"

Dickie Sebastian had ceased for the moment, and a few straggling couples emerged stealthily from the music-room, the first of whom was Mrs. Withers and Lord Marrible. Mrs. Withers would have been content, so it struck me, to kiss her hand to Agnes and pass on, for she had just been alluding to Aggie again, but since he came to a stop, she was obliged to wait also. He had already heard that he was "Jack," and his broad good-humoured face was a-chink with merriment as he spoke to my companion.

"Hallo, Aggie!" he said. "Been talking Secret Service on the stairs?"

"Mr. Goodenough and I," said Agnes carefully, "were waiting for Robbie. Do go and find him and bring him here by his golden hair."

"What, is Robbie here?" he asked, thereby conveying to me that he was an Oriolist. "I didn't see him. If Robbie is in a room it's not easy to miss him. I didn't even know he was in town."

"Of course he is," said Agnes. "Fancy not knowing if Robbie is in town. You might as well not know——"

"If the sun is shining," said I fervently.

"Quite. Lord Marrible, do go back and see if he isn't there. He and Mr. Goodenough and I are going back to his flat, and he is going to read to us. And then he is going to play the piano and then I suppose it will be time for breakfast before we have talked enough."

Mrs. Withers rose like a great salmon fresh from the sea, and rushed at this wonderful lure.

"I never heard anything so improper," she said. "You and—and Mr. Goodenough and Robbie Oriole! My dear Miss Lockett, who is chaperoning you?"

Agnes's face dimpled into the most delicious smile.

"Ah, we don't want any chaperon in the sunlight," she said, as John shouldered his way back into the music-room.

"Then let me drop you all at his flat," said Mrs. Withers. "I have my motor here, and I'm going home now. I am sure it is not out of my way."

Agnes nudged me with her elbow to indicate that I had to answer this.

"Robbie's car is here, many thanks," I said. "It's waiting for us. I saw it when I came in."

"And he plays the piano too?" asked Mrs. Withers.

Agnes laughed.

"Ah, I believe you know him all the time," she said, "and mean to repeat to him all the nice things that we say about him. You know him intimately, I believe, but if you tell me that he has already sent you those three sonnets he wrote as he flew to Cologne the other day, which he promised to read us to-night, I don't think I could bear it. Mr. Goodenough and I were promised the first hearing of them, and I believe he has sent them to you already."

"Indeed he hasn't," said Mrs. Withers in a social agony. "I really don't know Mr. Oriole, though I am dying to. I hoped you would have brought him to my little party last Thursday."

"Thursday, Thursday," said Agnes. "Yes, I remember: Robbie was up in the Lakes. Such a pity! He would have loved it, just the sort of party he adores."

Mrs. Withers's brow, that Greek brow with a fillet of crimson velvet across it, from which depended a splendid pearl, grew slightly corrugated, and made the pearl tremble. She prided herself on knowing all her engagements for a week ahead, but the recollection of them was difficult even to her.

"Sunday at lunch then," she said. "Will you both come and bring Mr. Oriole? Tell him how divine it would be if he would read us the Cologne sonnets."

"I'll tell Robbie," said Agnes, "but as for your chance of finding him disengaged, I couldn't promise anything. How his friends grab him when he appears! Ah, there's John—I mean Lord Marrible. Well?"

"He simply isn't here."

Agnes turned to me.

"Ah, now I remember," she said. "He told me that if he

couldn't get here by half-past ten, he wouldn't come at all, but would just send the car for us. What time is it now?"

"Eleven," said I.

"Oh, come quick, then," said she. "We've missed half an hour already."

Lord Marrible turned to Mrs. Withers.

"Well, you and I must console ourselves with supper," he said, "as Robbie hasn't asked us."

It was all very well for Agnes to say that we would go quickly, but Mrs. Withers just clung.

"But wouldn't he let me come too?" she said. "Mayn't I drop you at his door, Miss Lockett, and I would wait while you asked him if I might come in?"

Agnes's face dimpled again.

"My dear, if it were possible!" she said. "But with Robbie, however intimately you know him, you can't quite do that. You agree with me, Lord Marrible, I know. But if—if he gives me a copy of the Cologne sonnets, or lets me make one, you may guess to whom I will show it, unless he absolutely forbids me to show it to anybody. How tiresome it is that you don't know him!"

Mrs. Withers's pearl trembled again.

"Or if lunch on Sunday won't suit Mr. Oriole," she said, "I have got a few people to dinner on Tuesday and Wednesday, and if you would bring him then I should be more than charmed."

She remembered that her hospitable table was crammed on Wednesday, but there were two or three people who did not matter, and she could easily tell them that she expected them not that Wednesday but the next....

"Or if he would ring me up and suggest any time," she added.

Agnes laughed again.

"Too kind of you," she said, "and how rude of me to laugh! I laughed at the idea of Robbie telephoning. He can't bear any modern invention."

"But he is an airman, isn't he?" asked Mrs. Withers.

Never have I admired the quickness and felicity of the female mind more than at that critical moment which would have caused any mere man to stumble and bungle, and leave an unconvincing impression. There was not even the "perceptible pause" before Agnes answered.

"Ah, but Robbie says that flying is the effort to recapture bird-life of a million years ago," she said. "Birds and angels fly; it is not a modern discovery, but a celestial and ancient secret now being learned by us in our clumsy way. Robbie is lyrical about flying. But what bird or angel ever telephoned? Come, Mr. Goodenough, let us find that car."

"I forget how he reconciles himself to motoring," I said. I did not want to put Agnes in a fix, but only to delight my soul with another instance of feminine alacrity.

"He doesn't," said she brightly. "But then you have got to get to places quickly, and you can't fly through the streets of London yet."

"He sounds too marvellous," said Mrs. Withers ecstatically. "Sunday, Tuesday or Wednesday then. Any of them."

The discerning reader will easily have perceived by this time that both John Marrible and I were but wax in the inventive hands of Agnes, and flowed into the shapes that her swift fingers ordained for us. Occasionally we suggested little curves and decorations of our own, which she might or might not permit; but we had no independent will in the matter of Robert Oriole. She was the architect who built this splendid temple to an imaginary deity in whose honour Mrs. Withers, his deluded worshipper, swung unregarded censers of asparagus and salmon; at the most we were the cognisant choir and the organ....

During the next weeks which included the Sunday, Tuesday and Wednesday, on which Mrs. Withers's hospitality hungered for Robbie, the number of Oriolists greatly increased, and this secret society became positively masonic in clandestine fervour and fidelity. I could see at a glance, without grips of any kind, whether some friend or acquaintance who inquired after Robbie was a mason or not, for there was a gleeful solemnity about the initiated Oriolist which the profane crowd lacked.

There were many who now spoke of him, for Mrs. Withers in her frenzied efforts to capture him and show him at her house, asked everyone she met if he knew Robbie, and her large circle of uninitiated guests and acquaintances grew almost as excited about him as she. Those who knew, the initiates to whom these mysteries had been unveiled, answered casually enough when they were applied to by Mrs. Withers, but with that gleeful solemnity which revealed them to each other.

One morning Robbie would have been "stunting" over Richmond, or had lunched at the Ritz, or had been swimming in the Serpentine before breakfast, dropping in unexpectedly to entrance Agnes with the Brahms-Handel variations, or flying back to the Lakes in the afternoon, and the telephone messages that passed between the houses of the initiated were cryptic and yet comprehended utterances. Then on an ever-memorable day two

53

type-written copies of the Cologne sonnets circulated among the elect, and were secretly read in corners to the less fortunate.

On another day, Robbie must have called on me when I was out, for I found his card with his address, "Blaythwaite Fell," upon it, when I returned. He was not able to go to Mrs. Withers's house either on Sunday, Tuesday or Wednesday, but on Friday when she returned from a concert at which Royalty was present, she found a similar card with Agnes's on her table, and all the account her parlour-maid could give was that Miss Lockett had come to the door with "another gentleman" whom she had not seen before, for Lord Marrible had not previously come to the house.

Mrs. Withers, trembling with chagrin (for she had not been presented to Royalty at the concert, and had missed so much more by not stopping at home) telephoned to Agnes at once, only to learn that Robbie had that moment left by air for the Continent.

It is better to describe than to let the reader imagine for himself the state into which Mrs. Withers was brought during these days, because the imagination from excess of excited fancy would go wildly astray. For she did not grow one atom distraught or deranged; she became on the contrary more concentrated and businesslike than ever. She telephoned daily to Agnes and me to know whether Robbie—she always spoke of him now as Robbie—had got back from the Continent, and told us quite firmly that she would put off any other engagement in order to receive him at her house, or meet him at any other house.

But pending that consummation she remained as regular and as resonant as a cuckoo-clock, and struck her social hours with the same fluty regularity. She did not lose her appetite, or take to cocaine or opium-smoking or drown herself in the Thames, as imagination might expect, but kept her head, went up several times in an aeroplane in order to get used to it in case Robbie on his return suggested an expedition, and temporarily stole my copy of the Cologne sonnets.

I am not quite sure about this, but I missed them one afternoon when she had been having tea with me, and found next day that in my absence she had called and gone into my sitting-room to write a note to me. On my return I found the note prominently displayed, and the Cologne sonnets concealed in the blotting-book which I had unsuccessfully searched the evening before. The case is not proved against her, but certainly after that she could quote from the Cologne sonnets....

Then one morning, even while I was wondering what made Agnes keep Robbie so long on the Continent, I was rung up by her maid, and asked to go round to her at once. In answer to a further inquiry, "It's about Mr. Oriole, sir."

Full of some nameless apprehension, I started instantly on that bright June morning, feeling sure that at the least Robbie was the victim of some catastrophe. I was even prepared to learn that Robbie was dead, though I could not form the slightest conjecture as to what had led to this sudden demise. Or was Robbie engaged to be married, and had we to arrange about an elusive female of mysterious charm and antecedents?...

Well, it was not that, but it was even worse, for Agnes was engaged to John Marrible, who, with the selfishness of his sex, insisted that Robbie should die. He was with her and put his case. Agnes really seemed more taken up with Robbie than she was with him, and he demanded her undivided affection. For her part, she wanted to leave Robbie on the Continent for future emergencies, and promised not to think about him, but John objected to that. His head, he told us with a glance at her, was too full of other things, and he could not trust himself not to give the whole affair away by some inadvertence of happiness and pride. That glance settled it; Agnes took a half sheet of paper and wrote on it for a few minutes in silence.

"I will send it to the principal morning papers," she said, "and John shall pay for it. Listen! Will this do?

"ORIOLE.—On the 17th instant, very suddenly, at Mannheim, Robert, only son of the late William and Margaret Oriole, of Karachi, India. Age 31. Deeply lamented. No flowers.

'We will grieve not, only find
Strength in what remains behind.'"

That appeared next day, and I do not suppose that anybody lamented him more deeply than Mrs. Withers. She sent Agnes and me charming little notes of condolence and quoted from one of the Cologne sonnets, and asked if those touching lines in the notice of his death were by him.

A week or two later, I sat next Mrs. Withers at dinner, and Mr. Chapel was on her other side.

"Of course, you knew dear Robbie Oriole, Mr. Chapel," she said. "What a loss to poetry. Are not those Cologne sonnets the finest in your opinion since Keats? I was privileged to have a copy of them. You agree with me, do you not, Mr. Goodenough? Do you remember that marvellous one beginning, 'The clouds weep westwards under the scurrilous sky'?"

I hugged myself over not asking who had given her that privilege and sadly assented. She proceeded to talk to both of us, as her manner was at the dinner-table, with an intuition wrong in itself, but so excruciatingly right in general direction that it made me catch my breath.

"Yes, those sonnets," she said. "How amazingly feminine they are, both in their tenderness and bitterness. Or, perhaps, all I mean is that women will always appreciate them more than men. When I say them over to myself, as I so often do, I seem to see Robbie reading them to Aggie Lockett. Certainly, I thought, when she first spoke to me about Robbie, that she was absolutely devoted to him. Indeed, it gave me a little shock when I saw to-day that she was to marry Jack Marrible."

This was almost incredibly wonderful, for Mr. Chapel was one of our most fervent Oriolists. It was as full of points as a hedgehog; I could not count them all——

Then he turned on me the usual look of gleeful solemnity, and I knew we both wondered who would be the first to tell Aggie.

"Poor Robbie," he said. "I never knew anybody the least like him. He will be a sacred memory to us, will he not?"

Mrs. Withers shook her head, regretfully, smiling.

"And the last time he called," she said, "I was not at home. Of course, if he had only told me he was coming, I would have thrown over any engagement to be there, but, as you may not know, he would never use a telephone. It will always give me a little heartache to think that I was not there the last time."

Mr. Chapel let his eyes wander admirably before he caught mine again.

"It is only human to feel that," he observed in the best style.

IN THE DARK

Reginald Case, newly promoted to the rank of Captain in the 43rd Native Cavalry of the Indian Army, was picking his way back to his bungalow by the light of a somewhat ill-burning lantern from the regimental mess-room where he had dined. It was early in July, the long-delayed rains had broken at Haziri, in the Central Provinces, ten days before, and it was an imprudent man who would venture on a mere field-path like this at night without some illumination for his steps, lest inadvertently he might tread on a meditative and deadly kerait, with murder behind its stale small eyes, or step on the black coils of some hooded cobra. Only a few days before, Case had found one such in the bathroom of his bungalow, curled up on the mat within a few inches of his bare foot, when he went there to bathe before dinner, and he had no desire to give his nerves any further test of steadiness under such circumstances.

To-day there had been a break in the prodigious deluge, and all the afternoon the midsummer sun had blazed from a clear sky, causing all vegetable things to sprout with magical rapidity. This path, which yesterday had been a bare track over the fields, was now covered with springing herbs; the parade-ground, which for the last week had been but a sea of viscous mud, was clad in a mantle of delicate green blades, and the tamarisks and neem trees were studded with swelling buds among the dead and dripping foliage of the spring. A similar animation had tingled through the insect world, and as Case passed across the couple of fields that lay between the mess-room and his bungalow, a swarm of evil flies dashed themselves against the glass of his lantern. Overhead, since sunset, the clouds had gathered densely again across the vault of the sky, but to the east an arch of clear and star-lit heavens was dove-coloured with the approaching moonrise. Against it the shapes of silhouetted trees stood sharp and black in the windless and stifling calm.

It was a night of intolerable heat, and his two bulldogs, chained up in the veranda of his bungalow, with their dinner lying untouched beside them, could do no more by way of welcome to him than tap languidly with their tails on the matting in acknowledgment of his return. His bearer, not expecting him to be back so soon from the mess-room, was out, and he had to wait on himself, pulling out a long chair and table from his sitting-room, and groping for whisky and soda in his cupboard. The ice had run out, and after mixing and drinking a tepid peg, he went back to his bedroom and changed his hot dinner clothes for pyjamas and slippers. Cursing inwardly at the absence of his servant, he lit his lamp with a solitary match that he found on the table, and came out again into the veranda to think over, with such coolness as was capturable, the whole intolerable situation.

At first his mind hovered circling round outlying annoyances. He was dripping at every pore in this dark furnace of a night, the prickly heat covered his shoulders with a net of unbearable irritation, he had just lost heavily for the tenth successive evening at auction-bridge, his liver was utterly upset with the abominable weather, the lamp smelled, mosquitoes trumpeted shrilly round him. Here, more or less, was the outer and less essential ring of his discontent; to a happy and healthy man such inconveniences would have been of little moment, but in his present position they seemed portentously disagreeable. Then his mind, still hovering, moved a little inwards round a smaller and more intimate circle, surveying the calamities of the past six weeks. He had killed his favourite pony out pig-sticking, he was heavily in debt, and this morning only he had been talked to faithfully and frankly by his colonel on the text of slackness in respect of regimental duties. But still his mind did not settle down on his central misfortune—instinctively it shrank from it.

Thick and hot and silent the oppression of the night lay round him. Now and then one of his bulldogs stirred, or an owl hooted as its wings divided the motionless air, while farther away, in the bazaars of Haziri, a tom-tom beat as if it was the pulse of this stifling and feverish night. The clouds had grown thicker overhead, and every now and then some large drop of hot rain splashed heavily on the dry earth or hissed among the withered shrubs. Remote lightning winked on the horizon, followed at long intervals by drowsy thunder, and to the east, in the arch of sky that still remained unclouded, a tawny half-moon had risen, shapeless through the damp air, and illuminating the vapours with dusky crimson. Once more Case splashed the tepid soda-water over a liberal whisky, still pausing before he let his mind consciously dwell on that which lay as heavy over it as over the gasping earth this canopy of cloud.

The veranda where he sat was broad and deep, and two doors opened into it from the bungalow. One led into his own quarters, the other into those of his brother officer, Percy Oldham. He was away on leave up in the hills, but was expected back to-night, and Case knew that, before either of them slept, there would have to be talk of some kind between them. A year ago, when they had taken this bungalow together, they had been inseparable friends, so that the mess had found for them the nicknames of David and Jonathan; then, by degrees, growing impalpable friction of various kinds had estranged them, and to-night, when at length Case thought of Oldham, his mouth went dry with the intensity of his hate. And at the thought of him, his mind, hovering and circling so long, dropped like a stooping hawk into the storm-centre of his misery. He took from the table the letter he had found waiting for him in the rack at the mess-room that evening, and by the light of the fly-beleaguered lamp read it through again. It was quite short.

"Dear Case,—I shall get back late on Thursday night, and before we meet I think I had better tell you that I am engaged to Kitty Metcalf. I suppose we shall have to talk about it, though it might be better if we did not. For a man who is so happy, I am awfully sorry; that is all I can say about it. She wished me to tell you, though, of course, I should have done so in any case.—Yours truly,

"Percy Oldham."

Case read this through for the sixth or seventh time, then tore it into fragments, and again replenished his glass. It was barely six months ago that he had been engaged to this girl himself; then they had quarrelled, and the match had been broken off. But he found now that he had never ceased to hope that when he went up himself, later in the summer, to the hills, it would be renewed again. And at the thought his present discomfort, his debts, all that had occupied his mind before, were wiped clean from it. Oldham—they had talked of it fifty times—was to have been his best man.

Suddenly, out of the black bosom of the windless night, there came a sigh of hot air rustling the shrubs outside. It came into the veranda where he sat, like the stir of some corporeal presence, making the light of his lamp to hang flickering in the chimney for a moment, and then expire in a wreath of sour-smelling smoke. One of his dogs sat up for a moment growling, and then all was utterly still again. The arch of clear sky to the east had dwindled and become overcast, and the red moon showed but a faint blur of light behind the gathering clouds.

Case had used a solitary match to light his lamp, and did not know where, in his own bungalow, he might find a box. But he could get one for certain out of Oldham's bedroom, for he was a person of extremely orderly habits, and always kept one on a ledge just inside his bedroom door. Case got up and in the dark groped his way across the lobby out of which Oldham's bedroom opened, and feeling with his hand, immediately found the box on the ledge at the foot of his bed. Standing there, he lit a match, and his eye fell on the bed itself. It was covered with a dark blanket, and on the centre of it, coiled and sleeping, like a round pool of black water, lay a huge cobra. On the moment the match went out—it had barely been lit—and, closing the bedroom door, he went out again on to the veranda.

He did not rekindle his lamp, but sat, laying the forgotten match-box on his table, and looking out into the blackness of the yawning night. The wind that had extinguished his light had died away again, and all round he heard the heavy plump of the rain, which was beginning to fall heavily. Before five minutes were past, the sluices of the sky were fully open again, and the downpour had become torrential. The lightning, that an hour ago had but winked remotely on the horizon, was becoming more vivid, and the response of the thunder more immediate. At the gleam of the frequent flashes from the sky, the trees in front of the bungalow, the road, and the fields that lay beyond it, started into colour seen through the veil of the rain, that hung like a curtain of glass beads, firm and perpendicular, and then vanished again into the impenetrable blackness. He was not conscious of thought; it seemed only that a vivid picture was spread before his mind—the picture of a dark-blanketed bed on which, like a round black pool, there lay the coiled and sleeping cobra. The door of that room was shut, and a man entering it would no longer find, as he had done, a match-box ready to his hand, close beside the door.

For another hour he sat there, this mental picture starting from time to time into brilliant illumination, even as at the lightning flashes the landscape in front of him leaped into intolerable light and colour. The roar of the rain and the incessant tumult of the approaching thunder had roused the dogs, and by the flare of the storm Case could see that Boxer and his wife were both sitting tense and upright, staring uneasily into the night. Then simultaneously they both broke into chorus of deep-throated barking and strained at their chains. By the next flash Case saw what had roused their vigilance. The figure of a man with flapping coat was running at full speed from the direction of the mess-room towards the bungalow. He recognized who it was, and now the dogs recognized him, too, for their barking was exchanged for whimpers of welcome and agitated tails.

Oldham leaped the little hedge that separated the road from the fields and ran dripping into shelter of the veranda. In the gross darkness he could not see Case, and stood there, as he thought, alone, stripping off his mackintosh. Then, by the light of a fierce violet streamer in the clouds, he saw him.

"Hullo, Case," he said, "is that you?"

Oldham moved towards him as he spoke, and by the next flash Case saw him close at hand, tall and slim, with handsome, boyish face.

"You got my letter?" asked Oldham.

"Yes, I got your letter."

Case paused a moment.

"Do you expect me to congratulate you?" he asked.

"No, I can't say that I do. But I want to say something, and I hope you won't find it offensive. Anyhow, it is quite sincere. I am most awfully sorry for you. And I can't forget that we used to be the greatest friends. I hope you can remember that, too."

He sat down on the step that led into Case's section of the bungalow, and in the darkness Case could hear Boxer making affectionate slobbering noises. That kindled a fresh point of jealous hatred in his mind; both dogs, who obeyed him as a master, adored Oldham as a friend. Hotly burned that hate, and he thought again of the closed bedroom door and the black pool on the blanket. Then he spoke slowly and carefully.

"I quite remember it," he said, "and it seems to me the most amazing thing in the world. I can recall it all, all my—my love for you, and the day when we settled into this bungalow together, and the joy of it. I recall, too, that you have taken from me everything you could lay hands on, money, the affection of the dogs even——"

Oldham interrupted in sudden resentment at this injustice.

"As regards money, I may remind you, since you have chosen to mention it, that I have not succeeded in taking any away from you," he remarked.

Case was not roused by this sarcasm; he could afford, knowing what he knew, to keep calm.

"I am sorry for having kept you waiting so long," he said. "But you may remember that you begged me to pay you at my convenience. It will be quite convenient to-morrow."

"My dear chap," broke in Oldham again, "as if I would have mentioned it, if you hadn't!"

Case felt himself scarcely responsible for what he said; the tension of the storm, the infernal tattoo of the rain, the heat, the bellowing thunder, seemed to take demoniacal possession of him, driving before them the sanity of his soul.

"Perhaps you wouldn't mention it," he said, "until you had sold my debt to some Jewish money-lender."

In the darkness he heard Oldham get up.

"There is no use in our talking, if you talk like a madman," he said.

The sky immediately above them was torn asunder, and a flickering spear of intolerable light stabbed downwards, striking a tree not a hundred yards in front of the bungalow, and for the moment the stupendous crack of the thunder drowned thought and speech alike. Boxer gave a howl of protest and dismay, and nestled close to Oldham, while Case, starting involuntarily from his chair, held his hands to his ears until the appalling explosion was over.

"Rather wicked," he said, and poured himself out a dram of neat spirits.

That steadied him, and, recovering himself a little, he felt that he was behaving very foolishly in letting the other see the madness of his rage and resentment. It was far better that he should lull Oldham into an unsuspicious frame of mind; otherwise he might suspect, might he not, that something was prepared for him in his room? Others, subsequently, if they quarrelled, might guess that he himself had known what lay there ... but it was all dim and fantastic. Then the fancied cunning and caution of an unbalanced man who is at the same time ready to commit the most reckless violence took hold of him, and instantly he changed his tone. He must be quiet and normal; he must let things take their natural course, without aid or interference from himself.

"The storm has played the deuce with my nerves," he said, "that and the news in your letter, and the sight of you coming like a wraith through the rain. But I won't be a lunatic any longer. Sit down, Percy, and try to forgive all the wild things I have been saying. Of course, I don't deny that I have had an awful blow. But, as you have reminded me, we used to be great friends. She and I were great friends, too, and I can't afford to lose the two people I really care most about in the world, just because they have found each other. Let's make the best of it; help me, if you can, to make the best of it."

It was not in Oldham's genial nature to resist such an appeal, and he responded warmly.

"I think that is jolly good of you," he said, "and, frankly, I hate myself when I think of you. But, somehow, it isn't a man's fault when he falls in love. I couldn't help myself; it came on me quite suddenly. It was as if someone had come quickly up behind me and pitched me into the middle of it. At one moment I did not care for her; at the next I cared for nothing else."

Case had himself thoroughly in hand by this time. He even took pleasure in these reconciliatory speeches, knowing the completeness with which a revenge prepared without his planning should follow on their heels. Had a loaded pistol been ready to his hand, and he himself secure from detection, he would probably not have pulled the trigger on his friend, but it was a different matter that he should merely acquiesce in his walking in the dark into the room where death lay curled and ready to strike. That seemed to him to be the act of God; he was not responsible for it, he had not put the cobra there.

"I felt sure it must have happened like that," he said. "Besides, as you know, Kitty and I had quarrelled and had broken our engagement off. Of course, I hoped that some day we might come together again—at least, I know now that I hoped it. But that was nothing to do with you. You fell in love with her, and she with you. Yes, yes. Really, I don't wonder. Indeed—indeed, I do congratulate you—I congratulate you both."

Oldham gave a great sigh of pleasure and relief.

"It's ripping of you to take it like that," he said. "I hardly dared to hope you would. Thanks ever so much—ever so much! And now, do you know, I think I shall go to bed. I am dog-tired. I had a six hours' ride to the station this morning, and even up there it was hideously hot."

Case again reminded himself that he must behave naturally—not plan anything, but not interfere.

"Oh, you must have a drink," he said, "though I'm afraid there is no ice. I'll get you a glass and soda."

He came out into the veranda again with these requisites. Oldham was stifling a prodigious yawn.

"I'm half dead with sleep. Probably I shall chuck myself on my bed just as I am, to save the trouble of undressing."

Case felt his hand tremble as he put the glass down on the table.

"I know that feeling," he said. "Sometimes, when one is very sleepy, the sight of a bed is altogether too much for one. I dare say I shall do the same. Help yourself to whisky while I open the soda for you."

Oldham drank his peg and again rose.

"Well, I'm for bed," he said. "And I can't tell you what a relief it is to me to find you like this. By the way, about that bit of money. Pay me exactly when it's convenient to you—next year or the year after, if you like. I should be wretched if I thought you were putting yourself about over it. So good night, Reggie."

He turned to go, and it seemed to Case that hours passed and a thousand impressions were registered on his brain as he walked down the twenty-five feet of veranda that separated the two doors of entrance that led into their quarters. Outside, another change had come over the hot, tumultuous night, and, as if the very moon and stars were concerned in this pigmy drama, where but a single life out of the innumerable and infinitesimal little denizens of the world was involved, a queer triangular rent had opened in the rain-swollen sky, and a dim moon and a company of watery stars stared silently down, and to Case's excited senses they appeared hostilely witnessing. Ten minutes ago the rain had ceased as suddenly as if a tap had been turned off, and, except for the tom-tom that still beat monotonously in the town, a silence of death prevailed. The steam rose thick as sea-mist from the ground; above it a blurred etching of trees appeared and the roof of the mess-room. The grey unreal light shone full into the veranda, and he could see that Boxer was sitting bolt upright on his blanket-bed, looking at Oldham's retreating figure. Daisy was industriously scratching her neck with a hind-leg, and from the table a little pool of spilt soda-water was dripping on to the ground.

All this Case noticed accurately and intently, and, as yet, Oldham was not half-way down the veranda. Once he hung on his step and sniffed the hot, stale air. That was a characteristic trick; he wrinkled his nose up like a dog, showing his white teeth. Once he shifted his dripping mackintosh from right hand to left, holding it at arm's length. Then, as he turned to pass into the door, he made a little staccato sign of salutation to Case with his disengaged hand. Boxer appropriated that, and wagged a cordial tail in response.

Eagerly and expectantly, now that he had vanished from sight, Case followed his movements, visualizing them. He heard him shuffle his feet along the floor in the manner of a man feeling his way in the dark, and knew that he was drawing near to the closed bedroom door and the black interior. Oldham had said that he was very tired, that he was inclined just to throw himself on the bed and sleep, and the absence of matches and the added inconvenience of undressing in the dark would further predispose him to this. He would throw himself on the bed all in a piece, after the fashion of a tired man, and awake to fury the awful bedfellow, with the muscular coils and the swift death that lay crouched beneath its hood, which lay sleeping there. To-morrow there would be no debt for Case to pay, no gnawing of unsatisfied hate, and for Oldham no letter to his lady with the so satisfactory account of the evening's meeting.

Then from within came the rattle of a turned door-handle, and Case knew that the death-chamber stood open. There followed a pause of absolute stillness, in which Case felt utterly detached from and irresponsible for whatever might follow. Then came the jar of a closed door....

And that tore him screaming from his murderous dreams, from which, perhaps, he had awoke too late. He found himself, with no volition of his own, running down the veranda and calling at the top of his voice:

"Percy, Percy," he cried, "come out. There is a cobra on your bed!"

He heard the handle rattle and the door bang. Next moment he was on his knees in the dark lobby, clasping Oldham's legs in a torrent of hysterical sobbing.

THE FALSE STEP

Mrs. Arthur Bolney Ross, when, three years ago, she set sail, or, rather, set screw, for England, had no very clear idea of the campaign she intended to wage there, though a firm determination to win it, and had mentally arrived at no general plan beyond those preliminary manœuvres which our charming American invaders usually adopt when they first effect a landing on the primitive pavements of Piccadilly. She had, in fact, taken half a dozen rooms at the Ritz Hotel and a box on the grand tier of the Covent Garden Opera House. But she had also, for the six months preceding her expedition, secretly received daily lessons on the pronunciation and idioms of that particular (and, as she thought, peculiar) dialect of the English language which was in vogue among the section of the English-speaking race with whom she intended to have dealings.

Rightly or wrongly, she had decided that the screaming drawl of New York, which a few years before had so captivated the English upper classes, and had led to so many charming and successful marriages, was now out of date, and would enchant no longer. So instead of being content with her expressive native speech, she learned with almost passionate assiduity the mumbling English diction, the inaudible Victorian voice, which she rightly considered would be a novelty to those who had so largely abandoned it themselves in favour of a more strident utterance. But she did not, in mastering the Victorian voice and intonation, suffer her knowledge of her native tongue and its blatant delivery to wither from misuse; she but became bi-lingual, and schooled her vocal cords to either register without in the least confusing the two.

It was in this point that she showed herself a campaigner of no stereotyped order, but one who might go far, who intended in any case to go further than anybody else. The idea was brilliant. Others before her had become more English than the English, and had done well; others had remained more American than the Americans, and had done even better. But she, among the immense bales of her luggage, brought with her this significant little handbag, so to speak: she could sound American or English at will. She could say without stumbling, "Very pleased to make your acquaintance," or "How are you?" just as she pleased. And in this, so it seems to her historian, lay the germ of her success, and also the seeds of her final and irretrievable disaster, for in spite of her modulated voice and

66

acquired idiom, she remained American in thought, with the regal impulses of a queen in Newport.

In other respects she was not, on her first landing, different in kind from our ordinary hospitable invaders. She had a real Arthur Bolney Ross in the background, who was capable of being shown and tested, if, so to speak, she was "searched," but who, since his mind had in the course of years become nothing more nor less than a mint, out of which streams of bullion perpetually issued, preferred to be left alone for the processes of production. Amelie was excellent friends with him, when they had time and inclination to meet, and it always gave her a comfortable feeling to know that Arthur was in existence. If they had met very often, it is probable that they would have got on each other's nerves, and, since she had an immense fortune of her own, have considered the desirability of a divorce; but in the meantime Amelie decidedly liked the feeling of stability which her husband gave her. She did not think about him much, but she knew he was there.

Husbands, she had ascertained, were going to be fashionable in London this year, or, if not exactly fashionable, were going to be "worn" in the manner of some invisible but judicious part of the dress, like a cholera belt, or, as Amelie would have called it when she spoke American, a gripe-girdle. Pearls also were worn, though not so invisibly as husbands, and Amelie had five superb ropes of these, which could be verified by anybody, and never got on her nerves at all. She had also, among her general equipment, a very excellent sort of social godmother, Lady Brackenbury, who, for a remuneration that made no difference to Amelie, but a good deal to her, was prepared to exert herself to the utmost pitch of her very valuable capabilities in the matter of bringing people to see her and in taking her to see people, and in preventing the wrong sort of people from having any sort of access to her. Amelie was willing to put herself into Lady Brackenbury's hands with the complete confidence in which she would have entrusted her mouth to a reliable dentist, had her admirable teeth demanded any sort of adjustment. She could not have made a wiser choice: there was nobody, in fact, among possible godmothers in London, who would have been a sounder sponsor.

The two had met eighteen months before in New York, and subsequently, in the summer, Violet Brackenbury had spent a month with her friend at her cottage at Newport, which exteriorly resembled an immense Swiss chalet, and inside was like a terminus hotel. There, on ground for ever afterwards more historic than Marathon, had been fought the famous sixteen days' war, in which

67

Amelie had so signally defeated and deposed the reigning queen of the very smartest set of New York society.

The point to be decided, of course, was which of the two could give the most ludicrous, extravagant, and delirious parties, and thus be acclaimed sovereign among hostesses. Amelie, as challenger, had flung the gauntlet in the shape of a midnight lawn-tennis party, with hundreds of arc lamps hung above the courts, the nets covered with spangles, and the lines made of ground glass faintly illuminated by electric lights beneath, while, by way of contrast with this brilliance, a number of men dressed like mourners at a funeral, with top-hats and black scarves, picked up and presented the lawn-tennis balls to her guests in coffin-shaped trays. Here was a high bid for supremacy, and it was felt that Mrs. Cicero B. Dace would have to do something great in order to eclipse the brightness and originality of this entertainment. But bright and original she was, and when, two nights later, she gave her marvellous canary ball, it was thought that her throne had not yet tottered. On this occasion her admiring guests were thrilled to find that all round the walls of her ballroom had been planted mimosa trees, among the branches of which three thousand canaries had been let loose, after being doped with hard-boiled egg soaked in rum and water. These chirped and sang in a feverish and intoxicated manner. At the end of the ball the men of the party, dressed as huntsmen and armed with air-guns, shot these unfortunate songsters and presented the spoils to their partners in the cotillion.

Amelie had two answers to that—the first an indignant letter, printed in large type throughout the American press, denouncing this massacre, and the second another ball. The letter Mrs. Cicero B. Dace did not object to at all, since it but enhanced her notoriety, but she objected to the ball very much indeed, since Amelie's ingenious mind hit on the simple and exquisite plan of dispensing with the band, and having in its place a choir of three hundred singers, who, in batches of one hundred at a time, sang the dance tunes. The effect was contagious, and dancers joined in also, producing, as the press said, the "most stupendously lyrical effect since the days of Sappho."

Then Mrs. Cicero B. Dace sat down and thought again, lighting upon the famous idea of the auction ball, in which a real English Duke acted as auctioneer, and before each dance put up the ladies for auction, to be bid for by the men who wished to be their partners. But Amelie swiftly sent for Arthur Bolney Ross, and he and a friend of hers, who was backing her in this struggle for sovereignty, continued to bid for her for so long that, out of sinister compassion for her hostess, she stepped down from the rostrum

68

and refused to dance with either, for fear that there should be no more dancing for anybody. This completely spoiled the success of the auction ball, and while Mrs. Cicero B. Dace was still staggering from its failure, Amelie annihilated her altogether by giving her inimitable glacier ball on the hottest night of the year. A refrigerating apparatus was rigged up on the walls of her ballroom, and their entire surface thickly coated with real ice. Glass channels, fringed with blue gentians, were made round the margin of the floor, to carry off the melting water, while accomplished members of the band yodelled at intervals to carry out the Swiss illusion. She and the auctioneer Duke—whom she had captured from under the nose of Mrs. Cicero B. Dace—dressed in knickerbockers, with a rope round his shoulder and an ice-axe in his hand, led the cotillion, and Mrs. Cicero B. Dace, having in vain tried to point out that the gentians were three parts artificial flowers, retired at 1 A.M. in floods of tears.

Such were Amelie Ross's social achievements when, unlike Alexander the Great, she bethought herself that there were more worlds to conquer, and decided to extend her dominions over England. Her godmother, of course, knew her history, having, indeed, assisted at the history she had already made, and on the night of her arrival at the Ritz Hotel, dined with her there in her charming room looking over the Green Park, before going with her to her box at the opera. As regards this first appearance of her god-daughter, Violet Brackenbury had laid her plans very carefully, and explained them as they dined.

"I have asked nobody else at all, dear Amelie," she said, "because I want everybody to be wild to find out who you are, and nobody will be able to say. Curiosity is the best sauce of all."

Amelie became thoroughly American for a moment.

"My!" she said. "Don't you mean that your folk over here haven't seen hundreds and hundreds of pictures of me in the papers?"

"Probably not one, my dear. And I've only told one woman that you are coming. You are going to burst on everybody to-night, you and your lovely face, and your six feet of height, and your wonderful hair, and your wonderful pearls, and the most wonderful gown that you've got. I want all London for an hour or two to be wild to know who you are, and I have told the box-attendant to take your name off the door, and not to let anybody in between the acts. Afterwards I shall take you to the dance at Alice Middlesex's, which, luckily, ever so luckily, is to-night. She is the one person I have told."

"The Duchess of Middlesex?" asked Amelie.

"Yes; and she is quite certain to ask you if you know Lady Creighton, that dreadful countrywoman of yours who is climbing into London like a monkey and hopping about it like a flea. She tried to patronize Alice, and Alice won't get over it either in this world or the next. So tell her that Lady Creighton is not received in New York—which I believe is the case, isn't it?—and look very much surprised at the idea of knowing her. I can't tell you how important that is."

Amelie frowned slightly.

"But Elsie Creighton telephoned to me half an hour ago," she said, "asking me to lunch with her to-morrow to meet——"

"It doesn't matter whom she asked you to meet. If she asked you to meet the entire Royal Family, you would be wise to refuse. You don't want to climb into London on the top of a hurdy-gurdy."

"My! What's a hurdy-gurdy?" asked Amelie, whose English lessons had not taught her that word.

"Hurdy-gurdy? Street organ. It doesn't matter. You don't want to know people, if you understand; you want to make people want to know you. My plan is not that you should climb up, but that you should spread down."

Amelie instantly caught this.

"I see," she said. "I'm to begin at the top. But Elsie Creighton said there was a Prince coming to lunch to-morrow. I thought that was a good beginning."

"Not so good as the Creighton woman is bad. Did you accept, by the way?"

"Why, yes."

"Then telephone to-morrow exactly at lunch-time to say you are ill, and lunch with me very obviously downstairs in the restaurant. In fact, it couldn't have happened better. It will mark you off very definitely from her and her crowd. I don't mean to say that there are not charming people among it, but it would never do to enter London under her wing. Perhaps just at present, darling, you had better ask me before you accept invitations. It is so important to cut the right people."

Amelie was completely cordial over this.

"I expect that is what I have got to learn," she said. "And now for to-night—will my dress do?"

Lady Brackenbury regarded this admirable costume and shook her head.

"No, I don't think it will," she said. "It is lovely, but you want something more arresting. You, with your wonderful complexion, can stand anything. Orange, now—haven't you got a hit-in-the-face of orange? I want everybody to be forced to look at you, and you'll do the rest. You see I have made myself as plain and inconspicuous as possible, to act as a foil. It is noble of me, but then I am noble. And all the pearls, please, just all the pearls, with the big diamond fender on your head. To-morrow, at the French Embassy, you shall wear the simplest gown you have got, and one moonstone brooch, price three-and-sixpence."

Such was the opening of Amelie's amazing campaign, the incidents and successes of which followed swift and bewildering. Under Violet's capable guidance she began, not by collecting round her that brisk and hungry section of well-born London which is always ready to sing for its dinner, and by giving huge entertainments to bring together a crowd at all costs, but by attracting and attaching a small band of the people who mattered. Lady Brackenbury knew very well that even in the most democratic town in the world certain people, not necessarily Princes or Prime Ministers, were large pieces in the great haphazard game of chess; the crowd meantime, after whom Amelie secretly hankered, would only get more eager to be admitted. In particular, Lady Creighton starved for her entry. She asked Amelie to dine any Tuesday in June, when she was giving her series of musical parties, but Amelie found, to her great regret, that she was engaged on all those festive occasions. But she gave a musical party herself—London was prey this year to a disordered illusion that it liked music—and Melba and Caruso sang there—informally, so it seemed, just happening to sing—to not more than fifty people, who sat in armchairs at their ease, instead of elbowing each other in squashed and upright rows. In vain did Lady Creighton spread an assiduous report that the artists had sung out of tune and that the peaches were sour. Everyone knew that she had not been there, and that she alluded to another sort of fruit. Violet Brackenbury was successful in persuading Amelie not to send any account of this brilliant little affair to the papers, and to refuse all scraps to the writers for the press. But she was careful to provide for a far more telling publicity.

Gradually, craftily, a reef at a time, Violet allowed her friend to let out her sails. She left her flat at the Ritz and rurally installed herself in a spacious house in the middle of Regent's Park. There was a big field attached to the house, and, yielding to a severe attack of Americanism, which she thought it might be dangerous to suppress, Violet permitted her to give a haymaking party of the Newport type. Hay was brought in from the country and scattered over the field, and mixed up with roses and gardenias, while the guests on arrival were presented with delightful little ebony pitchforks with silver prongs, or cedar-wood rakes. But this symptom caused her a little uneasiness, for it was obvious that

Amelie thought her haymaking party a much brighter achievement than the previous concert.

The expansion continued. Amelie and her friend strolled into Christie's one morning, and found a tussle going on between two eminent dealers over the possession of a really marvellous string of pearls. At a breathless pause, after the first "Going!" that followed a fresh bid, Amelie said in her most ringing American voice, "I guess I'll sail in right now," and began bidding herself. The crowd of dilettante London, which delights in seeing other people spend large sums of money, parted for her, and she moved gloriously up the auction-room and took her stand just behind one of the Mosaic little gentlemen who wanted the pearls so badly.

The recognition of her spread through the place like spilled quicksilver, and the auctioneer, with an amiable bow, caused the pearls to be handed to her for her inspection. With them still in her hand, as if it was not worth while returning them to the tray, she sky-rocketed the price by three exalting bids, the third of which was as a fire-hose on the ardour of her competitors. Her cheque-book was fetched from her car outside, and she left the room a moment afterwards, having drawn her cheque on the spot, pausing only to clasp the pearls round her neck.... And Violet, with a strange sinking of the heart, felt as if her pet tiger-cub had tasted blood again after the careful and distinguished diet on which she had been feeding it.

Amelia had a fancy to leave London early in July, and give a few parties at an immense house she had taken near Maidenhead for the month. She had had some gondolas sent over from Venice, with their appropriate gondoliers, and London found it very pleasant to float about after dinner, while the excellent string band played in an illuminated barge that accompanied the flotilla. Exciting little surprises constantly happened, such as the arrival one evening of artists from the Grand Guignol, who played a couple of thrilling little horrors in the ballroom, while on another night the great Reynolds picture belonging to the Duke of Middlesex was found to have put in an appearance on the walls. Amelie said that it was her birthday present to her husband, and made no further allusion to it. The frame had gone to be repaired, and it was draped round in clouds of silvery-grey chiffon that extended half over the wall. And had Violet Brackenbury known the outrage that her friend had planned, the frenzy of suppressed Newportism that was ready to break forth, it is probable that she would gladly have returned the cheque which she had that morning received from Amelie.

As it was, she felt wholly at ease, and inclined to congratulate herself on the unique and signal character of Amelie's success. Never before, so she thought, had a woman so dominated the season; never, certainly, had one of her countrywomen so "mattered." And all this, with the exception, perhaps, of the haymaking party and the incident of the pearls at Christie's, had been gained in quiet, unsensational ways; and, lulled to content, she did not realize that the spirit that inspired the queen of hostesses was ready to flare up like an access of malarial fever. Poor unsuspecting godmother, who fondly believed that those gondolas from Venice, those Grand Guignol artists from Paris, this gem of Reynolds's pictures, were a safety-valve, not guessing that they were but as oil poured on the flame!

The cotillion that night was to begin at twelve. Amelie was leading it herself with one of the Princes, and the big ballroom was doubly lined with seated guests, when on the stroke of twelve she entered, dressed in exact facsimile of the glorious Reynolds. As she advanced with her partner into the middle of the room, the band in the gallery struck up, and simultaneously a tongue of fire shot through the flimsy draperies round the picture, instantly enveloping it in flames. The canvas blistered and bubbled, and in ten seconds the finest Reynolds in the world was a sheet of scorched and blackened rag.

The crowd leaped to its feet, but before the panic had time to mature, the cause of it was over. There was nothing inflammable within range of the swiftly-consumed chiffon, and only little fragments of burned-out ash floated on to the floor. But the fervent and instantaneous heat had done its work.

Then for a moment there was dead silence, and Amelie's voice was heard in its quietest, most English tones.

"Oh, isn't that a pity!" she said.

Then arose a sudden hubbub of talk, drowning the sound of the band, which, at a signal from Amelie, had started again.

* * * * *

Violet stood with her friend before the blackened canvas next morning in the empty room, drawing on her gloves.

"I don't think you understand yet the effect of what you have done," she said. "No one doubts that the fire was intentional, and— and I think that Lady Creighton will be of more use to you in the future than I can possibly be."

SPOOK STORIES

THE CASE OF FRANK HAMPDEN

There was a light visible from the chinks and crevices of drawn curtains in the window of Dr. Roupert's study as I passed it on my way back from dinner one night. He lived some six doors farther up the same street as I, and since it had long been a frequent custom for us to smoke the "go-to-bed" cigarette together, I rang and asked if he was at leisure. His servant told me that he had already sent a message across to my house, asking me to look in on him if I got home while the evening was not too far advanced for a casual conversational quarter of an hour; and accordingly I took off my coat, and went straight into the pleasant little front room, about which hung the studious fragrance of the books that lined it from floor to ceiling.

Arthur Roupert was not alone this evening; there was sitting on the near side of the fire, which sparkled prosperously in this clear night of early December frost, a young man whom I was sure I had never seen before. As I entered, he stopped in the middle of a sentence, turning towards the door, and I looked on the most handsome and diabolical face that I had ever beheld.

Simultaneously Roupert got up.

"I hoped you would look in," he said. "Let me introduce to you my cousin, Mr. Hampden, who is spending a day or two with me. This is Mr. Archdale, Frank, of whom I was speaking just now."

As the other rose, I saw that Roupert's almost foolishly amiable fox-terrier shrank away from where she had been sitting by her master's chair, instead of giving me her accustomed and effusive greeting, and retreated into a far corner of the room, where she sat quivering with raised hackles, and with vigilant eyes full of hate and terror fixed on young Hampden. His right arm was in a sling, and he held out his left hand to me.

"You must excuse me," he said, "but I am only just recovering from a broken arm. My cousin's dog doesn't approve of it; she would like to get her teeth into it."

"The oddest thing I ever saw, Archdale," said Roupert. "You know Fifi's usual amiability. Call her, Frank."

Frank Hampden whistled, and clicked his fingers together in an encouraging manner.

"Fifi—come here, Fifi!" he said.

For a moment I thought that this most confiding of ladies was going to fly at him. But apparently she could not find the courage for an attack, and, snapping and growling, retreated behind the window curtains.

"And that to me," said Hampden, licking his lips as he spoke. "Me, who adore dogs. Don't you, Mr. Archdale?"

As he said that I knew that he lied; that Fifi's detestation of him was met with a hatred quite as vivid but more controlled. I can no more account for that conviction than for the sense of hellish evil that my first glance at him had conveyed to me. He was quite young, twenty-two or twenty-three for a guess, and yet from behind the mask of that soft boyish face there looked out a spirit hard and malignant and mature, an adept in terrible paths. The impression was quite inexplicable but perfectly clear. Then, looking across to Roupert, I saw he was watching his cousin with eager intentness.

I had to answer the direct question he had put to me, but it required an effort to speak to him or to look at him.

"No; personally I don't care about dogs," I said. "I rather dislike them, and so enjoy a most unwelcome popularity among them. Fifi, for instance: your cousin will tell you how blind is her adoration for me!"

"See if Fifi will come to you if I stand by you," said Hampden. Fifi had half-emerged from her ambush behind the curtains, and I called to her. But she would not leave the retreat where her rage and terror had driven her. She gave a little apologetic whine, as if to signify that I was asking an impossible thing, and beat with her stumpy tail on the carpet.

"Now go back to your chair again, Frank," said Roupert.

Fifi needed no further invitation when he had left my neighbourhood. She bundled herself across the room to me, her thin white body curled like a comma, wriggling with delight and making incomprehensible little explanations of her previous conduct. But the moment that Hampden moved in his chair, she bolted away from me again.

He laughed and got up.

"Well, I think I shall go to bed now that you have come to keep Arthur company," he said. "By the way, where's your cat, Arthur? I haven't seen her about all day."

He was facing sideways to Roupert as he spoke, and I noticed that he did not turn his head towards him. This gave a certain casual cursory tone to his question, making it appear a mere careless inquiry.

"I haven't seen her either," said Roupert. "Perhaps, after taking counsel with Fifi, she has thought it prudent to fly from your baleful presence. Good night, Frank. Can you manage for yourself with your bandaged arm, or shall I come and help you?"

"Oh, I'm all right, thanks," he said; "good night. A kind good night, Fifi. We shall be good friends before long."

Arthur Roupert had retired some two years before from regular medical practice, in which, as all the world knows, he was undoubtedly the first authority on disease and aberrations of the brain and nervous system, devoting his attention more particularly to those riddles of obscure and baffling disorders to which he so often supplied strange and correct answers. He was possessed of an ample competence, and so, finding that his large professional practice did not permit him the leisure which was necessary for these exploratory studies, he had, though always willing to be consulted by his colleagues, thrown up an active career for one of research. He wanted to learn rather than to practise, and without precisely mistrusting the methods which had earned him so brilliant a success, had inferred the presence of huge fields of the unknown, huge expanses of further possibilities which would perhaps put utterly out of date the most advanced of theories and treatments hitherto recognized in his profession. At the time of his retirement he had once talked to me about the uncharted seas on to which he proposed to push forth.

"The most advanced of actual practitioners," he said, "are but groping in the dark on the threshold of real knowledge, feeling for the handle, fumbling for the bell. At the most, that is to say, in cases of brain disease and nerve disorder we try to get at the mind of the patient, and influence that, so that it, not we, may exert its healing power, and cure the imperfect functioning of the material part. Of course that is a tremendous step forward when we look at what medical science was twenty years ago, when doctors prescribed tonics, tonics to heal the physical damage caused by a disordered mind. But mind itself is but a very subordinate denizen in that house of mystery which we call man.

"Mind is no more than the servant who comes to the door, and takes your hat and coat, and tells you in a word or two how the patient has been. Mind is not the master of the house, whom you have really come to see, and who sits there alone, mortally sick, perhaps, and in terror and darkness for the master of the house is the spirit. We have got to examine him before we can touch the source of these diseases. For the farther that science advances, the more certain it is that there is a master sitting within to whom the mind is only the servant. As for the body, the tissues, the nerves, the grey matter, what shall we say that is? Why, it's no more than the servant's clothes, his jacket, or his boots. I'm not going to stay talking in the hall to 'mind,' the servant, any longer. I shall leave him there, and go straight up to the sick-chamber. I shall be called all sorts of names—charlatan, spiritualist, what you will—but I don't care two straws about that. Besides, I know quite well that my colleagues will still be glad to call me in when they are puzzled, and I hope to be better equipped to help them.... I won't reject any jungle-path without exploring it, not witchcraft, nor demoniacal possession, nor all the myths which science thinks she has exploded. In its first origin everything must be spiritual, be it comet or toothache or genius. Just as mental suggestion has taken the place of tonics, so must spiritual healing take the place of mental suggestion. The spirit is the original manifestation of God in man, and it is on prayer and on faith that the whole science of healing will some day rest. But first we have to investigate the conditions, the environment, the life...."

For these two years, then, which had followed his retirement, Roupert had given himself to these studies of occult and spiritual influences, learning about the healing powers contained in mental suggestion, and trying to get behind that into the more elemental and essential mysteries of man; leaving the servant, as he had said, in the hall of the house, while he went further into the presence of the master of the house. Often, during these "go-to-bed" cigarettes that multiplied themselves into the night, he told me tales that did not make going to sleep any easier. Nothing was too extravagant for his investigations; witchcraft, spiritualism, Satanism, the healing touch, and, above all, demoniacal possession were the subjects of this study that went deeper into the human organism than mind. There was no myth or exploded superstition that he did not examine, to see whether the explosion had been complete and shattering, or whether among the débris there did not remain some grains of solid stuff that were still solid, though science had affirmed that a puff of scattered smoke was all that was extant.... Consequently this evening, when Frank Hampden had gone to bed, I was quite prepared to find that Roupert had something to tell, some guess to hazard that had illumined his inquiries, the more so indeed because I had not seen him for some dozen nights.

"Did you receive the message I left at your house?" he asked abruptly as the door closed behind his cousin.

"No; I haven't been home. But your servant told me you had asked me to come in," said I.

"Yes, I did. You have done just what I wanted. In my note I asked you to come in and observe my cousin, and tell me your impression. I saw you couldn't help observing him, so now let us have the impression."

"Quite frankly? All?" I said.

"Of course."

"I never saw anyone so utterly terrible," I said.

"Terrible? Exactly how?" he asked.

The very intensity of my feeling about Hampden blurred the outline of it, and I paused trying to put a definite shape to it.

"Incomparably terrible," I said. "Murderous, I think: murderous for the fun of it. I felt like Fifi."

"I saw you did," he said; "and I suspect you are right, you and Fifi...."

He walked up and down the room once or twice, then sat down with the air of settling himself.

"Did you hear him ask about my cat?" he said. "He killed her last night; he buried her in the garden."

There was a grotesqueness, a ludicrousness even in this after the talk of murder, but that only added horror to it.

"What do you mean?" I asked.

"Precisely what I say. It so happened that I slept very badly last night, because, as a matter of fact, I was thinking about Frank, and wondering if I was on the horrible track which would show me what ailed him. About three in the morning I heard the door into the garden being opened: the window of my bedroom, which was open, is just above it. The idea of burglars occurred to me, and, without turning on my light, I went and looked out. There was bright clear starlight, and I saw Frank come out of the house carrying something white in his arm. He put it down to fetch a spade from the tool-house, and I saw what it was. He dug up a couple of plants with lumps of soil round their roots, working slowly, for he could only use one arm. He buried the cat in the excavation, and very carefully replanted the Michaelmas daisies over it. Then, more terribly yet, he knelt down by the grave, and I could hear him sobbing."

"Sobbing?" I asked.

"Yes. What he said to-night is, or was, perfectly true. He used to be devoted to dogs and, indeed, all animals, especially cats.... Now last night, out in the garden, he was in his dressing-gown. Well, when he came down to breakfast this morning he said his nose had been bleeding rather severely. He was uneasy about it, and I went up to his bedroom and found a good deal of blood in his slop-pail. His dressing-gown was lying on his bed, and there, too, was more blood and a quantity of cat's hairs. I told him not to think about it any more; there was nothing in the least alarming, and when he had gone out, in order to make quite sure, I dug up the Michaelmas daisies for the second time. Below, I found the body of my poor cat. He had cut its throat.... He would kill Fifi if he could; he is longing to."

"But the fellow is a fiend!" said I.

"For the present he is a fiend, or something very like it. He used not to be until the day on which he broke his arm. Pray God he will cease being what he is."

"Till the day he broke his arm?" I asked.

"Yes. Now do you want to hear the wildest and most extravagant tale, which I believe to be literally and awfully true?"

"Concerning this?" I asked.

"Of course. Also, are you disposed to sit up late to-night? There may be some confirmatory evidence about my story. I expect Reid, the medium, here at twelve. There is time for me to give you my theory before he comes."

"Till any hour," said I.

"Good. Then listen."

He spoke slowly, putting his hands over his eyes, as he so often does when he wants to shut out all external disturbances and concentrate himself on the history of a case.

"Two months ago," he said, "as you may possibly remember, a man called James Rolls was hanged at Beltonborough for the most atrocious murder of his wife. The deed apparently was quite objectless; there had been no quarrel, and after it was done he seemed sometimes to be distressed at the crime, sobbing and crying, sometimes to gloat over it, recounting it with gusto. There was no question whatever about his guilt, only about his sanity, and with regard to that these fits of remorse and enjoyment might be assumed in order to produce the impression that he was not accountable for his actions. He was examined by a Government expert, who asked me to come down with him and form my conclusion. We could neither of us find any other symptom of insanity about him. But there was a certain conjecture in my head about what we call the history of the case, and I stopped down at Beltonborough for a day or two in order to make further observations.

"As I was having an interview with him, I suddenly asked him this question, 'Did you begin by killing flies?' Usually he was rather sullen and silent, and often would not answer; but when I asked him this, his eye brightened, and he said, 'Yes, flies first, and then cats and dogs.' After that I could get nothing further out of him, but I had got what I expected to get. In all other respects he was, as far as I could judge, perfectly sane, and it was scarcely possible to call him a homicidal maniac, for he had never before shown signs of wanting to take human life. As it was, he had committed an atrocious murder, and had he been shut up as a homicidal maniac, I do not think there is any doubt that by this time he would have killed a warder.

"Now no man in a fit of rage is altogether sane, and yet we do not commute the sentence of those who have killed another when beside themselves with passion, and James Rolls had not even that extenuation. He was hanged.... But I feel convinced that Frank is suffering from an early stage of James Rolls's malady; I feel convinced also that the hanging of James Rolls infected him with it."

"The hanging of James Rolls caused it?" I asked.

"I do not doubt it, as you will see when I state my theory. But I hope to prove that my theory is correct, and I hope to cure my cousin."

Roupert sat up and looked at me while he said this; then he sank back in his chair again, and, as before, covered his eyes with his hands.

"Now for the theory," he said. "There is a very steep hill in Beltonborough with a sharp, dangerous corner just outside the prison gate. Practically at the moment when James Rolls was being taken to the scaffold, Frank came tearing down this hill on his bicycle to catch an early train to town. He skidded and fell just outside the prison, and sustained compound fracture of his right arm. It was important that he should be moved as little as possible, and they carried him straight into the prison infirmary, where chloroform was administered and the prison surgeon set his arm. It was a very bad fracture, and he was under the anæsthetic for a considerable time. And when he came round, he was changed.... It seemed as if another spirit had taken possession of his body. He was not the same person: from being a charming boy, he had become something hellish."

Roupert sat up again and looked at me.

"There is a theory," he said, "that in certain conditions, such as deep mesmeric trance, or under the stupefaction of some complete anæsthetic, the bonds that seem so indissolubly to unite a man's spirit to his mind and his body are strangely loosened. The condition approaches to that of temporary death: often under an anæsthetic the beat of the heart is nearly suspended, often the breathing is nearly suspended, and this happened to Frank under chloroform that morning. The connexion between his spirit and his body was loosened....

"There is another theory which you must consider also. It is proved, I think, beyond all doubt, that at the moment of death, particularly of sudden and violent death, the spirit, though severed from the body which it has inhabited, does not at once leave its vicinity, but remains hovering near to its discarded tenement, from which it has been expelled. Well, at that hour when Frank's spirit was maintaining but a relaxed hold on his body, another spirit, violent and strong, was close at hand—a spirit that had just been disembodied.... And I believe the spirit of James Rolls entered and took possession."

I felt then what I have felt before and since, namely, some stir of horror in my head that made my hair move. You can often see it in dogs (I had seen it to-night in Fifi) when terror or rage erects their hackles. But the experience was only momentary, and the flame of this thing, its awful and burning quality, licked hotly round me....

"And how is Reid to help?" I asked.

"He may be able to test for us part, at any rate, of my theory," said Roupert. "He is an extraordinarily powerful medium in the way of producing materialized forms of spirits, and I believe him to be honest and high-minded. Now if Frank's body is possessed by this murderous spirit, it is at least possible that Frank's own spirit, now unhoused and evicted, will be hovering near its rightful habitation. We will ask if the spirit of Frank Hampden is here. We will ask if it can assume material form. If Reid can produce this materialization, it will doubtless wear the appearance of Frank. We will try, anyhow.... Ah, no doubt that is Reid...."

A very gentle tapping sounded on the front door just outside the room, and Roupert got up.

"I told Reid not to ring," he said, "for fear that Frank should hear. I will let him in."

He left the room, and in another moment came back with the medium, a small, perfectly commonplace looking man, smug and prosperous. Then I met his eyes and thought him commonplace no longer. They seemed to look out and through and beyond.

In a few minutes Roupert, who had often sat with Reid before, explained what was wanted. He told him that we wished to know if the spirit of Frank Hampden was about, and, if so, whether we could communicate with it, or see it. That was all.

Reid asked only one question.

"Has Frank Hampden's spirit been long out of his body?" he said.

Roupert hesitated for a moment.

"I believe it to have been out of his body for about two months," he answered.

The electric light was put out, but the glow from the fire was bright enough to make a red twilight in the room. I could clearly see the profile of the medium, black against that illumination, the back of the chair in which he sat, the full face of Roupert, glints of reflected light on the glass of pictures, and, with perfect distinctness, Fifi, who had curled herself up on the hearthrug. Almost immediately the medium went into trance, and I saw his head bowed over his chest, and heard his breathing, which had been short and panting, as he passed into unconsciousness, grow quiet again. How long we sat there in silence, without anything supernormal occurring, I do not know, but it appeared to me not to be many minutes before a very loud rap sounded from the table, which began to quiver under our hands. Then Roupert asked:

"Is the spirit of Frank Hampden here?"

There was the assent of three raps.

"Shall we be able to see you?" he asked.

There were two raps, and, after a pause, a third.

Again we sat in silence, this time for a much longer period, and I think the clock on the mantelpiece twice chimed the quarter-hour. Then from the direction of the door there blew across the room a very cold current of air, and the curtains in the window stirred with it. Fifi, I imagine, felt it too, for she sat up, sneezed, and drew herself a little nearer to the fire. Simultaneously I was inwardly aware that there was something, somebody in the room which had not been there before. It had not entered through the door, for when the current of air began to blow I looked at it, and certainly it had not opened.

Then Roupert whispered.

"Look; it is coming."

The medium's head had fallen back, and over his chest, in the region of the heart, there appeared a faint, luminous area, inside which there was going on some energy, some activity. Whorls and spirals of grey, curling and intertwining and growing thicker and extending, began building themselves up in the air. For some little while I could not make out what it was that was thus taking shape in the red twilight; then as the materialization progressed, it defined itself into a human form swathed in some misty and opaque vesture. At the top, above shoulders now quite formed, there rose the outline of a head; features growing every moment more distinct fashioned

82

the face of it, and, pallid and silent, fading into darkness below, stood the head and torso of a human being.

The face was clearly recognizable; it was scarce an hour since I had looked on those features, but it wore so heart-broken an anguish in the curves of that beautiful mouth and in the tortured eyes, that my throat worked for very pity and compassion.

Then Roupert spoke.

"Frank," he said.

The head bowed, the lips moved, but I heard nothing.

"Why are you not in your body?" he asked.

This time there came a whisper just audible.

"I can't, I can't," he said. "Someone is there; someone terrible. For God's sake, help me!"

The white agonized face grew more convulsed.

"I can't bear it," it said.... "For God's sake, for God's sake!..."

I looked away from that face for a moment to the hearthrug where a sudden noise attracted my attention. Fifi was sitting bolt upright looking eagerly upwards, and the noise I heard was the pleased thumping of her tail.

Then she came cautiously forward, still gazing at the image which an hour before had driven her frenzied with rage and terror, uttering little anxious whinings, seeking attention. Finally she held out a paw, and gave the short whisper of a bark with which she demands the notice of her favourites.... And if I had been inclined to doubt before, I think that I would now have been convinced that here in some inscrutable manifestation was the true Frank Hampden.

Once more Roupert spoke.

"I will do all that man can do, Frank," he said, "and by God's grace we will restore you."

The figure slowly faded; some of it seemed withdrawn back into the medium, some to be dispersed in the dusk. Before long Reid's breath again grew quick and laboured, as he passed out of trance, and then drenched with sweat he came to himself.

Roupert told him that the séance had been successful, and then, turning on the light again, we all sat still while the medium recovered from his exhaustion. Before he left, Roupert engaged him to hold himself in readiness for a further séance next day, in case he was telephoned for; and when he had gone, we drew up our chairs to the fire, while Fifi went nosing about the room as if searching for traces of a friend. For a long time Roupert sat in silence, frowning heavily at the fire, asking me some question from time to time, to satisfy himself that our impressions had been identical. Then he appeared to make up his mind.

"I shall do it," he said; "at least, I shall make the attempt. That was Frank whom we saw just now; up to that point my theory is confirmed. Of course, there's a risk—there's an awful risk. But, Archdale, wouldn't anybody take any risk to cure the anguish we looked upon? That was a human spirit, man, disembodied but not dead, and it knows that its earthly habitation is being defiled and profaned by that murderous occupant. It sees the horrors that its own hands work; the brain that was its pleasant servant is planning worse things yet. I can't doubt that this is so. No reasonable man can doubt so incredible and so damnable a thing. But if the struggle that there must be is too much for the body that we seek to free, good Lord, what a tale for a coroner's inquest!"

"You mean that you risk your cousin's death?" I asked.

"Necessarily; who can tell what will happen? But that is not all. For of what nature is the spirit which we hope to expel from that poor lad's body? A strong and a desperate one, or it could never have taken possession of it. It will cling with all its force to the tenement which it has usurped, and if we drive it out, if God helps us to do that, what awful and evil power will once more be abroad! But we can't help that. There is holy justice and reparation to be done, and we can't count the cost. Now, let me think again!"

He got up and began pacing up and down the room, now muttering to himself, now speaking aloud as if in argument with me.

"It's a terrible risk for Reid, too," he said, "for Reid most of all, for he will be in deep trance; such power of faith as we can exert must defend him first of all.... Yet, we can't get at Rolls, I tell you, without the medium.... I must, of course, tell Reid everything, and ask him if he will take the risk.... He may refuse, though I don't think he will, for there's the courage of a saint in that man.... Then there's Frank, Frank's body, I mean. That must be absolutely unconscious when the operation takes place; no human nerves could stand it, nor with that fiend in possession would he consent to it.... Deep, the deepest possible unconsciousness.... By Jove, there's that new German drug, which appears safe enough, and it certainly produces a sleep that comes nearest of all to death; it seems to stupefy the very spirit itself.... Hyocampine, of course; don't tell me you haven't heard of it.... Tasteless too; it's a good thing that the criminal classes can't get hold of it.... Well, there we are.... Prayer and faith in an Almighty power.... Lighten our darkness, we beseech Thee, O Lord.... He does too, if our motives are right; that's one of the few facts we can be quite sure about.... You can run a lot of risks if you utterly believe that."

Suddenly the whole burden of perplexity and anxious thought seemed lifted off his mind.

"I'll go and see Reid to-morrow morning," he said. "I believe he will consent when he knows all. And you? Do you want to see the end of it? And look on the glory of God? Come if you like, but if you come, you must be strung up to the highest pitch of trust and serenity that you are capable of. Yes, do be here. You believe that all evil, however deadly and powerful, is altogether inferior in calibre and fighting power to good. Also I shall like a friend at my elbow. Perhaps I oughtn't to urge that as a reason, for I don't want any personal feeling to influence you. Only come if you want to witness the power of God, not Reid's, not mine; we are nothing at all except mere mossy channels."

For one moment he paused, and I knew that he was wavering himself, in the weakness of the flesh; but instantly he got hold of himself again.

"There's only one power that can't fail," he said. "Hell crashes into fragments against it."

Next morning I got a note from Roupert, saying that Reid consented, and asking me to come in to his house punctually at half-past two, if I had decided to be with him. When I arrived I found Roupert and Frank Hampden sitting over their coffee in the study. Hampden had just drunk his.

"Isn't there a home for cats somewhere in Battersea?" he was asking. "I'll go and find a new one for you, as yours appears to have vanished entirely."

He yawned.

"It's a feeble habit to go to sleep after lunch," he said, "but I really think I shall have a nap. I've got an astonishing inclination that way. Give me half an hour, will you, and then we'll go down to the cats' home, and get a large fat cat."

I guessed that Roupert had already given his cousin the dose of hyocampine, but just as the latter was pulling a chair round so that he need not face the light, he spoke.

"Make a proper job of it, Frank," he said, "and lie on the sofa. One always wakes feeling cramped if one goes to sleep in a chair."

Hampden's eyelids were already drooping, but he shuffled heavily across to the sofa.

"All right," he mumbled, "sorry for being so rude, Mr.—Mr. Archdale, but I must have just forty—I wonder why forty——"

And immediately he went to sleep.

Roupert waited a moment, but Hampden did not stir again. Then he went out, and returned with Reid, who had been waiting in his bedroom. All explanations had already been made, and in silence we darkened the room by drawing the thick curtains across the window. Only a little light came in from their edges, but, as last night, the firelight flickered on the walls. Then Roupert locked the door, and we took our places round the table.

"Into Thy hands, O Lord, we commend our spirits," he said.

Before many minutes were over the medium's head dropped forward, and after a little struggle he went into trance.

"The spirit of James Rolls," said Roupert.

In the silence that followed I could hear the slow breathing of Hampden as he slept in that remote unconsciousness. A chink of light from the window fell full on his face, and I could see it very distinctly. Then, I heard him breathing quicker, and a shudder passed through him, shaking the sofa where he lay. His face, hitherto serene and quiescent, began to twitch.

"He can't wake," whispered Roupert. "I gave him the full dose."

Then, not from the door at all, but from the direction of the sofa there came an icy blast of wind, and simultaneously a shattering rap from the table.

"Is that James Rolls?" asked Roupert.

Three raps answered him.

"Then in the name of God," said Roupert, in a loud, steady voice, "come from where you are, and be made manifest."

Suddenly Hampden began to groan. His mouth worked, and he ground his teeth together. A horrible convulsion seized his face, a distortion of rending agony, like that which sometimes seizes on a dying man whose body clings desperately to the spirit that is emerging from it. A rattle and a strangled gulping came from his throat, and the foam gathered on his lips.

"It is there that you are, James Rolls," said Roupert in a loud voice of exultation. "In the name of God, come out!"

The convulsions redoubled themselves; the body writhed and bent like that of a poisoned man. Then round the face, brightest about the mouth, there formed a pale greenish light, corrupt and awful. It began to wreathe itself into lines and curves, weaving and intertwining; it grew in height, like a luminous column built without hands, in the darkness; it defined itself into human form, until in the air just above the recumbent body it stood complete. With its emergence the convulsions and the groanings subsided, and at the end, when this wraith in semblance of a swathed man, with face of such murderous cruelty that I shuddered as I looked at it, stood fully fashioned and finished, the body of Frank Hampden lay quite still, in that sleep which was nearest of all to death.

Then Roupert's voice spoke again, clear and peremptory and triumphant.

"Begone, James Rolls!" he cried.

Very slowly the materialized spirit began to move, floating like a balloon in an almost windless air. Slowly it drifted towards us, with its eyes fixed on the unconscious medium and alight with awful purpose, its mouth curled into some sort of hellish smile. It came quite close to him, as if sucked there, and the edge of its outline began to extend towards him a feeler, as of a little whirlpool of water drawn down into a sink, till the end of it just touched him....

"In the name of the Holiest, and by the power of the Highest," shouted Roupert, "I bid you go to the place that He has appointed for you."

Then ... I can only describe what happened by saying that some shock, blinding, deafening, overwhelming every sense, shook the room. It leaped into a blaze of light, a thunder of sound rent the air, and yet I knew that all this came from within, was the echo of the spiritual crisis that raged round us made manifest to the bodily sense. And silence as of the frozen Polar night succeeded....

Then once again a light began to be built up over Hampden's body that lay utterly still beside the curtains. It fashioned itself, but only very faintly, into the outline of a man, and this seemed to be drawn inwards and absorbed by that motionless figure. We waited till it had disappeared altogether.

The medium stirred and struggled.

"It is over," he said, and laid his head on his arms.

Roupert got up and drew back the curtains. From outside the door came scratchings and whinings, and presently he unlocked it, and let Fifi in. She saluted everybody in her exuberant fashion; then came to the sofa, sniffed and jumped up on it, wagging her tail.

It was not till late in the afternoon that Frank Hampden came to himself. A beautiful spirit looked out of those jolly boyish eyes.

MRS. ANDREWS'S CONTROL

Mrs. Andrews was certainly Athenian by nature, and it was her delight not only to hear some new thing, but to put it into practice. Enjoying excellent health, she was able to take almost any liberties with her constitution, and for a long time was absorbed in the maelstrom of diets, each of which seemed to suit her to perfection. For a couple of months she adopted the Pembroke treatment, and droves of sheep were sacrificed to supply her with sufficient minced mutton, while the utmost resources of the kitchen boiler were needed to give her the oceans of hot water which she found it necessary to drink all day except at meals. Having obtained the utmost benefits derivable from this system, she nourished her ample and vigorous frame, by way of a change, on pyramids of grated nuts, carefully weighed out, and it cannot be doubted that she would enthusiastically have fed herself on chopped-up hard-boiled egg, like a canary, if she could have found any system of diet that inculcated such a proceeding.

Her husband, for all his mild and apparently yielding disposition, must at bottom have been a man of iron soul, for he absolutely refused to embark on any of these experiments, though he never dissuaded his wife from so doing, and stuck firmly, like a limpet, to his three solid and satisfactory meals, not disdaining minced mutton, nor even a modicum of milled nuts, when he felt that they would be agreeable, but adding them to his ordinary diet, without relying on them. The two, childless and middle-aged, lived in extreme happiness and comfort together, and no doubt Mrs. Andrews's enthusiasms, and the perennial amusement her husband derived from them, served to keep the sunlight of life shining on them. They were never bored and always busy, which, perhaps, even more than diet, secured them serenity of health.

But the time came when Mrs. Andrews, in an unacknowledged despair of feeling better and more vigorous physically than she always did, turned her Athenian mind towards mental and psychical fads. She began by telling the fortunes of her friends by means of cards, and, though she could always say how she knew, following the rules of her primer, that her husband had had scarlet fever when he was twenty-three, yet the fact that she knew it perfectly well without the help of the cards made the divination rather less amazing. She tried Christian Science, though only for a short time, since no amount of demonstration over false claims could rid her one day of the conviction that she had a raging toothache, whereas the dentist convinced her in a moment, by the short though agonizing application of the pincers, that he could remove the toothache, which had resisted all the precepts of her temporary creed.

An excursion into the realms of astrology succeeded this, and conjointly a study of palmistry, and at this point her husband, for the first time, began to take an interest in his wife's preoccupations. It certainly did seem very odd that his horoscope should testify to the identical events which the lines in his hand so plainly showed his wife, and certain apparent discrepancies were no doubt capable of explanation. When he knew that the right hand indicated what Nature meant him to be, and the left what he had made of himself, it could not but be gratifying to find he had lived so closely up to his possibilities, and it was pleasant, again, to find his wife so enthusiastic about his plump, pink palm.

"A most remarkable hand, dear," she said. "I never saw evidence of such pluck and determination. And look at your Mount of Jupiter! Splendid!"

Mr. Andrews did not know exactly what the Mount of Jupiter was, but he knew what pluck and determination were.

"Upon my word, my dear," he said, "there may be something in it. I will borrow your primer, if I may. And now about the future."

Mrs. Andrews was already peering eagerly into the future. This was as splendid as the Mount of Jupiter.

"Such a line of life!" she said. "Let me see, you are fifty-eight, are you not? Well, on it goes—sixty, seventy, eighty, without a break in it. Why, I declare it reaches ninety, Henry!"

This was very gratifying, and it showed only ordinary politeness on Henry's part to inquire into his wife's prospects.

"Ah, I haven't such a line as you, dear," she said. "But, after all, if I live in perfect health till I am eighty-two, which is what my hand tells me, I'm sure there's no reason to complain, and I for one shan't."

But when Mrs. Andrews had told the fortunes of her husband and all her friends, and secured them, on the whole, such charming futures, it was no wonder that she went further into matters more psychical and occult. A course of gazing into the most expensive crystal proved disappointing, since she could never see anything except the reflection of the objects in the room, while her husband, now actively taking part in these investigations, merely fell asleep when he attempted to see anything there. They both hoped that this might not be ordinary sleep, but the condition of deep trance which they found was one of the accompanying phenomena, and productive of great results; but these trances were so deep that no recollection of what occurred therein ever remained in his mind, with the exception of one occasion, on which he dreamed about boiled rabbit. As he had partaken of this disgusting provender at lunch that day, both Mrs. Andrews and he regarded this dream as retrospective in character, and as not possessed of prophetic significance.

It was about this time that they both became members of the Psychical Research Society, and their attention could not but be struck by the wonderful phenomena resulting from the practice of automatic writing. If you had a psychical gift in this direction—and it was now the settled conviction of both Henry Andrews and his wife that they had—all apparently that had to be done was to hold a pencil over a writing-pad conveniently placed, abstract your mind from the hand that held the pencil, and sit there to see what happened. The theory was that some controlling spirit might take possession of the pencil and dictate messages from the other world, which the pencil would record. Eager study of the psychical journals warned them that patient practice might be necessary before any results were arrived at, the reason being that the control must get used to the novel instrument of communication; and warning was given that they must not be discouraged if for a long time nothing was recorded on the paper except meaningless lines. But it appeared that most people, if they would only be patient enough, would be rewarded by symptoms of the presence of a control before very long, and when once a beginning was made, progress was apt to be very rapid. It was recommended also that practice should be regular, and, if possible, should take place at the same time every day.

The idea fired Mrs. Andrews at once.

"Upon my word, dear Henry," she said, "I think it is very well worth trying, for the crystal is yielding no results at all. Psychical gifts are possessed by everybody in some degree, so this very interesting article says, and if ours do not lie in the direction of crystal-gazing, it makes it all the more probable that we shall achieve something in automatic writing. And as for a regular time for practising it, what could be more pleasant than to sit out in the garden after tea, when you have come in from your golf, and enjoy these warm evenings, with the feeling that we are occupying ourselves, instead of sitting idle, as we are apt to do?"

Henry distinctly approved of the suggestion. He was often a little fatigued after his golf, though he was going to live till ninety, and the prospect of sitting quietly in a chair in the garden, instead of feeling that he ought to be weeding, was quite a pleasant one.

"Then shall we each sit with paper and pencil, dear?" he asked.

Mrs. Andrews referred to the essay that gave elementary instruction.

"Certainly," she said. "We will try that first. They say that two hands holding the pencil often produce extraordinary results, but we will begin, as they suggest, singly. I declare that my hand feels quite fidgety already, as if the control was just waiting for the means of communication to be prepared."

Everything in Mrs. Andrews's house was in apple-pie order, and it took her no time at all to find two writing-pads and a couple of sharpened pencils. With these she rejoined her husband on the paved walk, where they had had tea, outside the drawing-room, and, with pencil in hand, fixed her eye firmly on the top of the mulberry tree at the edge of the lawn, and waited. He, with left hand free for his cigarette, did the same, but his mind kept going back to the boiled rabbit he had dreamed of after crystal-gazing, which still seemed to him a very unusual occurrence, for, to the best of his recollection, he had never dreamed of boiled rabbit before.

Within a few days' time very promising developments had taken place. Almost immediately Mrs. Andrews had begun to trace angled lines on the paper, which, if they did not suggest anything else particular, were remarkably like the temperature chart of a very feverish patient. Her hand, seemingly without volition on her part, made energetic dashes and dabs all over the paper, and she felt a very odd tingling sensation in her fingers, which could scarcely be put down to anything else than the presence of the control.

Her husband, scarcely less fortunate, also began to trace queer patterns of irregular curves on his sheet, which looked very much as if they were words. But though they were like words, they were not any known words, whichever way up you attempted to read them, though, as Mrs. Andrews said, they might easily be Russian or Chinese, which would account for their being wholly meaningless to the English eye. Sheets of possible Russian were thus poured out by Mr. Andrews, and whole hospital records of fever charts on the part of his wife, but neither at present came within measurable distance of intelligibility. The control seemed incapable of making itself understood. Then on a memorable day Mr. Andrews's pencil evinced an irresistible desire to write figures, and after inscribing "one, two, one, two," a great many times, wrote quite distinctly 4958, and gave a great dash as if it had said its last word.

"And what 4958 indicates, my dear," said he, passing it over to Mrs. Andrews, "I think we must leave to the control to determine."

She looked at it a moment in silence; then, a great thought splendidly striking her, she rose in some excitement.

"Henry, it is as plain as plain," she said. "I am forty-nine; you are fifty-eight. Our ages are thus wonderfully conjoined. It certainly means that we must act together. Come and hold my pencil with me."

"Well, that is very curious," said Henry, and did as he was told.

At this point their experiments entered the second phase, and the pencil thus jointly held at once developed an intelligible activity. Instead of mere fever charts and numerals, it began to produce whole sentences which were true to the point of being positive truisms. Before they went to dinner that night, they were told, in a large, sprawling hand, that "Wisdom is more than wealth," and that "Fearlessness is best," and that "Hate blinds the eyes of Love." The very next day more unimpeachable sentiments were poured forth, and at the end was written, "From Pocky."

Pocky, then, was clearly the control; he became to Mr. and Mrs. Andrews an established personality with a mind stored with moral generalities. Very often some practical application could be made of his dicta, as, for instance, when Mr. Andrews was hesitating as to whether to invest quite a considerable sum of money in a rather speculative venture. But, recollecting that Pocky had said that "Wisdom is better than wealth," he very prudently refrained, and had the satisfaction of seeing the speculative concern come a most tremendous smash very soon after. But it required a good deal of ingenuity to fit Pocky's utterances into the affairs of daily life, and Mr. Andrews was getting a little tired of these generalities, when the curtain went up on the third phase.

This was coincident with the outbreak of the German war, when nothing else was present in the minds of husband and wife, and Pocky suddenly became patriotic and truculent. For a whole evening he wrote, "Kill them. Treacherous Germans. Avenge the scrap of paper," and very soon after, just when England generally was beginning to be excited over the rumour that hosts of Russians were passing through the country to the French battle-front, he made a further revelation of himself.

"The hosts of Russia are with you," he wrote, "Cossacks from the Steppes, troops of the Great White Tsar. Hundreds and thousands, Russia to England, England to France. The Allies triumph. From Pocksky." The pencil gave a great dash and flew from the fingers that held it.

It was all most clearly written, and in a voice that trembled with excitement, Mrs. Andrews read it out.

"There, my dear," she said, "I don't think we need have any further doubt about the Russians. And look how it is signed—not Pocky any longer, but Pocksky. That is a Russian name, if ever there was one!"

"Pocksky—so it is," said Mr. Andrews, putting on his spectacles. "Well, that is most wonderful. And to think that in those early days, when my pencil used to write things we couldn't read, you suggested it might be Russian!"

"I feel no doubt that it was," said Mrs. Andrews firmly. "I wish now that we had kept them, and my writing, too, which you used to call the fever charts. I dare say some poor fellow in hospital had temperatures like that."

Mr. Andrews did not feel so sure of this.

"That sounds a little far-fetched, dear," he said, "though I quite agree with you about the possibility of its being Pocksky who wrote through me. I wonder who he was? Some great general, probably."

You can easily imagine the excitement that pervaded Oakley in the weeks that followed, when every day brought some fresh butler or railway porter into the public press, who had told somebody who had told the author of the letter in question that he had seen bearded soldiers stepping out of trains with blinds drawn down, and shaking the snow off their boots. It mattered nothing that the whole romance was officially denied; indeed, it only made Mrs. Andrews very indignant at the suppression of war news.

"The War Office may say what it likes," she exclaimed, "and, indeed, it seems to make it its business to deny what we all know to be true. I think I must learn a few words of Russian, in case I meet any soldier with a beard—'God Save the Tsar!' or something of the kind. I shall send for a Russian grammar. Now, let us see what Pocksky has to tell us to-night."

That no further confirmation of Pocksky's announcements on this subject ever came to light was scarcely noticed by the automatic writers, for Pocksky was bursting with other news. He rather terrified his interpreters, when there was nervousness about possible Zeppelin raids, by saying: "Fires from the wicked ones in the clouds. Fourteen, twelve, fourteen, cellar best," since this could hardly mean anything but that a raid was to be expected on the fourteenth of December; and Mr. and Mrs. Andrews—and, indeed, a large number of their friends—spent the evening in their cellars, coming out again when it was definitely after midnight. But the relief at finding that no harm had been done speedily obliterated the feeling that Pocksky had misled them, and when, on Christmas Eve, he said, "Spirit of Peace descends," though certain people thought he meant that the War would soon be over, the truce on the Western Front for Christmas Day was more generally believed to bear out this remarkable prophecy.

All through the spring Pocksky continued voluble. He would not definitely commit himself over the course that Italy was to take, but, as Mrs. Andrews triumphantly pointed out, Italy would not definitely commit herself either, which just showed how right Pocksky was. He rather went back to the Pocky style over this, and said: "Prudence is better than precipitation; Italy prepares before making decision. Wisdom guides her counsels, and wisdom is ever best. From Pocksky." Intermittently the forcing of the Dardanelles occupied him.

Now, here a rather odd point arose. Mr. Andrews at this time had to spend a week in town, and only Mrs. Andrews held the pencil which the intelligence of Pocksky used to express himself with. In all these messages Pocksky spelled the name of the straits "Dardanels," which, for all I know, may be the Russian form. But two days ago Mrs. Andrews kindly sent me one of his messages, which I was glad to see was most optimistic in tone. She enclosed a note from herself, saying:

"You will like to see what Pocksky says about the Dardanels. Isn't he wonderful?"

So Mrs. Andrews, writing independently of Pocksky, spells Dardanelles the same way as Pocksky does when he controls the pencil. I cannot help wondering if the control is—shall we say?— quite complete. I wonder also how the straits will get themselves spelt when Mr. Andrews returns. It is all rather puzzling.

THE APE

Hugh Marsham had spent the day, as a good tourist should, in visiting the temples and the tombs of the kings across the river, and the magic of the hour of sunset flamed over earth and heaven as he crossed the Nile again to Luxor in his felucca. It seemed as if the whole world had been suddenly transferred into the heart of an opal, and burned with a myriad fiery colours. The river itself was of the green that beech trees are clad in at spring-time; the columns of the temple that stood close to its banks glowed as if lit from within by the flame of some perpetual evening sacrifice; the cloudless sky was dusky blue in the east, the blue of turquoise overhead, and melted into aqua-marine above the line of desert where the sun had just sunk. All along the bank which he was fast approaching under the press of the cool wind from the north were crowds of Arabs, padding softly home in the dust from their work, and chattering as sparrows chatter among the bushes in the long English twilights. Even the dust that hovered and hung and was dispersed again by the wind was rainbowed; it caught the hues from the river and the sky and the orange-flaming temple, and those who walked in it were clad in brightness.

Here in the South no long English twilight lingered, and as he walked up the dusky fragrant tunnel of mimosa that led to the hotel, night thickened, and in the sky a million stars leaped into being, while the soft gathering darkness sponged out the glories of the flaming hour. On the hotel steps the vendors of carpets and Arabian hangings, of incense and filigree work, of suspicious turquoises and more than suspicious scarabs were already packing up their wares, and probably recounting to each other in their shrill incomprehensible gabble the iniquitous bargains they had made with the gullible Americans and English, who so innocently purchased the wares of Manchester. Only in his accustomed corner old Abdul still squatted, for he was of a class above the ordinary vendors, a substantial dealer in antiques, who had a shop in the village, where archæologists resorted, and bought, sub rosa, pieces that eventually found their way into European museums. He was in his shop all day, but evening found him, when serious business hours were over, on the steps of the hotel, where he sold undoubted antiquities to tourists who wanted something genuine.

The day had been very hot, and Hugh felt himself disposed to linger outside the hotel in this cool dusk, and turn over the tray of scarabs which Abdul Hamid presented to his notice. He was a wrinkled, dried-up husk of a man, loquacious and ingratiating in manner, and welcomed Hugh as an old customer.

"See, sir," he said, "here are two more scroll-scarabs like those you bought from me before the week. You should have these; they are very fine and very cheap, because I do no business this year. Mr. Rankin, you know him? of the British Museum, he give me two pounds each last year for scroll-scarabs not so fine, and to-day I sell them at a pound and a half each. Take them; they are yours. Scroll-scarabs of the twelfth dynasty; if Mr. Rankin were here he pay me two pounds each, and be sorry I not ask more."

Hugh laughed.

"You may sell them to Mr. Rankin then," he said. "He comes here to-morrow."

The old man, utterly unabashed, grinned and shook his head.

"No; I promised you them for pound and a half," he said. "I am not cheat-dealer. They are yours—pound and a half. Take them, take them."

Hugh resisted this unparalleled offer, and, turning over the contents of the tray, picked out of it and examined carefully a broken fragment of blue glaze, about an inch in height. This represented the head and shoulders of an ape, and the fracture had occurred half-way down the back, so that the lower part of the trunk, the forearms which apparently hung by its sides, and the hind legs were missing. On the back there was an inscription in hieroglyphics, also broken. Presumably the missing piece contained the remainder of the letters. It was modelled with extreme care and minuteness, and the face wore an expression of grotesque malevolence.

"What's this broken bit of a monkey?" asked Hugh carelessly.

Abdul, looking much like a monkey himself, put his eyes close to it.

"Ah, that's the rarest thing in Egypt," he said, "so Mr. Rankin he tell me, if only the monkey not broken. See the back? There it says: 'He of whom this is, let him call on me thrice'—and then some son of a dog broke it. If the rest was here, I would not take a hundred pounds for it; but now ten years have I kept half-monkey, and never comes half-monkey to it. It is yours, sir, for a pound it is yours. Half-monkey nothing to me; it is fool-monkey only being half-monkey. I let it go—I give it you, and you give me pound."

Hugh Marsham felt in one pocket, then in another, with no appearance of hurry or eagerness.

"There's your pound," he said casually.

Abdul peered at him in the dusk. It was very odd that Hugh

did not offer him half what he asked, instead of paying up without bargaining. He regretted extremely that he had not asked more. But the little blue fragment was now in Hugh's pocket, and the sovereign glistened very pleasantly in his own palm.

"And what was the rest of the hieroglyphic, do you think?" Hugh asked.

"Eh, Allah only knows the wickedness and the power of the monkeys," said Abdul. "Once there were such in Egypt, and in the temple of Mut in Karnak, which the English dug up, you shall see a chamber with just such monkeys sitting round it, four of them, all carved in sandstone. But on them there is no writing; I have looked at them behind and before; they not master-monkeys. Perhaps the monkey promised that whoso called on him thrice, if he were owner of the blue image of which gentleman has the half, would be his master, and that monkey would do his bidding. Who knows? It is of the old wickedness of the world, the old Egyptian blackness."

Hugh got up. He had been out in the sun all day, and felt at this moment a little intimate shiver, which warned him that it was wiser to go indoors till the chill of sunset had passed.

"I expect you've tried it on with the half-monkey, haven't you?" he said.

Abdul burst out into a toothless cackle of laughter.

"Yes, effendi," he said. "I have tried it a hundred times, and nothing happens. Else I would not have sold it you. Half-monkey is no monkey at all. I have tried to make boy with the ink-mirror see something about monkeys, but nothing comes, except the clouds and the man who sweeps. No monkey."

Hugh nodded to him.

"Good-night, you old sorcerer," he said pleasantly.

As he walked up the broad flagged passage to his room, carrying the half-monkey in his hand, Hugh felt with a disengaged thumb in his waistcoat pocket for something he had picked up that day in the valley of the tombs of the kings. He had eaten his lunch there, after an inspection of the carved and reeking corridors, and, as he sat idly smoking, had reached out a lazy hand to where this thing had glittered among the pebbles. Now, entering his room, he turned up the electric light, and, standing under it with his back to the window, that opened, door fashion, on to the three steps that led into the hotel garden, he fitted the fragment he had found to the fragment he had just purchased. They joined on to each other with the most absolute accuracy, not a chip was missing. There was the complete ape, and down its back ran the complete legend.

The window was open, and at this moment he heard a sudden noise as of some scampering beast in the garden outside. His light streamed out in an oblong on to the sandy path, and, laying the two pieces of the image on the table, he looked out. But there was nothing irregular to be seen; the palm trees waved and clashed in the wind, and the rose bushes stirred and scattered their fragrance. Only right down the middle of the sandy path that ran between the beds, the ground was curiously disturbed, as by some animal, heavily frolicking, scooping and spurning the light soil as it ran.

The midday train from Cairo next day brought Mr. Rankin, the eminent Egyptologist and student of occult lore, a huge red man with a complete mastery of colloquial Arabic. He had but a day to spend in Luxor, for he was en route for Merawi, where lately some important finds had been made; but Hugh took occasion to show him the figure of the ape as they sat over their coffee in the garden just outside his bedroom after lunch.

"I found the lower half yesterday outside one of the tombs of the kings," he said, "and the top half by the utmost luck among old Abdul's things. He told me you said that if it was complete it would be of the greatest rarity. He lied, I suppose?"

Rankin gave one gasp of amazed surprise as he looked at it and read the inscription on the back. Marsham thought that his great red face suddenly paled.

"Good Lord!" he said. "Here, take it!" And he held out the two pieces to him.

Hugh laughed.

"Why in such a hurry?" he said.

"Because there comes a breaking-point to every man's honesty, and I might keep it, and swear that I had given it back to you. My dear fellow, do you know what you've got?"

"Indeed I don't. I want to be told," said Hugh.

"And to think that it was you who only a couple of months ago asked me what a scarab was! Well, you've got there what all Egyptologists, and even more keenly than Egyptologists all students of folk-lore and magic black and white—especially black—would give their eyes to have found. Good Lord! what's that?"

Hugh was sitting by his side in a deck-chair, idly fitting together the two halves of the broken image. He too heard what had startled Rankin; for it was the same noise as had startled him last night, namely, the scampering of some great frolicsome animal, somewhere close to them. As he jumped up, severing his hands, the noise ceased.

"Funny," he said, "I heard that last night. There's nothing; it's some stray dog in the bushes. Do tell me what it is that I've got."

Rankin, who had surged to his feet also, stood listening a moment. But there was nothing to be heard but the buzzing of bees in the bushes and the chiding of the remote kites overhead. He sat down again.

"Well, give me two minutes," he said, "and I can tell you all I know. Once upon a time, when this wonderful and secret land was alive and not dead—oh, we have killed it with our board-schools and our steamers and our religion—there was a whole hierarchy of gods, Isis, Osiris, and the rest, of whom we know a great deal. But below them there was a company of semi-divinities, demons if you will, of whom we know practically nothing. The cat was one, certain dwarfish creatures were others, but most potent of all were the cynocephali, the dog-faced apes. They were not divine, rather they were demons, of hideous power, but"—and he pointed a great hand at Hugh—"they could be controlled. Men could control them, men could turn them into terrific servants, much as the genii in the 'Arabian Nights' were controlled. But to do that you had to know the secret name of the demon, and had yourself to make an image of him, with the secret name inscribed thereon, and by that you could summon him and all the incarnate creatures of his species.

"So much we know from certain very guarded allusions in the Book of the Dead and other sources, for this was one of the great mysteries never openly spoken of. Here and there a priest in Karnak, or Abydos, or in Hieropolis, had had handed down to him one of those secret names, but in nine cases out of ten the knowledge died with him, for there was something dangerous and terrible about it all. Old Abdul here, for instance, believes that Moses had the secret names of frogs and lice, and made images of them with the secret name inscribed on them, and by those produced the plagues of Egypt. Think what you could do, think what he did, if infinite power over frog-nature were given you, so that the king's chamber swarmed with frogs at your word. Usually, as I said, the secret name was but sparingly passed on, but occasionally some very bold advanced spirit, such as Moses, made his image, and controlled——"

He paused a moment, and Hugh wondered if he was in some delirious dream. Here they were, taking coffee and cigarettes underneath the shadow of a modern hotel in the year A.D. 1912, and this great savant was talking to him about the spell that controlled the whole frog-nature in the universe. The gist, the moral of his discourse, was already perfectly clear.

"That's a good joke," Hugh said. "You told your story with extraordinary gravity. And what you mean is that those two blue bits I hold in my hand control the whole ape-nature of the world? Bravo, Rankin! For a moment, you and your impressiveness almost made me take it all seriously. Lord! You do tell a story well! And what's the secret name of the ape?"

Rankin turned to him with the shake of an impressive forefinger.

"My dear boy," he said, "you should never be disrespectful towards the things you know nothing of. Never say a thing is moonshine till you know what you are talking about. I know, at this moment, exactly as much as you do about your ape-image, except that I can translate its inscription, which I will do for you. On the top half is written, 'He, of whom this is, let him call on me thrice—'"

Hugh interrupted.

"That's what Abdul read to me," he said.

"Of course. Abdul knows hieroglyphics. But on the lower half is what nobody but you and I know. 'Let him call on me thrice,' says the top half, and then there speaks what you picked up in the valley of the tombs, 'and I, Tahu-met, obey the order of the Master.'"

"Tahu-met?" asked Hugh.

"Yes. Now in ten minutes I must be off to catch my train. What I have told you is all that is known about this particular affair by those who have studied folk-lore and magic, and Egyptology. If anything—if anything happens, do be kind enough to let me know. If you were not so abominably rich I would offer you what you liked for that little broken statue. But there's the way of the world!"

"Oh, it's not for sale," said Hugh gaily. "It's too interesting to sell. But what am I to do next with it? Tahu-met? Shall I say Tahu-met three times?"

Rankin leaned forward very hurriedly, and laid his fat hand on the young man's knee.

"No, for Heaven's sake! Just keep it by you," he said. "Be patient with it. See what happens. You might mend it, perhaps. Put a drop of gum-arabic on the break and make it whole. By the way, if it interests you at all, my niece Julia Draycott arrives here this evening, and will wait for me here till my return from Merawi. You met her in Cairo, I think."

Certainly this piece of news interested Hugh more than all the possibilities of apes and super-apes. He thrust the two pieces of Tahu-met carelessly into his pocket.

"By Jove, is she really?" he said. "That's splendid. She told me she might be coming up, but didn't feel at all sure. Must you really be off? I shall come down to the station with you."

While Rankin went to gather up such small luggage as he had brought with him, Hugh wandered into the hotel bureau to ask for letters, and seeing there a gum-bottle, dabbed with gum the fractured edges of Tahu-met. The two pieces joined with absolute exactitude, and wrapping a piece of paper round them to keep the edges together, he went out through the garden with Rankin. At the hotel gate was the usual crowd of donkey-boys and beggars, and presently they were ambling down the village street on bored white donkeys. It was almost deserted at this hottest hour of the afternoon, but along it there moved an Arab leading a large grey ape, that tramped surlily in the dust. But just before they overtook it, the beast looked round, saw Hugh, and with chatterings of delight strained at his leash. Its owner cursed and pulled it away, for Hugh nearly rode over it, but it paid no attention to him, and fairly towed him along the road after the donkeys.

Rankin looked at his companion.

"That's odd," he said. "That's one of your servants. I've still a couple of minutes to spare. Do you mind stopping a moment?"

He shouted something in the vernacular to the Arab, who ran after them, with the beast still towing him on. When they came close the ape stopped and bent his head to the ground in front of Hugh.

"And that's odd," said Rankin.

Hugh suddenly felt rather uncomfortable.

"Nonsense!" he said. "That's just one of his tricks. He's been taught it to get baksheesh for his master. Look, there's your train coming in. We must get on."

He threw a couple of piastres to the man, and they rode on. But when they got to the station, glancing down the road, he saw that the ape was still looking after them.

Julia Draycott's arrival that evening speedily put such antique imaginings as the lordship of apes out of Hugh's head. He chucked Tahu-met into the box where he kept his scarabs and ushapti figures, and devoted himself to this heartless and exquisite girl, whose mission in life appeared to be to make as miserable as possible the largest possible number of young men. Hugh had already been selected by her in Cairo as a decent victim, and now she proceeded to torture him. She had no intention whatever of marrying him, for poor Hugh was certainly ugly, with his broad, heavy face, and though rich, he was not nearly rich enough. But he had a couple of delightful Arab horses, and so, since there was no one else on hand to experiment with, she let him buy her a side-saddle, and be, with his horses, always at her disposal. She did not propose to use him for very long, for she expected young Lord Paterson (whom she did intend to marry) to follow her from Cairo within a week. She had beat a Parthian retreat from him, being convinced that he would soon find Cairo intolerable without her; and in the meantime Hugh was excellent practice. Besides, she adored riding.

101

They sat together one afternoon on the edge of the river opposite Karnak. She had treated him like a brute beast all morning, and had watched his capability for wretchedness with the purring egoism that distinguished her; and now, as a change, she was seeing how happy she could make him.

"You are such a dear," she said. "I don't know how I could have endured Luxor without you; and, thanks to you, it has been the loveliest week."

She looked at him from below her long lashes, through which there gleamed the divinest violet, smiling like a child at her friend. "And to-night? You made some delicious plan for to-night."

"Yes; it's full moon to-night," said he. "We are going to ride out to Karnak after dinner."

"That will be heavenly. And, Mr. Marsham, do let us go alone. There's sure to be a mob from the hotel, so let's start late, when they've all cleared out. Karnak in the moonlight, just with you."

That completely made Hugh's mind up. For the last three days he had been on the look out for a moment that should furnish the great occasion; and now (all unconsciously, of course) she indicated it to him. This evening, then. And his heart leaped.

"Yes, yes," he said. "But why have I become Mr. Marsham again?"

Again she looked at him, now with a penitent mouth.

"Oh, I was such a beast to you this morning," she said. "That was why. I didn't deserve that you should be Hugh. But will you be Hugh again? Do you forgive me?"

In spite of Hugh's fixing the great occasion for this evening, it might have come then, so bewitching was her penitence, had not the rest of their party on donkeys, whom they had outpaced, come streaming along the river bank at this moment.

"Ah, those tiresome people," she said. "Hughie, what a bore everybody else is except you and me."

They got back to the hotel about sunset, and as they passed into the hall the porter handed Julia a telegram which had been waiting some couple of hours. She gave a little exclamation of pleasure and surprise, and turned to Hugh.

"Come and have a turn in the garden, Hughie," she said, "and then I must go down for the arrival of the boat. When does it come in?"

"I should think it would be here immediately," he said. "Let's go down to the river."

Even as he spoke the whistle of the approaching steamer was heard. The girl hesitated a moment.

"It's a shame to take up all your time in the way I'm doing," she said. "You told me you had letters to write. Write them now; then—then you'll be free after dinner."

"To-morrow will do," he said. "I'll come down with you to the boat."

"No, you dear, I forbid it," she said. "Oh, do be good, and write your letters. I ask you to."

Rather puzzled and vaguely uncomfortable, Hugh went into the hotel. It was true that he had told her he had letters that should have been written a week ago, but something at the back of his mind insisted that this was not the girl's real reason for wanting him to do his task now. She wanted to go and meet the boat alone, and on the moment an unfounded jealousy stirred like a coiled snake in him. He told himself that it might be some inconvenient aunt whom she was going to meet, but such a suggestion did not in the least satisfy him when he remembered the obvious pleasure with which she had read the telegram that no doubt announced this arrival. But he nailed himself to his writing-table till a couple of very tepid letters were finished, and then, with growing restlessness, went out through the hall into the warm, still night. Most of the hotel had gone indoors to dress for dinner, but sitting on the veranda with her back to him was Julia. A chair was drawn in front of her, and facing her was a young man, on whose face the light shone. He was looking eagerly at her, and his hand rested on her knee. Hugh turned abruptly and went back into the hotel.

He and Julia for these last three days had, with two other friends, made a very pleasant party of four at lunch and dinner. To-night, when he entered the dining-room, he found that places were laid here for three only, and that at a far-distant table in the window were sitting Julia and the young man whom he had seen with her on the veranda. His identity was casually disclosed as dinner went on; one of his companions had seen Lord Paterson in Cairo. Hugh had only a wandering ear for table-talk, but a quick glancing eye, ever growing more sombre, for those in the window, and his heavy face, as he noted the tokens and signs of their intimacy, grew sullen and savage. Then, before dinner was over, they rose and passed out into the garden.

Jealousy can no more bear to lose sight of those to whom it owes its miseries than love can bear to be parted from the object of its adoration, and presently Hugh and his two friends went and sat, as was usual with them, on the veranda outside. Here and there about the garden were wandering couples, and in the light of the full moon, which was to be their lamp at Karnak to-night when the "tiresome people" had gone, he soon identified Julia and Lord Paterson. They passed and repassed down a rose-embowered alley,

103

hidden sometimes behind bushes and then appearing again for a few paces, and each sight of them, each vanishing of them again served but to confirm that which already needed no confirmation. And as his jealousy grew every moment more bitter, so every moment Hugh grew more and more dangerously enraged. Apparently Lord Paterson was not one of the "tiresome people" whom Julia longed to get away from.

Presently his two companions left him, for they were starting now to ride out to Karnak, and Hugh sat on, smoking and throwing away half consumed an endless series of cigarettes. He had ordered that his two horses, one with a side-saddle, should be ready at ten, and at ten he meant to go to the girl and remind her of her engagement. Till then he would wait here, wait and watch. If the veranda had been on fire, he felt he could not have left it to seek safety in some place where he was unable to see the bushy path where the two strolled. Then they emerged from that on to the broader walk that led straight to where he was sitting, and after a few whispered words, Lord Paterson left her there, and came quickly towards the hotel. He passed close by Hugh, gave him (so Hugh thought) a glance of amused derision, and went into the hotel.

Julia came quickly towards him when Lord Paterson had gone.

"Oh, Hughie," she said. "Will you be a tremendous angel? Lord Paterson—yes, he's just gone in, such a dear, you would delight in him—Lord Paterson's only here for one night, and he's dying to see Karnak by moonlight. So will you lend us your horses? He absolutely insists I should go out there with him."

The amazing effrontery of this took Hugh's breath away, and in that moment's pause his rage flamed within him.

"I thought you were going out with me?" he said.

"I was. But, well, you see——"

She made the penitent mouth again, which had seemed so enchanting to him this afternoon.

"Oh, Hughie, don't you understand?" she said.

Hugh got up, feeling himself to be one shaking black jelly of wounded anger.

"I'm not sure if I do," he said. "But no doubt I soon shall. Anyhow, I want to ask you something. I want you to promise to marry me."

She opened her great childlike eyes to their widest. Then they closed into mere slits again as she broke out into a laugh.

"Marry you?" she said. "You silly, darling fellow! That is a good joke."

Suddenly from the garden there sounded the jubilant scamper

of running feet, and next moment a great grey ape sprang on to the veranda beside them, and looked eagerly, with keen dog's eyes, at Hugh, as if intent on obeying some yet unspoken command. Julia gave a little shriek of fright and clung to him.

"Oh, that horrible animal!" she cried. "Hughie, take care of me!"

Some sudden ray of illumination came to Hugh. All the extraordinary fantastic things that Rankin had said to him became sober and real. And simultaneously the girl's clinging fingers on his arm became like the touch of some poisonous, preying thing, snake-coil, or suckers of an octopus, or hooked wings of a vampire bat. Something within him still shook and trembled like a quicksand, but his conscious mind was quite clear and collected.

"Go away," he said to the ape, and pointed into the garden, and it scampered off, still gleefully spurning and kicking the soft sandy path. Then he quietly turned to the girl.

"There, it's gone," he said. "It was just some tame thing escaped. I saw it, or one like it, the other day on the end of a string. As for the horses, I shall be delighted to let you and Lord Paterson have them. It is ten now; they will be round."

The girl had quite recovered from her fright.

"Ah, Hughie, you are a dear," she said. "And you do understand?"

"Yes, perfectly," said he.

Julia went to dress herself for riding, and presently Hugh saw them off from the gate, with courteous wishes for a pleasant ride. Then he went back to his bedroom and opened the little box where he kept his scarabs.

An hour later he was walking out alone on the road to Karnak, and in his pocket was the image of Tahu-met. He had formed no clear idea of what he was meaning to do; the immediate reason for his expedition was that once again he could not bear to lose sight of Julia and her companion. The moon was high, the feathery outline of palm-groves was clearly and delicately etched on the dark velvet of the heavens, and stars sat among their branches like specks of golden fruit. The caressing scent of bean-flowers was wafted over the road, and often he had to stand aside to let pass a group of noisy tourists mounted on white donkeys, coming riotously home from the show-piece of Karnak by moonlight. Then, striking off the road, he passed beside the horseshoe lake, in the depths of whose black waters the stars burned unwaveringly, and by the entrance of the ruined temple of Mut. And then, with a stab of jealousy that screamed for its revenge, he saw, tied up to a pillar just within, his own horses. So they were here.

He gave the beasts a wide berth, lest, recognizing him, they should whinny and perhaps betray his presence, and, creeping in the shadow of the walls behind the row of great cat-headed statues, he stole into the inner court of the temple. Here for the first time he caught sight of the two at the far end of the enclosure, and as they turned, white-faced in the moonlight, he saw Paterson kiss the girl, and they stood there with neck and arms interlaced. Then they began walking towards him again, and he stepped into a dark chamber on his right to avoid meeting them.

It had that strange stale animal odour about it that hangs in Egyptian temples, and with a thrill of glee he saw, by a ray of moonlight that streamed in through the door, that by chance he had stepped into the shrine round which sit the dog-faced apes, whose secret name he knew, and whose controlling spell lay in his breast-pocket. Often he had felt the underworld horror that dwelt here, as a thing petrified and corpse-like; to-night it was petrified no longer, for the images seemed tense and quivering with the life that at any moment he could put into them. Their faces leered and hated and lusted, and all that demoniac power, which seemed to be flowing into him from them, was his to use as he wished. Rankin's fantastic tales were bursting with reality; he knew with the certainty with which the night-watcher waits for the day, that the lordship of the spirit of apes, incarnate and discarnate, would descend on him as on some anointed king the moment he thrice pronounced the secret name. He was going to do it too; he knew also that all he hesitated for now was to determine what orders their lord should give. It seemed that the image in his breast-pocket was aware, for it throbbed and vibrated against his chest like a boiling kettle.

He could not make up his mind what to do; but fed as with fuel by jealousy, and love, and hate, and revenge, his sense of the magical control he wielded could be resisted no longer, but boiled over, and he drew from his pocket the image where was engraven the secret name.

"Tahu-met, Tahu-met, Tahu-met," he shouted aloud.

There was a moment's absolute stillness; then came a wild scream of fright from his horses, and he heard them gallop off madly into the night. Slowly, like a lamp turned down and then finally turned out, the blaze of the moon faded into utter darkness, and in that darkness, which whispered with a gradually increasing noise of scratchings and scamperings, he felt that the walls of the narrow chamber where he stood were, as in a dream, going farther and farther away from him, until, though still the darkness was impenetrable, he knew that he was standing in some immense space. One wall, he fancied, was still near him, close behind him, but the space which was full of he knew not what unseen presences, extended away and away to both sides of him and in front of him. Then he was aware that he was not standing, but sitting, for beneath his hands he could feel the arms as of some throne, of which the seat's edge pressed him just below his knees. The animal odour he had noticed before increased enormously in pungency, and he sniffed it in ecstatically, as if it had been the scent of beanfields, and mixed with it was the sweetness of incense and the savour as of roast meat. And at that the withdrawn light began to glow once more, only now it was not the whiteness of the moon, but a redder glow as of flames that aspired and sank again.

He saw where he was now. He was seated on a chair of pink granite, and a little in front of him was a huge altar, on which limbs smoked. Overhead was a low roof supported at intervals by painted pillars, and the whole of the vast floor was full of great grey apes, squatting in dense rows. Sometimes they all bowed their heads to the ground, sometimes, as by a signal, they raised them again, and myriads of obscene expectant eyes faced him. They glowed from within, as cats' eyes glow in the dusk, but with an infinity of hellish power. All that power was his to command, and he gloried in it.

"Bring them in," he said, and no more. Indeed, he was not sure if he said it; it was just his thought.

But as if he spoke the soundless language of animals, they understood, and they clambered and leaped over each other to do his bidding. Then a huddled wave of them surged up in front of where he sat, and as it broke in foam of evil eyes and paws and switching tails, it disclosed the two whom he had ordered to be brought before him.

"And what shall I do with them?" he asked himself, cudgelling his monkey-brain for some infamous invention.

"Kiss each other," he said at length, in order to inflame the brutality of his jealousy further, and he laughed chatteringly, as their white trembling lips met. He felt that all remnants of humanity were draining from him; there was but a little left in his whole nature that could be deemed to belong to a man. A hundred awful schemes ran about through his brain, as sparks of fire run through the charred ashes of burnt paper.

And then Julia turned her face towards him. In the hideous entry that she had made in that wave of apes her hair had fallen down and streamed over her shoulders. And at that, the sight of a woman's hair unbound, the remnant of his manhood, all that was not submerged in the foulness of his supreme apehood, made one tremendous appeal to him, like some final convulsion of the dying, and at the bidding of that impulse his hands came together and snapped the image in two.

Something screamed; the whole temple yelled with it, and mixed with it was a roaring in his ears as of great waters or hurricane winds. He stamped on the broken image, grinding it to powder below his heel, and felt the ground and the temple walls rocking round him.

Then he heard someone not far off speaking in human voice again, and no music could be so sweet.

"Let's get out of the place, darling," it said. "That was an earthquake, and the horses have bolted."

He heard running steps outside, which gradually grew fainter. The moon shone whitely into the little chamber with the grotesque stone apes, and at his feet was the powdered blue glaze and baked white clay of the image he had ground to dust.

"THROUGH"

Richard Waghorn was among the cleverest and most popular of professional mediums, and a never-failing source of consolation to the credulous. That there was fraud, downright, unadulterated fraud mixed up with his remarkable manifestations it would be impossible to deny; but it would have been futile not to admit that these manifestations were not wholly fraudulent. He had to an extraordinary degree that rare and inexplicable gift of tapping, so to speak, not only the surface consciousness of those who consulted him, but, in favourable circumstances, their inner or subliminal selves, so that it frequently happened that he could speak to an inquirer of something he had completely forgotten, which subsequent investigation proved to be authentic.

So much was perfectly genuine, but he gave, as it were, a false frame to it all by the manner in which he presented these phenomena. He pretended, at his séances, to go into a trance, during which he was controlled sometimes by the spirit of an ancient Egyptian priest, who gave news to the inquirer about some dead friend or relative, sometimes more directly by that dead friend or relative who spoke through him.

As a matter of fact, Waghorn would not be in a trance at all, but perfectly conscious, extracting, as he sat quiescent and with closed eyes, the knowledge, remembered or even forgotten, that lurked in the mind of his sitter, and bringing it out in the speech of Mentu, the Egyptian control, or of the lost friend or relative about whom inquiry was being made. Fraudulent also, as purporting to come from the intelligence of discarnate spirits, were the pieces of information he gave as to the conditions under which those who had "passed over" still lived, and it was here that he chiefly brought consolation to the credulous, for he represented the dead as happy and busy, and full of spiritual activities. This information, to speak frankly, he obtained entirely from his own conscious mind. He made it up, and we cannot really find an excuse for him in the undoubted fact that he sincerely believed in the general truth of all he said when he spoke of the survival of individual personality.

Finally, deeply dyed with fraud, and that in crude, garish colours, were the spirit-rappings, the playing of musical boxes, the appearance of materialized spirits, the smell of incense that heralded Cardinal Newman, all that bag of conjuring tricks, in fact, which disgraces and makes a laughing-stock of the impostors who profess to be able to bring the seen world into connection with the unseen world. But to do Waghorn justice, he did not often employ those crude contrivances, for his telepathic and thought-reading gifts were far more convincing to his sitters. Occasionally, however, his powers in this line used to fail him, and then, it must be confessed, he presented his Egyptian control with every trapping and circumstance of degrading device.

Such was the general scheme of procedure when Richard Waghorn, with his sister as accomplice in case mechanical tricks were necessary, undertook to reveal the spirit world to the material world. They were a pleasant, handsome pair of young people, gifted with a manner that, if anything, disarmed suspicion too much, and while futile old gentlemen found it quite agreeable to sit in the dark holding Julia's firm, cool hand, similarly constituted old ladies were the recipients of thrilling emotions when they held Richard's, the touch of which, they declared, was strangely electric. There they sat while Richard, breathing deeply and moaning in his simulated trance, was the mouthpiece of Mentu and told them things which, but for his indubitable gift of thought-reading, it was impossible for him to know; or, if the power was not coming through properly, they listened, hardly less thrilled, to spirit-rappings and musical boxes and unverifiable information about the conditions of life where the mortal coil hampers no longer. It was all very interesting and soothing and edifying. And then one day there occurred an irruption of something wholly unexpected and inexplicable.

Brother and sister were dining quietly after a busy, but unsatisfactory day when the tinkling summons came from the telephone, and Richard found that a loud voice, belonging, so it said, to Mrs. Gardner, wanted to arrange a sitting alone for next day. No address was given, but he made an appointment for half-past two, and without much enthusiasm went back to his dinner.

"A stranger," he said to his sister, "with no address and no reference or introduction. I hope I shall be in better form to-morrow. There was nothing but rappings and music to-day. They are boring, and also they are dangerous, for one may be detected at any time. And I got an infernal blow on my knuckles from that new electric tapper."

Julia laughed.

"I know. I heard it," she said. "There was quite a wrong noise in one of the taps as we were spelling out 'silver wing.'"

He lit his cigarette, frowning at the smoke.

"That's the worst of my profession," he said. "On some days I can get right inside the mind of the sitter, and, as you know, bring out the most surprising information; but on other days—to-day, for

110

instance—and there have been many such lately—there's a mere blank wall in front of me. I shall lose my position if it happens often; nobody will pay my fees only to hear spirit-rappings and generalities."

"They're better than nothing," said Julia.

"Very little. They help to fill up, but I hate using them. Don't you remember, when we began investigating, just you and I alone, how often we seemed on the verge of genuine supernatural manifestations? They appeared to be just round the corner."

"Yes; but we never turned the corner. We never got beyond mere thought-reading."

He got up.

"I know we didn't, but there always seemed a possibility. The door was ajar; it wasn't locked, and it has never ceased to be ajar. Often when the mere thought-reading, as you call it, is flowing along most smoothly, I feel that if only I could abandon my whole consciousness a little more completely, something, somebody would really take control of me. I wish it would; and yet I'm frightened of it. It might revenge itself for all the frauds I've perpetrated in its name. Come, let's play piquet and forget about it all.

It was settled that Julia should be present next day when the stranger came for her sitting, in order that if Richard's thought-reading was not coming through any better than it had done lately, she should help in the rappings and the luminous patches and the musical box. Mrs. Gardner was punctual to her appointment, a tall, quiet, well-dressed woman who stated with perfect frankness her object in wishing for a séance and her views about spirit-communication.

"I should immensely like to believe in spirit-communication," she said, "such as I am told you are capable of producing; but at present I don't."

"It is important that the atmosphere should not be one of hostility," said Waghorn in his dreamy, professional manner.

"I bring no hostility," she said. "I am in a state, shall we say, of benevolent neutrality, unless"—and she smiled in a charming manner—"unless benevolent neutrality has come to mean malevolent hostility. That, I assure you, is not the case with me. I want to believe." She paused a moment.

"And may I say this without offence?" she asked. "May I tell you that spirit-rappings and curious lights and sounds of music do not interest me in the least?"

They were already seated in the room where the séance was to be held. The windows were thickly curtained, there was only a glimmer of light from the red lamp, and even this the spirits would very likely desire to have extinguished. If this visitor took no interest in such things, Waghorn felt that he and his sister had wasted their time in adjusting the electric hammer (made to rap by the pressure of the foot on a switch concealed in the thick rug underneath the table) behind the sliding-panel, in stringing across the ceiling the invisible wires on which the luminous globes ran, and in making ready all the auxiliary paraphernalia in case the genuine telepathy was not on tap. So with voice dreamier than before and with slower utterance as he was supposed to be beginning to sink into trance, he just said:

"I can't foretell the manner in which they may choose to make their presence known."

He gave one loud rap, which perfectly conveyed the word "No" to his sister, indicating that the conjuring tricks were not to be used. Subsequently, if really necessary, he could rap "Yes" to her, and the music and the magic lights would be displayed. Then he began to breathe quickly and in a snorting manner, to show that the control was taking possession of him.

"My brother is going into trance very quickly," said Julia, and there was dead silence.

Almost immediately a clear and shining lucidity spread like sunshine, after these days of cloud, over Waghorn's brain. Every moment he found himself knowing more and more about this complete stranger who sat with hand touching his. He felt his subconscious brain, which had lately lain befogged and imperceptive, sun itself under the brilliant clarity of illumination that had come to it, and in the impressive bass in which Mentu was wont to give vent to his revelations he said:

"I am here; Mentu is here."

He felt the table rocking beneath his hands, which surprised him, since he had exerted no pressure on it, and he supposed that Julia had not understood his signal, and was beginning the conjuring tricks. One hand of his was in hers, and by the pressure of his finger-tips he conveyed to her in code, "Don't do it." Instantly she answered back, "I wasn't."

He paid no more heed to that, though the table continued to oscillate and tip in a very curious manner, for his mind was steeped in this flood of images that impressed themselves on his brain.

"What shall Mentu tell you to-day?" he went on, with pauses between the sentences. "Someone has come to consult Mentu. It is a lady, I can see her. She wears a locket round her neck, below her coat, with a piece of black hair under glass between the gold."

He felt a slight jerk from Mrs. Gardner's hand, and in finger-tip code said to Julia, "Ask her."

Julia whispered across the table:

"Is that so?"

"Yes," said Mrs. Gardner, and Waghorn heard her take her breath quickly. He just remembered that she was not in mourning; but that made no difference. He knew, not guessing, that Mrs. Gardner wished to know something from the man or woman on whose head that hair once grew which was contained in the locket that rested unseen below her buttoned jacket. Then the next moment he knew also that this was a man's hair. Thereafter the flood of sun and precise mental impressions poured over him in spate of bright waters.

"She wants to know about the boy whose hair is in the locket. He is not a boy now. He is, according to earth's eyes, a grown man. There is a D; I see a D. Not Dick, not David. There is a Y. It is Denys. Not Saint Denys, not French. English Denys—Denys Bristow."

He paused a moment, and heard Mrs. Gardner whisper:

"Yes; that is right."

Waghorn gave vent to Mentu's jovial laugh.

"She says it is right," he said. "How should not Mentu be right? Perhaps Mentu is right, too, when he says that Denys is her brother? Yes; that is Margaret Bristow who sits here, though not Margaret Bristow now. Margaret——"

Waghorn saw the name quite clearly, but yet he hesitated. It was not Gardner at all. Then it struck him for the first time that nothing was more likely than that Mrs. Gardner had adopted a pseudonym. He went on:

"Margaret Forsyth is Denys's sister. Margaret wants to know about Denys. Denys is coming. He will be here in a moment. He has spoken of his sister before. He did not call her Margaret. He called her Q—he called her Queenie. Will Queenie speak?"

Waghorn felt the trembling of her hand; he heard her twice try to speak, but she was unable to control the trembling in her voice.

"Can Denys speak to me?" she said in a whisper. "Can he really come here?"

Up to this moment Waghorn had been enjoying himself immensely, for after the days in which he had been unable to get into touch with this rare and marvellous gifts of consciousness-reading, it was blissful to find his mastery again, and, besieged with the images which Margaret Forsyth's contact revealed to him, he had been producing them in Mentu's impressive voice, revelling in his restored powers. Her mind lay open to him like a book; he could read where he liked on pages familiar to her and on pages which had remained long unturned. But at this moment, as sudden as

113

some qualm of sickness, he was aware of a startling change in the quality of his perceptions. Fresh knowledge of Denys Bristow came into his mind, but he felt that it was coming not from her, but from some other source. Some odd buzzing sang in his ears, as when an anæsthetic begins to take effect, and opening his eyes, he thought he saw a strange patch of light, inconsistent with the faint illumination of the red lamp, hovering over his breast. At the same moment he heard, though dimly, for his head was full of confused noise, the violent rapping of the electric hammer, and already only half conscious, felt an impotent irritation with his sister for employing these tricks. He struggled with the oncoming of the paralysis that was swiftly invading his mind and his physical being, but he struggled in vain, and next moment, overwhelmed with the onrush of a huge, enveloping blackness, he lost consciousness altogether. The trance that he had often simulated had invaded him, and he knew nothing more.

He came to himself again, with the feeling that he had been recalled from some vast distance. Still unable to move, he sat listening to the quick panting of his own breath before he realized what the noise was. His face, from which the sweat poured in streams, rested on something cold and hard, and presently, when he opened his eyes, he saw that his head had fallen forward upon the table. He felt utterly exhausted and yet somehow strangely satisfied. Some amazing thing had happened.

Then as he recovered himself he began to remember that he had been reading Mrs. Gardner's, or Mrs. Forsyth's mind when some power external to himself took possession of him, and on his left he heard Julia's voice speaking very familiar words.

"He is coming out of his trance," she said. "He will be himself again in a moment now."

With a sense of great weariness he raised his head, disengaged his hands from those of the two women, and sank back in his chair.

"Draw back the curtains," he said to Julia, "and open the window. I am suffocating."

She did as he told her, and he saw the red rays of the sun near to its setting pour into the room, while the breeze of sunset refreshed the air. On his right still sat Mrs. Forsyth, wiping her eyes, and smiling at him; and having opened the window, Julia came back to the table, looking at him with a curious, anxious intentness.

Then Mrs. Forsyth spoke.

"It has been too marvellous," she said. "I cannot thank you enough. I will do exactly as you, or, rather, Denys, told me about the test; and if it is right, I will certainly leave my house to-morrow, taking my servants with me. It was so like Denys to think of them, too."

To Waghorn this meant nothing whatever; she might have been speaking Hebrew to him. But Julia, as she often did, answered for him.

"My brother knows nothing of what happened in his trance," she said.

Mrs. Forsyth got up.

"I will go straight home," she said. "I feel sure that I shall find just what Denys described. May I telephone to you about it at once?"

"Yes, pray do," said Julia. "We shall be most anxious to hear."

Richard got up to show her out, but having regained his feet, he staggered, and collapsed into his chair again. Mrs. Forsyth would not hear of his attempting to move just yet, and Julia, having taken her to the door, returned to her brother. It was usual for him, when the sitting was over, to feign great exhaustion, but the realism of his acting to-day had almost deceived her into thinking that something not yet experienced in their séances had occurred. Besides, he had said such strange, detailed, and extraordinary things. He was still where she had left him, and there could be no reason, now that they were alone, to keep up this feigned languor.

"Dick," she said, "what's the matter? And what happened? I couldn't understand you at all. Why did you say all those things?"

He stirred and sat up.

"I'm better," he said. "And it is you who have to tell me what happened. I remember up to a certain point, and after that I lost consciousness completely. I remember thinking you were rocking the table, and I told you not to."

"Yes; but I wasn't rocking it. I thought you were."

"Well, it was neither of us, then," said he. "I was vexed because Mrs. Gardner—Mrs. Forsyth had said she didn't want that sort of thing, and I was reading her as I never read any one before. I told her about the locket and the black hair, I got her brother's name, I got her name and her nickname Queenie. Then she asked if Denys could really come, and at that moment something began to take possession of me. I think I saw a light as usual over my breast, and I think I heard a tremendous rapping. Did you do either of those, or did they really happen?"

Julia stared at him for a moment in silence.

"I did neither of those," she said; "but they happened. You must have pressed the breast-pocket switch and trod on the switch of the hammer."

He opened his coat.

"I had not got the breast-pocket switch," he said, "and I certainly did not tread on the hammer-switch."

Julia moved her chair a little closer to him.

"The hammer did not sound right," she said. "It was ten times louder than I have ever heard, and the light was quite different somehow. It was much brighter. I could see everything in the room quite distinctly. Go on, Dick."

"I can't. That's all I know until I came to, leaning over the table and bathed in perspiration. Tell me what happened."

"Dick, do you swear that is true?" she asked.

"Certainly I do. Go on."

"The light grew, and then faded again to a glimmer," she said, "and then suddenly you began to talk in a different voice: it wasn't Mentu any longer. Mrs. Forsyth recognized it instantly, and I thought what wonderful luck it was that you should have hit on a voice that was like her brother's. Then it and she had a long talk; it must have lasted half an hour. They reminded each other how Denys had come to live with her and her husband on their father's death. He was only eighteen at the time and still at school. He was killed in a street accident, being run over by a bicycle two days before her birthday. All this was correct, and I thought I never heard you mind-reading so clearly and quickly; you hardly paused at all."

Julia was silent a moment.

"Dick, don't you really know what followed?" she asked.

"Not in the smallest degree," he said.

"Well, I thought you had gone mad," she said. "Mrs. Forsyth asked for a test, something that was not known to her, and never had been known to her, and you gave it instantly. You laughed, Denys laughed, the voice that spoke laughed, and told her to look behind the row of books beside the bed in the room that was still known as Denys's room, and she would find tucked away a little cardboard box with a gold safety-pin set with a pearl. He had bought it for her birthday present, and had hidden it there till the day came. He was killed, as I told you, two days before. And she, half sobbing, half laughing, said, 'O Denys, how deliciously secretive you used to be!'"

"And is that what she is going to telephone about?" asked Waghorn.

"Yes, Dick. What made you say all that?"

"I don't know, I tell you. I didn't know I said it. And was that all? She said something about leaving her house to-morrow and taking the servants. What did that mean?"

"You got very much distressed. You told her she was in danger. You said——" Julia paused again. "You said there was something coming, fire from the clouds, and a rending. You said her country house, which I gathered was down somewhere near Epping, would be burst open by the fire from the clouds to-morrow night. You made her promise to leave it and take the servants with her. You said her husband was away, which again is the case. And she asked if you meant Zeppelins, and you said you did."

Waghorn suddenly got up.

"'You meant,' 'you said,' 'you did,'" he cried. "What if it's 'he meant,' 'he said,' 'he did'?"

"It's impossible," she said.

"Good Lord! What's impossible?" he asked. "What if I really am that which I have so long pretended to be? What if I am a medium, one who is the mysterious bridge between the quick and the dead? I'm frightened, but I'm bound to say I'm horribly interested. All that you tell me I said when I was in trance never came out of Mrs. Forsyth's mind. It wasn't there. She didn't know about the pearl pin; she had never known it. Nor had I ever known it. Where did it come from, then? Only one person knew, the boy who died ten years ago."

"It yet remains to be seen whether it is true," said she. "We shall know in an hour or two, for she is motoring straight down to her house in the country."

"And if it turns out to be true, who was talking?" said he.

The sunset faded into the dusk of the clear May evening, and the two still sat there waiting for the telephone to inform them whether the door which, as Waghorn had said, had seemed so often ajar, and never quite closed, was now thrown open, and light and intelligence from another world had shone on his unconscious mind. Presently the tinkling summons came, and with an eager curiosity, below which lurked that fear of the unknown, the dim, mysterious land into which all human creatures pass across the closed frontier, he went to hear what news awaited him.

"Trunk call," said the operator, and he listened.

Soon the voice came through.

"Mr. Waghorn?" it said.

"Yes."

"I have found the box in exactly the place described. It contained what we had been told it would contain. I shall leave the house, taking all the servants away, to-morrow."

Two mornings later the papers contained news of a Zeppelin raid during the night on certain Eastern counties. The details given were vague and meagre, and no names of towns or villages where bombs had been dropped were vouchsafed to the public. But later in the day private information came to Waghorn that Forsyth Hall, near Epping, had been completely wrecked. No lives, luckily, were lost, for the house was empty.

CAT STORIES

"PUSS-CAT"

It was during the month of May some nine years ago that the beginning of the events that concerned Puss-cat took place. I was living at the time on the green outskirts of a country town, and my dining-room at the back of the house opened on to a small garden framed in brick walls some five feet high. Breakfasting there one morning, I saw a large black and white cat, with a sharp but serious face, observing me with studied attention. Now at the time there was an interregnum, and my house was without a mistress (in the shape of a cat), and it at once struck me that I was being interviewed by this big and pleasing stranger, to see if I would do. So, since there is nothing that a prospective mistress likes less than premature familiarity on the part of the householder whom she may be thinking of engaging, I took no direct notice of the cat, but continued to eat my breakfast carefully and tidily. After a short inspection, the cat quietly withdrew without once looking back, and I supposed that I was dismissed, or that she had decided, after all, to keep on her present household.

In that I proved to be mistaken: she had only gone away to think about it, and next morning, and for several mornings after that, I was subjected to the same embarrassing but not unfriendly scrutiny, after which she took a stroll round the garden to see if there were any flower-beds that would do to make ambushes in, and a convenient tree or two to climb should emergencies arise. On the fourth day, as far as I remember, I committed an error, and half-way through breakfast went out into the garden, to attempt to get on more familiar terms. The cat regarded me for a few moments with pained surprise, and went away; but after I had gone in again, she decided to overlook it, for she returned to her former place, and continued to observe. Next morning she made up her mind, jumped down from the wall, trotted across the grass, entered the dining-room, and, arranging herself in a great hurry round one hind-leg, which she put up in the air like a flagstaff, proceeded to make her morning toilet. That, as I knew quite well, meant that she thought I would give satisfaction, and I was therefore permitted to enter upon my duties at once. So I put down a saucer of milk for her, which she very obligingly disposed of. Then she went and sat by the door, and said "A-a-a-a," to show that she wished the door to be opened for her, so that she might inspect the rest of the house. So I called down the kitchen stairs, "There is come a cat, who I think means to stop. Don't fuss her." In this manner the real Puss-cat—though I did not know that—entered the house.

Now here I must make a short defence for my share in these things. I might, by a hasty judgment, be considered to have stolen her who soon became Puss-cat's mamma, but anyone who has any real knowledge of cats will be aware that I did nothing of the kind. Puss-cat's mamma was clearly dissatisfied with her last household and had, without the least doubt, made up her mind to leave them all and take on a fresh lot of servants; and if a cat makes up her mind about anything, no power on earth except death, or permanent confinement in a room where neither doors nor windows are ever opened, will stop her taking the contemplated step. If her last (unknown) household killed her, or permanently shut her up, of course, she could not engage fresh people, but short of that they were powerless to keep her. You may cajole or bully a dog into doing what you want, but no manner of persuasion will cause a cat to deviate one hair's breadth from the course she means to pursue. If I had driven her away she would have gone to another house, but never back to her own. For though we may own dogs and horses and other animals, it is a great mistake to think that we own cats. Cats employ us, and if we give satisfaction they may go so far as to adopt us. Besides, Puss-cat's mamma did not, as it turned out, mean to stay with me altogether: she only wanted quiet lodgings for a time.

So our new mistress went discreetly downstairs and inspected kitchen, scullery, and pantry. She spent some time in the scullery, so I was told, and felt rather doubtful. But she quite liked the new gas-stove in the kitchen, and singed her tail at it, as nobody had told her that lunch was a-cooking. Also she found a mouse-hole below the wainscoting, which appeared to decide her (for, as we soon found out, she liked work), and she trotted upstairs again and sat outside the drawing-room door till somebody opened it for her. I happened to be inside, with Jill, a young lady of the fox-terrier breed, and, of course, did not know that Puss-cat's mamma was waiting. Eventually I came out and saw her sitting there. Jill saw her, too, and eagerly ran up to her only to talk, not to fight, for Jill likes cats.

But Puss-cat's mamma did not know that, so, just in case, she slapped Jill smartly first on one side the head, and then on the other. She was not angry, but only firm and strong, and wished that from the first there should be no doubt whatever about her position. Having done that, she allowed Jill to explain, which Jill did with twitchings of her stumpy tail and attitude provocative of gambols. And before many minutes were up, Puss-cat's mamma was kind enough to play with her. Then she suddenly remembered that she had not seen the rest of the house, and went upstairs, where she remained till lunch-time.

It was the manner in which she spent the first morning that gave me the key to the character of Puss-cat's mamma, and we at once settled that her name had always been Martha. She had annexed our house, it is true, but in no grabbing or belligerent spirit, but simply because she had seen from her post on the garden wall that we wanted somebody to look after us and manage the house, and she could not help knowing how wonderful she was in all things connected with a mistress's duties. Every morning when the housemaid's step was heard on the stairs during breakfast (she had a very audible step), Martha, even in the middle of fish or milk, ran to the door, said "A-a-a-a" till it was opened, and rushed after her, sitting in each bedroom in turn to see that the slops were properly emptied and the beds well and truly made. In the middle of such supervision sometimes came other calls upon her, the front-door bell would ring, and Martha had to hurry down to see that the door was nicely opened. Then perhaps she would catch sight of somebody digging in the garden, and she was forced to go out in this busiest time of the morning, to dab at the turned-up earth, in order to be sure that it was fresh. In particular, I remember the day on which the dining-room was repapered. She had to climb the step-ladder to ascertain if it was safe, and sit on the top to clean herself. Then each roll of paper had to be judged by the smell, and the paste to be touched with the end of a pink tongue. That made her sneeze (which must be the right test for paste), and she allowed it to be used. That day we lunched in the drawing-room, and it is easy to imagine how busy Martha was, for the proceeding was very irregular, and she could not tell how it would turn out. Meal-times were always busy: she had to walk in front of every dish as it was brought in, and precede it as it was taken out, and to-day these duties were complicated by the necessity of going back constantly to the real dining-room to see that the paper-hangers were not idling. To make the rush more overpowering, Jill was in the garden wanting to play (and to play with Jill was one of Martha's duties) and some young hollyhocks were being put in, certain of which, for inscrutable reasons, had to be dug up again with strong backward kicks of the hind-legs.

She had settled that there was but one cat, which was, of course, herself. Occasionally alien heads looked over the wall, and the cries of strangers sounded. Whenever that happened, whatever the stress of housework might be, Martha bounded from house into garden to expel and, if possible, kill the intruder. Once from my bedroom window I saw a terrific affair. Martha had been sitting as good as gold among hair-brushes and nail-scissors, showing me how to shave, when something feline moving in the garden caught her eye. Not waiting for the door to be opened, she made one leap of it out of the window into the apple-tree, and whirled down the trunk, even as lightning strikes and rips its way to the ground, and next moment I saw her, with paw uplifted, tearing tufts of fur from the next-door tabby. She was like one of those amazing Chinese grotesques, half-cat, half-demon, and wholly warrior. Shrill cries rent the peaceful morning air, and Martha, intoxicated with vengeance, allowed the mishandled tabby to escape. Then with awesome face and Bacchanalian eye she ate the tufts of bloodstained fur, rolling them on her tongue and swallowing them with obvious difficulty, as if performing some terrible, antique and cannibalistic rite. And all this from a lady who was so shortly to be confined. But it was no use trying to keep Martha quiet.

A second minute inspection of her house was necessary before she decided which should be the birth-chamber. She spent a long time in the wood-shed that morning, and we hoped that it was going to be there; she spent a long time in the bath-room, and we hoped it wasn't. Eventually she settled on the pantry, and when she had quite made up her mind we made her comfortable. Next morning three dappled little blind things were there. She ate one, for no reason, as far as we could judge, but that she was afraid that Jill wanted to. So, as it was her kitten, not Jill's, she ate it.

With all respect for Martha, I think that here she had mistaken her vocation. She should never have gone in for being a mother. The second kitten she lay down upon with fatal results. Then, being thoroughly disgusted with maternity, she went away and never was seen any more. She deserted the only child she had not killed; she deserted us who had tried so hard to give satisfaction; and in the basket there was left, still blind, still uncertain whether it was worth while to live at all, Puss-cat.

Puss-cat was her mother's own child from the first, though with much added. She wasted no time or strength in bewailing her orphaned condition, but took amazing quantities of milk administered on a feather. Her eyes opened, as eyes should do, on the seventh day, and she smiled at us all, and spat at Jill. So Jill licked her nose with anxious care, and said quite distinctly, "When you are a little older, I will be always ready to do whatever you like." Jill says the same sort of thing to everybody except the dustman.

Soon after, Puss-cat arose from her birth-bed and staggered across the pantry. Even this first expedition on her own feet was not made without purpose, for in spite of frequent falls she went straight up to a blind-tassel, and after looking at it for a long time, tested it with a tiny paw to make sure of it, thus showing, while scarcely out of the cradle, that serious purpose which marked her throughout her dear life. Her motto was, "Do your work," and since she remained unmarried in spite of many very eligible offers, I think that her unnatural mother must have impressed upon her, in those few days before she deserted her, that the first duty of a cat is to look after the house, and that she herself didn't think much of maternity. Puss-cat inherited also, I suppose, her fixed conviction that she ought to have been, even if she was not, the only cat in the world, and she would allow no one of her own race within eyeshot of house or garden. Some of her duties, though they were always conscientiously performed, I think rather bored her, but certainly she brought to the expulsion of cats an exquisite sense of enjoyment. On the appearance of any one of her own nation she would go hastily into ambush with twitching tail and jerking shoulder-blades, teasing and torturing herself with the postponement of that rapturous stealthy advance across the grass, if the quarry was looking the other way, or the furious hurling of herself through the air, if a frontal attack had to be delivered. And I often wondered that she did not betray her ambush by the rapture and sonorousness of her purring, as the supreme moment approached.

Jill, I am afraid, gave her a lot of worry over this duty of the expulsion of aliens, for Jill would sooner play with an alien than expel it, and her plan was to gambol up to the intruder with misplaced welcome. It is true that the effect was just the same, because a trespassing cat, seeing an alert fox-terrier rapidly approaching, seldom, if ever, stops to play, so that Jill's method was really quite effective, too. But Puss-cat had high moral purpose behind her: she wanted not only to expel, but to appal and injure, and like many moralists of our own species, she enjoyed her fulminations and onslaughts quite tremendously. She liked punishing other cats, because she was right and they were wrong, and vigorous kicks and bites would help them perhaps to understand that.

But though Puss-cat resembled her mother in the matter of

the high sense of duty and moral qualities, she had what Martha lacked: that indefinable attraction which we call charm, and a great heart. She was always pleased and affectionate, and went about her duties with as near an approach to a smile as is possible for the gravest species of animal. Martha, for instance, played with Jill as a part of her duty, Puss-cat made a pleasure out of it and played with the ecstatic abandon of a child. Indeed, I have known her put dinner a quarter of an hour later, because she was in the lovely jungle of long grass at the end of the garden, and was preparing to give Jill an awful fright. This business of the jungle deserves mention, not because it was so remarkable in itself, but because it was so wonderful to Puss-cat.

The jungle in question was a space of some dozen yards, where in spring daffodils grew in clumps of sunshine and fritillaries hung their speckled bells. There were pæonies also planted in the grass, and a briar-rose, and an apple-tree; nothing, as I have said, was remarkable in itself, but it was fraught with amazing possibilities to the keen imagination of Puss-cat. At the bottom of this strip of untamed jungle the lawn began, and it was one of Puss-cat's plans to hide at the edge of the jungle, flattening herself out till she looked like a shadow of something else. If luck served her, Jill, sooner or later in the pursuit of interesting smells, would pass close to the edge of the jungle without seeing her. The moment Jill had gone by, Puss-cat would stretch out a discreet paw, and just touch Jill on the hind-quarters. Jill, of course, had to turn round to see what this inexplicable thing meant, and on the moment Puss-cat would fling herself into the air and descend tiger-like on Jill's back. That was the beginning of the game, and it contained more vicissitudes than a round of golf. There were ambushes and scurryings innumerable, assaults from the apple-tree, repulsions from behind the garden roller, periods of absolute quiescence, suddenly and wildly broken by swift flanking movements through the sweet-peas, and at the end a failure of wind and limb, and Jill would lie panting on the bank, and Puss-cat, having put off dinner, proceed to clean herself for her evening duties. She had to be smart at dinner-time, whether we were dining alone, or whether there was a dinner-party, for she was never a tea-gown cat, and she dressed for her dinner, even if we were dining out. She was not responsible for that; what she was responsible for was to be tidy herself.

Puss-cat, without doubt, was a plain kitten; but again, like many children of our own inferior race, she grew up to be a very handsome cat. With great chic she did not attempt colours, but was pure black and white. Across her broad, strong back there was a black saddle, but the saddle, so to speak, had slewed round and made a black band across her left side. There was an arbitrary patch of black, too, on her left cheek, a black band on her tail, and a black tip to it. Otherwise she was pure white, except when she put out a pink tongue below her long, snowy whiskers. But her charm—the outstanding feature of Puss-cat—was independent of this fascinating colouring. Martha, for instance, had been content that dishes were carried into the dining-room, and subsequently carried out. That and no more was her notion of her duties towards dinner. But Puss-cat really began where Martha ended. Like her, she preceded the soup, but when those who were present had received their share, she always went round with loud purrings to each guest, to congratulate them and hope that they liked it. For this process, which was repeated with every dish, she had a particular walk, stepping high and treading on the tips of her toes. This congratulatory march was purely altruistic: she did not want soup herself; she was only glad that other people had got it. Then when fish came, or bird, she would make her congratulatory tour just the same, and then sit firmly down and say she would like some too. Occasionally she favoured some particular guest with marked regard, and sometimes almost forgot her duties as mistress of the house, choosing rather to sit by her protégée and purr loudly, so that a dish would already be half-eaten before she went her round to see that everyone was pleased with his portion. Finally, when coffee was brought, she went downstairs to the kitchen and retired for the night, usually sharing Jill's basket, where they lay together in a soft slow-breathing heap of black and white.

Puss-cat, like the ancient Greeks, was never sick or sorry; never sick, because of her robust and stalwart health; never sorry, because she never did anything to be sorry for. From living with Jill, and never seeing a cat, except for those short and painful interviews which preceded expulsion from the garden, she grew to have something of the selfless affection of a dog, and when I came home after an absence she would run out into the street to meet me, stiff-tailed, and really not attending to the debarkation of luggage, but intent only on welcoming me home. Eight busy, happy years passed thus, and then one bitter February morning, Pussy-cat disappeared.

The weeks went on, and still there came no sign of her, and when winter had passed into May I gave up all hopes of her return, and got a fresh cat, this time a young blue Persian with topaz-coloured eyes. Another month went by, and Agag (so-called from his delicate walk) had established himself in our affections, on account of his extraordinary beauty, rather than from any charm of character, when the second act of the tragedy opened.

I was sitting at breakfast one morning, with the door into the garden thrown wide, and Agag was curled up on a chair in the window (for, unlike Puss-cat and Martha, he did no housework at all, being of proud and aristocratic descent), when I saw coming slowly across the lawn a cat that I scarcely recognized. It was lean to the point of emaciation, its fur was disordered and dirty, but it was Puss-cat come home again. Then suddenly she saw me, and with a little cry of joy ran towards the open door. Then she saw Agag, and, weak and thin as she was, she woke at once to her old sense of duty, and bounded on to his chair. Never before in her time had a cat got right into the house, and such a thing, she felt determined, should not occur again. Round the room and out into the garden raged the battle before I could separate them—Puss-cat inspired by her sense of duty, Agag angry and astonished at this assault of a mere gutter-cat in his own house. At last I got hold of Puss-cat and took her up in my arms, while Agag cursed and swore in justifiable indignation. For how could he tell that this was Puss-cat?

They never fought again, but it was a miserable fortnight that followed, and all the misery was poor Puss-cat's. Agag, in spite of his beauty, had no heart, and did not mind how many cats I kept, so long as they did not molest him, or usurp his food or his cushion. But Puss-cat, though she understood that for some inscrutable reason she had to share her house with Agag, and not fight him, was a creature of strong affections, and her poor little soul was torn with agonies of jealousy. Jill, it is true, who was always treated with contemptuous unconsciousness by Agag, was certainly pleased to see her friend again, and had not forgotten her; but Puss-cat wanted so much more than Jill could give her. She took on her old duties at once, but often when she escorted the fish into the dining-room and found Agag asleep on his chair, she would be literally unable to go through with them, and would sit in a corner by herself, looking miserably and uncomprehendingly at me. Then perhaps the smell of fish would wake up Agag, and he would stretch himself and stand for a moment with superbly-arched back on his chair, before he jumped down, and with loud purrings rubbed himself against the legs of my chair to betoken his desire for food, or even would jump up on to my knees. That was the worst of all for Puss-cat, and she would often sit all dinner through in her remote corner, refusing food, and unable to take her eyes off the object of her jealousy. While Agag was present, no amount of caresses or attentions offered to her would console her, so that, when Agag had eaten, we usually turned him out of the room. Then for a little while Puss-cat had respite from her Promethean vulture; she would go her rounds again to see that everybody was pleased, and escort fresh dishes in with high-stepping walk and erect tail.

We hoped, foolishly perhaps, that in course of time the two would become friends; else, I think, I should have at once tried to find another home for Agag. But indeed, short of that, we did all we could do, lavishing attentions on dear Puss-cat, and trying to make her feel (which indeed was true) that we all loved her, and only liked and admired Agag. But while we still hoped, Puss-cat had had more than she could bear, and once again she disappeared. Jill missed her for a little while, Agag not at all. But the rest of us miss her still.

THERE AROSE A KING

Agag, though of undoubtedly royal blood, was never a real king. He was no more than one of the Hyksos, a shepherd-king, bound by the limitations of his race, and no partaker in its magnificence. Naturally, he did not work as the late housekeeper had done (and no one expected that of him), but he had neither the splendour nor the vivacity, possessed, let us say, by Henry VIII. or George IV., to make up for his indolence in affairs of state. Henry VIII., anyhow, busied himself in marriages, whereas Agag was merely terrified at the idea of wooing, not to say winning, any of the princesses that were brought to his notice; and they, on their part, only made the rudest faces at him. Again George IV., though unkingly in many respects, used to plunge about in the wild pursuit of pleasure, and was supposed to have a kind heart. Agag, on the contrary, never plunged: a cushion and some fish and plenty of repose were the sum of his desires, and as for a kind heart, he never had a heart at all. An unkind heart would have given him some semblance of personality, but there was not the faintest room to suppose that any emotion, other than the desire for food and sleep and warmth, came within measurable distance of him. He died in his sleep, probably of apoplexy, after a large meal, and beautiful in death as in life, was buried and forgotten. I have never known a cat so completely devoid of character, and I sometimes wonder whether he was a real cat at all, and not some sort of inflated dormouse in cat's clothing.

There followed a republican régime in this matter of cats. We went back, after Agag, to working cats, who would sit at mouse-holes for hours together, pounce and devour, and clean themselves and sleep, but among them all there was no "character" which ever so faintly resembled even Martha, far less Puss-cat.

I suppose the royalty of Agag, stupid and dull though he was, had infected me with a certain snobbishness as regards cats, and secretly—given that there were to be no more of those splendid plebeians, like Puss-cat—I longed for somebody who combined royal descent (for the sake of beauty and pride) with character, good or bad. Nero or Heliogabalus or Queen Elizabeth, or even the Emperor William II. of Germany would have done, but I didn't want George I. on the one side or a mere mild President of a small republic on the other.

Just after Agag's death I had moved up to London, and for a time there was this succession of unnoticeable heads of the state.

They were born—those presidents of my republic—from respectable hard-working families, and never gave themselves out (though they knew quite well that they were the heads of the state) to be anything else but what they were: good, hard-working cats, with, of course, not only a casting, but a determining vote on all questions that concerned them or anybody else.

We were democratic in those days, and I am afraid "freedom broadened slowly down" from president to president. We were loyal, law-abiding citizens under their rule, but when our president was sitting at the top of the area steps, taking the air after his morning's work, it used to be no shock to me to see him tickled on the top of his head by people like tradesmen coming for orders, or a policeman or a nursery-maid. The president, in these circumstances, would arch a back, make poker of a tail, and purr. Being at leisure and unoccupied with cares of State, he did not pretend to be anything but bourgeois. The bourgeoisie had access to him; he would play with them, without any sense of inequality, through the area railings. There was a nursery-maid, I remember, whom our last president was very much attached to. He used to make the most terrific onslaughts at her shoelaces.

But now all that régime is past. We are royalist again to the core, and Cyrus, of undoubtedly royal descent, is on the throne. The revolution was accomplished in the most pacific manner conceivable. A friend, on my birthday, two years ago, brought a small wicker basket, and the moment it was opened the country, which for a month or two had been in a state of darkest anarchy, without president or any ruler, was a civilized state again, with an acknowledged king. There was no war; nothing sanguinary occurred. Only by virtue of the glory of our king we became a great Power again. Cyrus had arranged that his pedigree should come with him; this was much bigger than Cyrus, and, being written on parchment (with a large gold crown painted at the head of it), was far more robust than he whose ancestors it enumerated. For his majesty, as he peered over the side of the royal cradle, did not seem robust at all. He put two little weak paws on the edge of his basket and tried to look like a lion, but he had no spirit to get farther. Then he wrinkled up his august face, and gave a sneeze so prodigious that he tumbled out of the basket altogether, and by accident (or at the most by catarrh) set foot in the dominions where he still reigns. Of course, I was not quite so stupid as not to recognize a royal landing, though made in so unconventional a manner; it was only as if George IV., in one of his numerous landings on some pier (so fitly commemorated by the insertion of a large brass boot print), had

128

fallen flat on his face instead, and was commemorated by a full-length brass, with top-hat a little separate.

Babies of the human species, it is true, are all like each other, and I would defy any professor of Eugenics or of allied and abstruse schools of investigation to say, off-hand, whether a particular baby, divorced from his surroundings, is the Prince of Wales or Master Jones. But, quite apart from his pedigree, there was never any question at all about Cyrus. There was no single hair on his lean little body that was not of the true and royal blue, and his ears already were tufted inside with downy growth, and his poor little eyes, sadly screened by the moisture of his catarrh, showed their yellow topaz irises, that were never seen on Master Jones. So he tumbled upside down into his new kingdom, and, recovering himself, sat up and blinked, and said, "Ah-h-h." I took him up very reverently in both hands, and put him on my knee. He made an awful face, like a Chinese grotesque instead of a Persian king, but anyhow it was an Oriental face. Then he put a large paw in front of his diminutive nose and went fast asleep. It had been a most fatiguing sneeze.

Royal Persian babies, as you perhaps know, must never, after they have said good-bye to their royal mammas, be given milk. When they are thirsty they must have water; when they are hungry they have little finely chopped-up dishes of flesh and fish and fowl. As Cyrus slept, little chopped-up things were hastily prepared for him, and when he woke, his food and drink were waiting his royal pleasure. They seemed to please him a good deal, but at a crucial moment, when his mouth was quite full, he sneezed again. There was an explosion of awful violence, but the Royal baby licked up the fragments.... We knew at once that we had a tidy king to rule over us.

Cyrus was two months old when he became king, and the next four months were spent in growing and eating and sneezing. His general manner of life was to eat largely and instantly fall asleep, and it was then, I think, that he grew. Eventually a sneeze plucked him from his slumber, and this first alarum was a storm-cone, so to speak, that betokened the coming tornado. Once, after I began to count, he sneezed seventeen times.... Then, when that was over, he sat quiet and recuperated; then he jumped straight up in the air, purred loudly, and ate again. The meal was succeeded by more slumber, and the cycle of his day was complete.

His first refreshment he took about seven in the morning—as soon as anybody was dressed—and an hour later, heavily slumbering, he was brought up to my room when I was called, buttoned up in my servant's coat, and placed on my bed. He at once guessed that there must be a pleasant warm cave underneath the bedclothes, and, with stampings and purrings, penetrated into this abyss, curled himself against my side, and resumed his interrupted slumbers. After a while I would feel an internal stirring begin in my bed, and usually managed to deposit the king on the floor before his first sneeze. His second breakfast, of course, had come upstairs with my hot water, and after the sneezing was over he leaped into the air, espied and stalked some new and unfamiliar object, and did his duty with his victuals. He then looked round for a convenient resting-place, choosing one, if possible, that resembled an ambush, the definition of which may be held to be a place with a small opening and spaciousness within.

That gave us the second clue (tidiness being the first) towards the king's character. He had a tactical mind, and should make a good general. As soon as I observed this, I used to make an ambush for him among the sheets of the morning paper, providing it with a small spy-hole. If I scratched the paper in the vicinity of the spy-hole, a little silver-blue paw made wild dabs at the seat of the disturbance. Having thus frustrated any possible enemy, he went to sleep.

But the ambush he liked best was a half-opened drawer, such as he found one morning for himself. There among flannel shirts and vests he made himself exceedingly comfortable, pending attacks. But before he went to sleep he made a point of putting out a small and awe-inspiring head to terrify any marauding bands who might be near. This precaution was usually successful, and he slept for the greater part of the morning.

For six months he stuffed and sneezed and slept, and then, one morning, like Lord Byron and the discovery of his fame, Cyrus woke and discovered the responsibilities of kingship. His sneezing fits suddenly ceased, and the Cyropaidaia (or education of Cyrus) began. He conducted his own education, of course, entirely by himself; he knew, by heredity, what a king had to learn, and proceeded to learn it. Hitherto the pantry and my bedroom were the only territories of his dominion that he had any acquaintance with, and a royal progress was necessary. The dining-room did not long detain him, and presented few points of interest, but in a small room adjoining he found on the table a telephone with a long green cord attached to the receiver. This had to be investigated, since his parents had not told him about telephones, but he soon grasped the principle of it, and attempted to get the ear-piece off its hook, no doubt with a view to issuing orders of some kind. It would not yield to gentle methods, and, after crouching behind a book and wriggling his body a great deal, he determined to rush the silly thing. A wild leap in the air, and Cyrus and the green cord and the receiver were all mingled up together in hopeless confusion.... He did not telephone again for weeks.

The drawing-room was less dangerous. There was a bearskin on the floor, and Cyrus sat down in front of the head, prepared to receive homage. This, I suppose, was duly tendered, because he tapped it on the nose (as the King entering the City of London touches the sword presented by the Lord Mayor), and passed on to the piano. He did not care about the keyboard, but liked the pedals, and also caught sight of a reflection of himself in the black shining front of it.

This was rather a shock, and entailed a few swift fandango-like steps with fore-paws waving wildly in the air. Horror! The silent image opposite did exactly the same thing; ... it was nearly as bad as the telephone. But the piano stood at an angle to the wall, offering a suitable ambush, and he scampered behind it. And there he found the great ambush of all, for the back cloth of the piano was torn, and he could get completely inside it. Tactically, it was a perfect ambush, for it commanded the only route into the room from the door; but his delight in it was such that whenever he was ambushed there, he could not resist putting his head out and glaring, if anybody came near, thus giving the secret completely away. Or was it only indulgence towards our weak intellects, that were so incapable of imagining that there was a king inside the piano?

The exploration of the kitchen followed; the only point of interest was a fox-terrier at whom the king spat; but in the scullery there was a very extraordinary affair—namely, a brass tap, conveniently placed over a sink, half-covered with a board. On the nozzle of this tap an occasional drop of water appeared, which at intervals fell off. Cyrus could not see what happened to it, but when next the drop gathered he put his paw to it and licked it off. After doing this for nearly an hour he came to the conclusion that it was the same water as he drank after his meals. The supply seemed constant, though exiguous; ... it might have to be seen to. After that he just looked in at the linen cupboard, and the door blew to while he was inside. He was not discovered till six hours later, and was inclined to be stiff about it.

Next day the Royal progress continued, and Cyrus discovered the garden (forty feet by twenty, but large enough for Mr. Lloyd George to have his eye on it, and demand a valuation of the mineral rights therein). But it was not large enough for Cyrus (I don't know what he expected), for after looking at it closely for a morning, he decided that he could run up the brick walls that bounded it. This was an infringement of his prerogative, for the king is bound to give notice to his ministers, when he proposes to quit the country, and Cyrus had said nothing about it. Consequently I ran out and pulled him quietly but firmly back by the tail, which was the only part of him that I could reach. He signified his disapproval in what is called "the usual manner," and tried to bite me. Upon which I revolted and drove the king indoors, and bought some rabbit wire. This I fastened down along the top of the wall, so that it projected horizontally inwards. Then I let the king out again and sat down on the steps to see what would happen.

Cyrus pretended that the walls were of no interest to him, and stalked a few dead leaves. But even a king is bounded, not only by rabbit wire, but by the limitations of cat-nature, which compelled him to attempt again what he has been thwarted over. So, after massacring a few leaves (already dead), he sprang up the wall, and naturally hit his nose against the rabbit wire, and was cast back from the frontier into his own dominions. Once again he tried and failed, appealed to an obdurate prime minister, and then sat down and devoted the whole power of his tactical mind to solving this baffling affair. And three days afterwards I saw him again run up the wall, and instead of hitting his nose against the rabbit wire, he clung to it with his claws. It bent with his weight, and he got one claw on the upper side of it, then the other, wriggled round it, and stood triumphant with switching tail on the frontier.

So in turn I had to sit and think; but, short of building up the whole garden wall to an unscalable height, or erecting a chevaux de frise on the top of it, I had a barren brain. After all, foreign travel is an ineradicable instinct in cat-nature, and I infinitely preferred that the king should travel among small back-gardens than out of the area gate into the street. Perhaps, if he had full licence (especially since I could not prevent him) to explore the hinter-lands, he might leave the more dangerous coast alone.... And then I thought of a plan, which perhaps might recall my Reise-Kaiser, when on his travels. This I instantly proceeded to test.

Now I had been told by my Cabinet that the one noise which would pluck the king out of his deepest slumber, and would bring him bouncing and ecstatic to the place where this sound came from, was the use of the knife-sharpener. This, it appeared, was the earliest piece of household ritual performed in the morning, when Cyrus was hungriest, and the sound of the knife-sharpener implied to him imminent food. I borrowed the knife-sharpener and ran out into the garden. Cyrus was already four garden walls away, and paid not the slightest attention to my calling him. So I vigorously began stropping the knife. The effect was instantaneous; he turned and fled along the walls that separated him from that beloved and welcome noise. He jumped down into his own dominion with erect and bushy tail ... and I gave him three little oily fragments of sardine-skin. And up till now, at any rate, that metallic chirruping of the sharpened knife has never failed. Often I have seen him a mere speck on some horizon roof, but there appears to be no incident or interest in the whole range of foreign travel that can compete with this herald of food.

On the other hand, too, if Cyrus is not quite well (this very seldom happens), though he does not care for food, he does not, either, feel up to foreign travel, and, therefore, the knife-sharpener may repose in its drawer. Indeed, there are advantages in having a greedy king that I had never suspected....

As the months went on and Cyrus grew larger and longer-haired, he gradually, as befitted a king who had come to rule over men, renounced all connexion with other animals, especially cats. He used to lie perdu in a large flower-pot which he had overturned (ejecting the hydrangea with scuffles of backward-kicking hind legs), and watch for the appearance of his discarded race. If so much as an ear or a tail appeared on the frontier walls, he hurled himself, his face a mask of fury, at the intruder. The same ambush, I am sorry to say, served him as a butt for the destruction of sparrows. He did not kill them, but brought them indoors to the kitchen, and presented them, as a token of his prowess as a hunter, to the cook. Dogs, similarly, were not allowed, when he sat at the area gate. Once I saw, returning home from a few doors off, a brisk Irish terrier gambol down my area steps (Cyrus's area steps, I mean), and quickened my pace, fearing for Cyrus, if he happened to be sitting there. He was sitting there, but I need not have been afraid, for before I had reached the house a prolonged and dismal yell rent the air, and an astonished Irish terrier shot up, as from a gun, through the area gate again with a wild and hunted expression. When I got there I found Cyrus seated on the top step calm and firm, delicately licking the end of his silvery paw.

Once only, as far as I remember, was Cyrus ever routed by anything with four legs, but that was not a question of lack of physical courage, but a collapse of nerves in the presence of a sort of hobgoblin, something altogether uncanny and elfin. For a visitor had brought inside her muff an atrocious little griffon, and Cyrus had leaped on to this lady's knee and rather liked the muff. Then, from inside it, within an inch or two of Cyrus's face, there looked out a half-fledged little head, of a new and nerve-shattering type. Cyrus stared for one moment at this dreadful apparition, and then bolted inside the piano-ambush. The griffon thought this was the first manœuvre in a game of play, so jumped down and sniffed round the entrance to the ambush. Panic-stricken scufflings and movements came from within.... Then a diabolical thought struck me: Cyrus had never yet been in his ambush when the piano was played, and the griffon being stowed back again in the muff, for fear of accidents, I went very softly to the keys and played one loud chord. As the Irish terrier came out of the area gate, so came Cyrus out of his violated sanctuary....

Cyrus was now just a year old; his kitten-coat had been altogether discarded; he already weighed eleven pounds, and he was clad from nose to tail-tip in his complete royal robes. His head was small, and looked even smaller framed in the magnificent ruff that curled outwards from below his chin. In colour he was like a smoky shadow, with two great topaz lights gleaming in the van; the tips of his paws were silvery, as if wood-ash smouldered whitely through the smoke. That year we enjoyed a summer of extraordinary heat, and Cyrus made the unique discovery about the refrigerator, a large tin box, like a safe, that stood in the scullery. The germ of the discovery, I am afraid, was a fluke, for he had snatched a steak of salmon from the tray which the fishmonger had most imprudently left on the area steps, and, with an instinct for secrecy which this unusual treasure-trove awoke in him, he bore it to the nearest dark place, which happened to be the refrigerator. Here he ate as much as it was wise to gobble at one sitting, and then, I must suppose, instead of going to sleep, he pondered. For days he had suffered from the excessive heat; his flower-pot ambush in the garden was unendurable, so also was his retreat under my bedclothes. But here was a far more agreeable temperature.... This is all the reconstruction of motive that I can give, and it is but guesswork. But day after day, while the heat lasted, Cyrus sat opposite the refrigerator and bolted into it whenever he found opportunity. The heat also increased his somnolence, and one morning, when he came up to breakfast with me, he fell asleep on the sofa before I had time to cut off the little offering of kidney which I had meant to be my homage. When I put it quite close to his nose he opened his mouth to receive it, but was again drowned in gulfs of sleep before he could masticate it. So it stuck out of the corner of his mouth like a cigarette. But eventually, I knew, he "would wake and remember and understand."

And now Cyrus is two years old, and has reigned a year and ten months. I think he has completed his own education, and certainly he has cleared his frontiers of cats, and, I am afraid, his dominion of sparrows. One misguided bird this year built in a small bush in his garden. A series of distressing unfledged objects were presented to the cook.... He has appropriated the chair I was accustomed to use in my sitting-room, and he has torn open the new back-cloth that I had caused to be put on my piano. I dare say he was right about that, for there is no use in having an ambush if you cannot get into it. In other ways, too, I do not think he is strictly constitutional. But whenever I return to his kingdom after some absence, as soon as the door is open Cyrus runs down the steps to meet me (even as Puss-cat used to do) and makes a poker of his tail, and says "Ah-h-h-h." That makes up for a good deal of what appears to be tyranny. And only this morning he gave me a large spider, precious and wonderful, and still faintly stirring....

CRANK STORIES

THE TRAGEDY OF OLIVER BOWMAN

Oliver Bowman was sitting opposite his sister after dinner, watching her cracking walnuts in her strong, firm hands. The wonder of it never failed: she put two walnuts in her palms, pressed her hands together as if in silent prayer, and then there was a great crash and pieces of walnut-shell flew about the table. It was a waste of energy, no doubt, since close beside her were the nut-crackers that gave the nut-eater so great a mechanical advantage; but then his sister had so much energy that it would have been not less ridiculous to accuse the sea of wasting energy because it broke in waves on the shore. Presently she would drink a couple of glasses of port and begin smoking in earnest.

"And then?" asked Oliver, who was exhibiting a fraternal interest in the way in which Alice had passed her day.

"Then I had tea at an A B C shop, and walked round the Park. Lovely day: you ought to have come out."

"I had a little headache," said Oliver. He spoke in a soft voice, which occasionally cracked and went into a high key, as when a boy's voice is breaking. That had happened to him some fifteen years ago, since he was now thirty; but he had made a habit of dropping into falsetto tones, as being an engaging remnant of youthfulness.

"A good walk in the sun and wind would have made that better," said his sister.

"But I don't like the sun," said he petulantly, "and you know I detest the wind."

"What did you do, then?" she asked.

"I read a story by Conrad about a storm at sea. I quite felt as if I was going through it all without any of the inconveniences of it. That is the joy of a well-written book: it enlarges your experiences without paying you out for them."

Alice dusted the fragments of walnut-shell from her fingers, poured out a glass of port, and lit a cigarette.

"I would sooner do any one thing myself than read about any twenty," she observed. "I should hate to get my experiences secondhand, already digested for me, just as I should hate to wear secondhand clothes or eat peptonized food. They've got to be mine, and I've got to do them—I mean digest them—myself."

Oliver refused port, and took a very little coffee with a good deal of hot milk in it.

"Considering Nature has been making men and women for so many million years, it's odd how often she makes mistakes about them," he said. "She constantly puts them into the wrong envelope: she puts a baby girl into a baby boy's envelope, and a baby boy into a baby girl's. You ought to have been a boy, Alice, and I ought to have been a girl."

Alice could not resist another walnut or two, and the crashings began again.

"That may be true," she said; "but that's not really the point. A woman may be a real woman and yet want to do things herself. The real mistake that Nature makes is to give people arms and legs and a quantity of good red blood, and not give them the desire of using them."

"Or to give them an imagination without the desire of using it," remarked Oliver.

"I'm glad I have none," said Alice firmly. "I never imagine what a thing is going to be like. I go and do the thing, and then I know."

They passed into the drawing-room next door, which seemed to bear out Oliver's criticism on Nature's mistakes, because the room had been furnished and decorated in accordance with his tastes, and with one exception was completely a woman's room. Everything in it was soft and shaded and screened sideways and draped. But in one corner was a turning-lathe with an unshaded electric light directly over it.

Oliver walked across to an easy-chair by the fireplace, and took down an embroidered bag that hung on a painted screen there. It contained a quantity of coloured wools, and an embroidery tambour. He was employed just now on making a chair-back in petit point, and could easily fill in areas of uniform colour by electric light, though daylight was necessary for matching shades of wool. The design was a perfectly unreal rustic scene with a cottage and a tree and a lamb and a blue sky and a slightly lighter blue lake. It realized completely to him what the country ought to be like, and what the country never was like. Instead of the lamb there was in real life a barking dog and a wasp; instead of a blue lake a marsh, which oozed with mud and dirtied your boots; instead of a clean

137

white cottage, a pig-sty or a cowshed where stupid animals breathed heavily through their noses at you. Oliver hated the country in consequence, and never left town unless it was to immure himself from Saturday till Monday in a very comfortable house with central heating, or to spend a few weeks in some other town; but it was delightful to sit in his own pleasant room, and with coloured wools make a picture of what the country should be. In the foreground of his piece were clumps of daffodils, which he copied from those that stood on a table near him, for there ought always to be daffodils in the foreground.

Alice occupied herself for half an hour or so with an active foot on the treadle of her lathe, and made loud buzzing noises with steel tools and boxwood. Then, as usual, she went to bed very early, after a short struggle to read the evening paper, and left Oliver to himself. These were the hours which he liked best of all the day, for there was no chance of being interrupted and no prospect of having to go out of doors or perform any action in which he would come in contact with real life in any form. Alice's lathe was silent, and all round him were soft, shaded objects and his piece of needlework. But though he disliked the rough touch of life more than anything in the world, there was nothing he liked better than to imagine himself in the hubbub and excitement of adventure without stirring from his chair.

Sometimes, as he had done this afternoon, he would read a story of the sea, and thus, without terror of shipwreck or qualms of nausea, listen to the crash of menacing waves and the throb of the racing screw. Sometimes he would spend an hour in the country, while his unerring needle made daffodils and lambs; or, with a strong effort of the imagination, travel across France to the delightful shores of the Riviera with a vividness derived from the Continental Bradshaw. A sniff at the lemon brought in with a tray of wafer biscuits and a siphon could give him the effect of a saunter through the lemon groves outside Nice, and the jingle of money in his pocket recalled the Casino at Monte Carlo, where he saw himself amassing a colossal fortune in a single night, and losing it all again. As a matter of fact, he never set foot in the real Temple of Chance, because there were so many bold females there who looked at his handsome face with such friendly, if not provocative, glances. For though in imagination he was a perfect Don Juan, the merest glance of interest from a female eye would send him scurrying back like a lost lamb to the protective austerity of Alice.

To-night it seemed to him that the habits and instincts of years came about him in crowds, asking him to classify them and construct a definite theory about them for use in practical life, and suddenly, in a flash of illumination, he saw the cohering principle on which he had acted so long without consciously formulating it. He had always hated real people, real experiences, the sun, the wind, the rain, but equally had he loved the counterfeits of them as presented by Art in its various forms, and by the suggestions that a lemon or a continental Bradshaw or a piece of wool-work could give him. The theory that held all these things together was that life for him consisted of imagination, not of experience, and the practical application of that was to study and soak himself in the suggestions that gave him the sting of experience, without any sordid contact with life. To make a fortune (or lose one) at Monte Carlo would have implied setting cheek to jowl with bold, bad people, and risking a great deal of money. It was infinitely better to study the time-table of the trains to Monte Carlo, sniff a lemon, and jingle his money in his pocket; while if he wanted the sense of the hot, smoke-laden, scent-heavy atmosphere, he must smoke a cigarette and sprinkle his handkerchief with musk or frangipane. A pack of cards thrown about the table would assist the illusion, and he could say, "Faites vos jeux, messieurs et mesdames," in the chanting monotone of the croupiers.

From that night his horizons began to expand, and he wondered at himself for the blindness in which he had hitherto spent his life. The London streets, in spite of the wind and the sun and the rain and the fog, woke into a teeming life of their own, and pelted suggestions at him as the crowd pelted confetti at mi-carême. He began not to dislike the crowded pavements, for he no longer took any notice of the real people who were there, so absorbing had become the shop windows which gave him the material which he translated into dreams. Hitherto, when he had passed a fish shop he had held his breath, so that the objectionable smell of it might not vex him; now, he inhaled it with a gusto as adding to the vividness of M. Pierre Loti's "Pêcheur d'Islande," He would stand before a fish shop for five minutes at a time, and be no longer in Bond Street, but in the hold of his boat or on the quay at Paimpol. Even the boy in the shop who went out with a flat tray on his shoulder was mon frère Yves, and Oliver almost spoke to him in French. Next door was a shop filled with Japanese screens and carved jade and branches of paper cherry-blossom, and lo! his fishing experiences were whisked away, and he was living in the land of Madame Chrysanthème.

But it was only for a short while that the shop windows were, so to speak, coloured illustrations in books written by other men, for he soon discarded these second-hand canvases, and constructed out of them and the wealth of suggestive material that lay broadcast round him new and amazing adventures of his own. His senses, and in particular his sense of smell, grew every day more acute, for daily he was keenly on the look out for a sight or sound, a touch or smell, that would be to him a hint out of which he could evolve some fantastic imagination that lived henceforth in his brain as the memory of an actual experience lives in the brain of those who, like his sister, must know that a thing has happened to them before they can call it their own.

But of all the senses, that of smell supplied him with the vividest hints: the aromatic odour, for instance, that came out of the door of a chemist's shop would launch him on a brain adventure which lasted the whole length of a stroll down Piccadilly, in which he felt himself suffering from some acute and mysterious disease that baffled the skill of doctors, and led them to administer all manner of curious drugs in the hope of bringing him alleviation. Then when he had soaked the honey from this painful experience— for however disagreeable such an illusion would have been in real life, it had in those vivid unrealities the thrill and excitement of such without any of its inconveniences—the sight of a jeweller's window blazing with gems would scatter the clouds of his approaching demise, and muffle the sound of his own passing bell with the strains of a ball-room band. He would spring from his death-bed, and, experiencing a new incarnation and a change of sex, would be the central figure, queen in her own right, of some great State ball.

She—he, that is to say—was unmarried, and as she wove the chain of the royal quadrille, the hands of half a dozen aspirants to be her prince-consort communicated their hopes in the pressure of finger-tips. A tiara to which the one in the shop window supplied the clue was on her golden-haired head, ropes of pearls clinked as she moved, a great diamond four times the size of the solitary splendour that winked on the dark blue velvet there, scintillated on her breast, and to each of her lovers, the Grand Duke Peter, the Archduke Francis, the Prince Ignatius, she gave the same mysterious little smile, that, while she disdained their passion, yet expressed some faint vibrating response. All men seemed rather alike to her, and she gave a little sigh, half contemptuous of their adoration, half curious about the desire that made them so divinely discontent. To-night she had determined to choose one of them, for, queen though she was, she must conform to the usage of the world, and besides—besides, the thought of bearing a child of her own made some secret nerve ecstatically ache within her. She must choose....

Then, even while Oliver was hesitating between the Archduke Francis and Prince Ignatius, he would catch sight of a flower-seller by the fountain in Piccadilly Circus, and straightway he would be in

140

the country of his petit point again, where lambs were white and lakes blue; or the sight of a draped model with a waxwork head would switch him off into a new amorous adventure with a lady in an orange-coloured dress, just like that, and the point of an infinitesimal shoe peeping seductively from below its hem.

By degrees, this particular figure, standing in royal state alone behind the plate-glass window in Regent Street, began to exercise a controlling influence on his imagination, and he would hurry by the rows of shops which lay on his route without constructing independent romances out of the hints they gave him, and only glancing at them to see what suggestions they supplied as regards Her. He gave her, for instance, the tiara which he had worn when he was queen in his own right; he presented her with some lemon-coloured gloves that reached to her elbow; he bought her daffodils from Piccadilly Circus; and, rather more tentatively, he endowed her with a black hat with Gloire-de-Dijon roses in it; and standing there in front of her, he would hold up to his nose the handkerchief on which he had poured wallflower scent, which he was sure she would use, and inhale a sweetness that really seemed to come from her through the plate-glass window. All other shops which could not contribute to her embellishment became uninteresting again, and once more he would hurry with held breath past the fishmonger, for if was clearly unsuitable to present her with kippers, raw salmon, or even live lobsters. Then, standing a little sideways, not directly in front of her, her eyes met his, and though usually they seemed lost in reverie, occasionally they would meet his own in a way that sent his heart thumping in his throat. Always she wore the same faint, unfathomable smile, reminding him of Leonardo's "Monna Lisa," and it seemed to him that the reason for which Nature had brought him into the world was that he should penetrate into the thoughts that set that red mouth so deliciously ajar. It must surely be on his own lips that it would close.... Her loveliness, while she was kind, made the whole world lovely to him, and his whole nature seemed to awake.

His constant day-long walks about London had wonderfully improved his health; he no longer feared the sun and the wind, and got quite bronzed in complexion. Still more remarkable was, so to speak, the psychical bronzing of his mind, the suntan of virility that overspread it; everything was shot with interest for him, and he even got Alice to show him how to work the lathe. For this was no pining and lovelorn affection; it was quite a hopeful affair, and though, when alone, he might sigh and turn over and back again on his bed, the brilliance and upright carriage of the object of his adoration stung him into a manly robustness. She would not like him to go sighing and sheltering himself about the world.

It was no wonder that Alice noticed and applauded the change in him.

"Something has happened to you, Oliver," she said one night at dinner, while they were cracking walnuts together, for he had aspired to that accomplishment, though it hurt his soft hands very much. "Something has happened to you. I wonder if I can guess what it is?"

He felt quite secure of the secrecy of his passion, and cracked two walnuts.

"I'm quite certain you can't," he said. "Lord, that did hurt!"

"Well, I shall do no harm then if I try," said she. "I believe you've fallen in love."

The convoluted kernels dropped from Oliver's fingers.

"What makes you think that?" he asked.

"My dear, it's obvious to a woman's eyes. I always told you that what you needed was to fall in love. You don't do wool-work any more; you walk instead of sitting in an easy-chair. Some day, if you go on like this, you will play golf."

"Gracious! Am I as bad as that?" exclaimed he, startled into an irony that gave his case away.

Alice clapped her hands delightedly.

"Ah! I am right then!" she cried. "My dear, do tell me who she is? Shall I go and call on her? Have I ever seen her?"

Oliver felt a curious diplomatic pleasure in giving true information which he knew would deceive.

"Yes; I feel sure you have seen her," he said, remembering that Alice had her dresses made at the shop where his divinity deified the window. "I can't say that you know her."

"Oh, who is she?" cried Alice. "Is she a girl? Is she a woman? Will she marry you?"

"No; I don't suppose so," said he.

Alice's face fell.

"Is she somebody else's wife, then?" she asked. "I hope not. But I don't know that it matters. It is the fact of your having fallen in love which has improved you so immensely. I've noticed that an unhappy romance is just as good for people as a humdrum success which ends in christening mugs and perambulators."

Oliver got up.

"You are rather coarse sometimes, dear Alice," he observed.

Oliver's romance and his growing robustness lasted for some few days after Alice had guessed his secret, and then an end came to it more horrible than any that his wildest imaginations could have suggested to him. One day he had seen in a celebrated furrier's a sable stole that would most delightfully protect his lady's waxen neck from the inclemencies of a shrewd May morning, and he hurried along, while that was still vivid to his eye, in order to visualize it round her neck. There was a crowd of women in front of her window, and he edged his way in with eyes downcast, as was his wont, so that she might burst splendidly upon him at short range. Then, full of devotion and sable stole, he raised them.

She was not there. In her place was a bold-faced creature in carmine, with lustful, wicked eyes like the females at Monte Carlo. His healthy outdoor life stood him in good stead at that moment, for he did not swoon or address shrill ejaculations to his Maker. He just staggered back one step, as if he had received a blow in the chest, then rallied his failing forces again....

All day he walked from dressmaker to dressmaker, seeking to find her; and when he was too much fatigued to pursue his way on foot any longer, he went to his club, and by the aid of a London directory ascertained the addresses of a couple of dozen more shops farther afield where she might possibly be found. These he visited in a taxi, but without success, and returned home to his flat a quarter of an hour before dinner, where, utterly exhausted, he went to sleep in his chair. Naturally, he dreamed about her, in a vague nightmarish manner, and she seemed to be in trouble.

He awoke with a start, and for a moment thought that, like Pygmalion, he had brought his Galatea to life, for there she stood in front of him in the dusk. At least, her orange dress stood there.

"My dear Oliver," said Alice's voice, "aren't you ready for dinner yet? Make me some compliment on my new tea-gown...."

After that miserable adventure he resolved to have no more to do with the serious or emotional side of life, and in the words of one of our modern bards "he held it best in living to take all things very lightly." He had consecrated all the power of his imagination on one great passion, and now his dream was exploded and Alice had got the tea-gown! Almost worse than that was that the divine orange vesture of his beloved had begun to multiply in a most unseemly manner in the shops of quite inferior dressmakers, and half a dozen times a day he could feel his breath catch in his throat as for a moment he thought he saw in some other window the wraith of her who was for ever lost to him. But while this stung and wounded him, it yet probably helped to cure him, and a few weeks later he was immersed again in the minor joys of life, visiting Capri and the Bay of Naples, when he saw the cages of quails in the poulterers' shops, going again to Court balls opposite the jeweller's, tossing with the fishing fleet on moonlit nights off the Cornish coast opposite the fishmonger's, or spending hours in the country over his embroidery frame.

One day a smart shower drove him into the portals of Micklethwait's Stores in Knightsbridge, where the most exotic of purchasers can find their curious wants supplied, and all at once it struck him that these incessant peregrinations of the streets made up a very diluted form of life. Here all possible fountains of desire and adventure scintillated under one roof, and you had but to take a step out of the Arctic winter of the fur department to find yourself in the hot summer weather of straw hats, or playing a match against the heads of the profession in the room where billiard balls and tables were sold.

Though he would never fall seriously in love again, he could have some pleasant flirtations in the ladies' underwear department, or, if his mood was Byronic, he would go to the games department and think of the nursery he would have furnished for his growing family if the beloved in the orange dress had remained faithful to him, and not given her tea-gown to Alice, whom it strangely misbecame. With a stifled groan he would tear himself away from that, and, surrounded by paper and envelopes and red-tape and sealing-wax, spend an hour as Secretary of State for Foreign Affairs, conducting abstruse diplomatic operations with the perfidious Turk, and worsting him at every turn in the tangled game.

So underneath those lofty roofs and terra-cotta cupolas, he began to live a life of which the variety and extravagance baffles description. A chance shower had originally taken him there (for on such small accidents does our destiny depend), but now rain or fine, hot or cold, he was the first in the morning to pass through the swing doors and, with a couple of hurried intervals for meals, the last to leave in the evening. Whether August burned the torrid pavements outside, or whether the fog gripped the town in its grimy hand, there was always the same warm, calm atmosphere inside laden with a hundred aromatic scents and teeming with rich suggestions of love and athletics and chemistry and travel. Often in the morning he would be tempted to go straight to the department of tea-gowns and other more intimate feminine apparel, but he kept a firm hold on himself and transacted business in the stationery department, or spent a studious hour in the book-room first.

Nor did he neglect his exercise, and in the games department he knocked up a hundred runs at cricket, or had a brisk game of hockey, or played a round of golf, a pursuit to which he was now passionately attached owing to the strange suggestive forms of niblicks and brassies. Or, artistically inclined, he would wander among paint-boxes, palettes, and sketching umbrellas by the shore of some windless sea, and then hurry away to a counter behind which were discreet bathing costumes for both sexes, and spend a pleasant quarter of an hour in mixed bathing. This always gave him an appetite, and he tripped off to the cooked foods department, popping in at the bakery on the way, and had a delicious lunch off crisp country bread, with a pot of caviare and a couple of slices of galantine, washed down with a glass of Chablis from the wine department. Then perhaps after a whiff of roasting coffee from the grocery department, he would put on some clean ducks with a grey silk tie (haberdashery), in which he put a pear-shaped pearl pin (jewellery), and then, fresh and cool, spent a half-hour of airy badinage with the agreeable ladies, "whose presence," as he recollected Mr. Pater saying, "so strangely rose" beside the chiffon and millinery. His constant passage through the various departments provoked no suspicion in the minds of the shop-walkers and attendants that he was one of the light-fingered brigade, for from time to time he made small purchases and always paid ready cash, and it occurred to no one that here was an opportunity of studying, first-hand, the rapid development of one of the strangest and most harmless monomaniacs who had ever pursued his innocent way outside the protective walls of a lunatic asylum.

After such a delicious lunch it was no wonder that when he went back to his flat he could make but small pretence at eating, for in imagination he had fared so delicately and well that the lumps of muscular mutton and robust beef provided by Alice's catering made no appeal to him. She might wonder at the smallness of his appetite, but she could not feel the slightest anxiety about that, so bright of eye and alert of limb was he under the spell of the happy busy life crowded with incident, that now was his.

After lunch he would sit with her a little, talking in the most vivid and interesting manner on the topics of the moment, and then, looking at his watch, would silently remind himself that he was giving a pianoforte recital at three, and, if he was already a little late, would call a taxi to take him back to the Stores, while he suppled and gave massage to his fingers as he drove.

He was by this time in an advanced state of his agreeable insanity, for he had lost all control over his imagination, the workings of which were entirely in the hands of the suggestions that external objects made to it. It was just in this that the completeness of his enjoyment of life lay. It was in this, too, that there lay such discomfort and suffering as was his. The sight of a "dental case" in a window, with its rows of gleaming teeth and rose-coloured gums and palates, was sufficient to give him a violent stab of pain in his teeth, for the suggestion implied that he would have to get them all taken out before he attained to the acquisition of those foreign splendours. But he had learned by this time the position of all the shops between his flat and the Stores which displayed these and similar dolorous exhibitions, and his eye would instinctively avert itself from doctors' door-plates or shops where were sold ear-trumpets, and pitch, with the precision of a bird on a twig, on cheerful and harmonious windows. He no longer, in fact, lived a self-governing life of his own, but was no more than thistledown in a wind before the suggestions that the outside world made to his disordered senses. And then, as was bound to happen sooner or later, came the crash.

That day he saw for the first time, close beside the lift in the boot department, through which he passed by accident, for boots conveyed nothing at all to him, a black door slightly ajar, and thinking, with a pang of delight, that some fresh world of experiences might be about to burst upon him, he entered. His first impression was of some lovely garden full of white flowers arranged in wreaths, as if in garden beds, and all covered with glass cases. Then he saw that though his first impression had been of gleaming whites, the predominant note was black. There were black cloaks, black scarves, black hats, black-edged cards.... And then, with a sudden icy pang at his heart, he saw straight in front of him a large oblong box with glass sides, on the top of which were nodding ostrich plumes. Simultaneously there advanced out of the gloom a small man in black clothes, with neat side-whiskers, clearly dyed. He came towards him, rubbing his hands in a professional and sympathetic manner.

"Is there anything we can do for you, sir?" he asked.

Oliver's teeth chattered in his head, and his eyes rolled heavenwards. Then he spun round and fell in a heap on the floor. He was dead.

PHILIP'S SAFETY RAZOR

Up to the time of Philip's obsession there cannot have been in all the world a happier couple than he and his wife. As everybody knows, the ecstasy of life has its home in the imagination, and Philip and Phœbe Partington lived almost exclusively in those realms which were illumined by the light that never was on sea or land. I do not absolutely affirm that sea and land would have been the better for that light; all that I insist on was that the Partington effulgence certainly never was there. It was a remunerative light also, and out of the proceeds they bought a quantity of false Elizabethan furniture and a motor-car. A spin in the motor-car after the ecstatic labour of the morning cleared Phœbe's head, and they dined together in an Elizabethan room with rushes on the floor. That cleared Phœbe's head, too, for nothing in the world could be remoter from the setting of her imaginative life than anything Elizabethan. She and her husband lived in an opulent and lurid present, which, in its turn, was just as remote from contemporary life as most people know it, as were the "spacious days" that had left their spurious traces on the dining-room.

They were the most industrious of artists and often had as many as three feuilletons running simultaneously in provincial papers, and the manner of their activity was this. Every morning, directly after breakfast, Philip sat in the dining-room, and until one o'clock proceeded to turn into narrative the very complete and articulated skeleton of the tale which Phœbe manufactured in the drawing-room. The imaginative gift was hers; there was not a situation in the world which she could not contemplate unwinking, like an eagle staring into the sun, and these she passed on to her husband, whose power of putting them into narrative was as unrivalled as his wife's in conceiving them.

Picture him, then, with his plump, amiable face bent over Phœbe's imaginings, a perennial pipe in his mouth, and, invariably, two or three little tufts of cotton-wool struck on to his cheek or chin, where he had cut himself shaving that morning. Occasionally, but very rarely, he had to go into the drawing-room to ask the elucidation of some situation: how, for instance, was Algernon Montmorency to leap lightly out of the window, and so regain his motor-car, when Phœbe had laid the scene in the top room of the moated tower of Eagles Castle? But Phœbe could always suggest a remedy which cost the minimum of readjustment, and ten minutes afterwards Algernon would be thundering along the road with the lurid Semitic moneylender in close pursuit. But for such occasional interruption and the periodical lighting of his pipe he would not pause for a second till the morning's work was over. He never hesitated for a word, for he had at his command the entire vocabulary of English clichés, and he often got through two instalments before lunch. At one precisely the parlourmaid came in, and groping through the fog of tobacco-smoke, opened all the windows and began to lay the table. Upon which Philip washed off his tufts of cotton-wool, snatched Phœbe from her imaginative visions, and strolled in the garden with her till the gong summoned them to the recuperative spell of a mutton chop and a glass of blood-making Australian Burgundy.

After lunch they drove in the motor-car, returning for tea, and from tea till dinner they read over aloud and discussed their morning's work. In this way Philip made acquaintance with the subject-matter he would be employed on next morning, and Phœbe learned how that which she had written yesterday had turned out. Philip had never any criticism to make: his wife's imagination seemed to him one of the most glorious instruments ever devised for the delectation of the literary, and she often said that of all contemporary novelists her husband was the only man capable of handling the situations she poured out in this unending flood. After dinner they played patience, went early to bed, and awoke with an unquenchable zest for the labour and rewards of another day.

It is impossible to figure a happier or a more harmonious existence. In imagination they roamed over the entire world without the expense or inconvenience of foreign travel: their spirits ranged through the whole gamut of human emotion, and whatever adversities the Algernon and Eva of the moment went through, their creators and interpreters knew in their heart of hearts that all was going to end well, for otherwise they would speedily have lost their pinnacled eminence as writers of serial stories in the daily press. It is true that Philip's voice often shook as he read, and that Phœbe's eyes were dim as she listened to the written tale of the remarkable disasters and misunderstandings through which the children of her brain had to pass; but these were but luxurious and sterile sorrows. In fact, the greatest trial that ever came to them during these halcyon years was when the editor of one of the papers in which the tale was running wrote to say that it was so popular that he insisted on having at least another fortnight of it, instead of bringing it to an end in two more instalments.

That entailed a vast deal of work, for Phœbe had to search the file to find out by what constructive carpentering she could engineer an episode that would be of the requisite length; for the last instalment of all, when the severed were reunited, must naturally be left for the end. But she never failed to manage it somehow, and even when tribulation was great, and for the moment she could not conceive how to spin the story out, her cloud had a silver lining, for all this difficult work was due to the story's amazing popularity. Or sometimes some ill-mannered reader would write to the newspaper office to point out that St. Peter's Church at Rome did not stand on a "commanding eminence," or ask more information about the "glittering spires" on the Acropolis at Athens, or demur to the "pellucid waters of the Nile in flood, as it rolled down in blue cataracts studded with milk-white foam." But otherwise their life flowed on in an unbroken succession of literary triumphs and domestic happiness.

Then suddenly without any warning whatever the curtain was rung up on a psychological tragedy; for Philip, by some species of spiritual infection from his wife, began to develop an imagination. It did not at first threaten to attack what Phœbe in a Gallic moment had once called their "vie intérieure," by which she meant their literary labours, but was directly concerned only with the present of a safety razor which she had made him on his birthday, in order to save cotton-wool and his life-blood. This safety razor consisted of a neat little sort of a rake into which razor blades were fitted. Each of these, when blunted by use, was to be thrown away and a fresh one inserted, and that morning, Philip, finding that his blade had begun to lose its edge, tossed it lightly and airily out of his dressing-room window, from which it fell into a herbaceous border which ran along the house. The new blade gave the utmost satisfaction, and precisely at nine-thirty he lit his first pipe and began his work for the day on Phœbe's scenario.

The dining-room was just below his dressing-room, and at that moment there came a rustle from the herbaceous bed, and Phœbe's adorable Persian cat leaped on to the window-sill from outside, and proceeded to make its toilet in the warm May sunshine. And at that precise and fatal moment Philip Partington's imagination began to work. It stirred within him like the first faint pang of a toothache. For some quarter of an hour he refused to recognize its existence, and proceeded to clothe in suitable language the flight of Eva up the frozen Thames in an ice-ship. Not knowing exactly what an ice-ship was, and being aware that his readers would be similarly ignorant, he evolved a beautiful one out of his inner consciousness that "skimmed along" on a single runner like a skate. It was not, he reflected, any less likely that it should keep its balance than that a bicycle should....

149

Suddenly he laid down his pen. His imagination was beginning to hurt him. It would be a terrible thing if Phœbe's cat, while it prowled though the herbaceous bed, stepped on the blade of the safety razor. Blunt though it was for shaving purposes, it would easily inflict a cruel wound on Tommy's paw. When his work was done, he must really hunt for the blade, and bestow it in some safer place.

He took up his pen again and wrote, "Ever faster through the deepening winter twilight sped the ice-ship, and Eva controlling the tiller in her long taper fingers, watched the dusky banks fly past her. 'Oh, God,' she murmured, 'grant that I may be in time!' The woods of Richmond...."

The cat had finished its toilet and jumped down again into the herbaceous bed. Philip heard a faint mew, and his awaking imagination told him that Tommy had cut his foot already. With a spasm of remorse he ran out into the garden and began a frenzied search for the razor-blade which with such culpable carelessness he had thrown away. A quarter of an hour's search was rewarded by its discovery, and as there was no blood on the edge of it he thankfully assumed that he had not been punished (nor Tommy either) for his thoughtlessness. He unfortunately stepped on a fine calceolaria, and regained the gravel path with the blade in his hand.

He locked it up in the drawer of his knee-hole table, where he kept his will and his pass-book and his cheque book, and with a free mind returned to Eva, perilously voyaging on the ice past the woods of Richmond, and praying that she should be "in time." But suddenly, and for the first time in their dual and prosperous career as feuilleton writers, Philip found himself finding a certain want of actuality in Phœbe's imaginings. They lacked the bite of such realism as he had found illustrated in the poignancy of his own search for the discarded razor-blade in the herbaceous border. There was emotion, real human emotion, though only concerned with the paws of a cat and a razor, whereas Eva's taper fingers on the tiller of this remarkable craft seemed to want the solidity of mortal experience. But it would never do to lose faith in Phœbe's inventions, for it was his faith in them that lent him his unique skill as interpreter and chronicler of them. And, anyhow, the razor-blade was safely inaccessible now to any cat on its pleasure excursions, and he turned his mind back to the woods of Richmond.

With the unexpectedness of a clock loudly chiming, his imagination began to work again. What if he should suddenly die even as he sat there at his table! Phœbe alone knew where his will was kept, and he saw her, blind with tears, unlocking the drawer and groping with trembling hand among its contents. Suddenly she

150

would start back with a cry of pain, and withdraw her hand, on which the fast-flowing blood denoted that she had severed an artery or two, and would bleed to death in a few seconds, as had happened to a most obnoxious Marquis in the tale, "Kind hearts are more than coronets."

Next moment he had unlocked the drawer, and gingerly holding the dread instrument of Phœbe's death between finger and thumb, looked wildly round for some secure asylum for the hateful thing. Long he stood there in hesitation; then, mounting a set of "library steps," deposited it on the top of the tall bookcase which held the complete file of all the newspapers in which their tales had appeared. Then he set to work again on Eva, who presently ran her ice-boat ashore below the Star and Garter hotel. But half the morning had already gone, and he had scarcely yet made a beginning of the morning's work.

Phœbe was unusually buoyant at lunch time to-day, but for once her cheerfulness failed in shedding sunshine on Philip.

"My dear, I have got over such a difficult point," she said. "Do you remember how Moses Isaacson got Algernon to sign the paper which acknowledged that he was not Lord St. Austell's legitimate son?"

"Yes, yes," said Philip feverishly, trying to recall the exact happening of those miserable events.

"Well, all that was written in invisible ink, and all he thought he signed was the lease of Eagles Castle. There! And look, here is the first dish of asparagus."

"And how about the lease?" asked Philip.

"It was written in water-colour ink, and, of course, Moses Isaacson washed it off afterwards."

"Capital!" said Philip. "That does the trick."

There was silence for a minute or two as the novelists ate the fresh asparagus, and then Phœbe said:

"To-morrow, dear, you will have to come and work with me in the drawing-room. The maids must begin their spring cleaning, and indeed it should have been done a month ago. We will have lunch and dinner in the hall while they do this room, and the day after they will do the drawing-room, and I will do my work with you here."

Philip's fingers were stealing towards the last stick of asparagus, but at this they were suddenly arrested.

"Ah, spring cleaning!" he said with assumed cheerfulness. "They just dust the books, I suppose, and sweep the floor."

She laughed. She had Eva's celebrated laugh, which was like a peal of silver bells.

"Indeed, they do much more than that," she said. "Every book is taken out and dusted; they move all the furniture, and clean it all, back and front and top and bottom. But you won't know a thing about it, except that our dear Elizabethan dining-room will look so spick and span that Elizabeth herself might have dinner in it. Some day we must do an historical novel, you and I. Think what a setting we have here!"

Though the day was so deliciously warm, it felt rather chilly in the evening, or so Philip thought, and a fire was lit in the drawing-room. Phœbe had a slight headache, and thus it was quite natural that she should go to bed early, leaving her husband sitting up. As soon as he had heard the door of her bedroom close, he went softly to the dining-room, and again mounting the library-steps, took down the razor-blade from the cache which this morning had seemed so secure, and went back with it into the drawing-room. It would have been terrible if Jane, the housemaid, who always sang at her work, should to-morrow have suddenly interrupted her warblings with a wild scream, as she dusted the top of the bookcase. Perhaps the razor-blade would have embedded itself in her hand; perhaps, even more tragically, her flapping duster would have flicked it into her smiling and songful face, and have buried it deep in her eye or her open mouth. But now this gruesome domestic tragedy had been averted by Philip's ingenious perception of the chilliness of the evening, and with a sigh of relief he dropped the fatal blade into the core of the fire.

He went softly up to bed, feeling very tired after this emotional day. Now that his anxiety was allayed he would have liked to tell Phœbe how silly he had been, for never before had he had a secret from her. But then one of Phœbe's most sacred idols in life was her husband's stern masculine common sense that (like Algernon's) was never the prey of foolish fears and unfounded tremors. He hated the idea of smashing up this cherished image of Phœbe's, and determined to keep his unaccountable failing to himself. Phœbe should never know. Besides, it would vex her very much to be told that her present to him had occasioned him such uneasiness.

He fell asleep at once, and woke in the grey dawn of the morning to the sound, as it were, of clashing cymbals of terror in his brain.... The housemaid would clear up the fireplace in the drawing-room, and there among the ashes, like a snake in the grass, would be the keen tooth of the razor-blade. Perhaps already Philip was too late, and before he could get down a cry of pain would ring through the silent house, betokening that Jane's life-blood was already spreading over the new Kidderminster carpet, and he sprang from his bed and with bare feet went hurriedly down to the drawing-room.

Thank God he was in time, and a minute afterwards he was on his way up to bed again with the razor-blade still dusty with ashes, but as sharp as ever, in an envelope taken from Phœbe's table. Temporarily, he put it between his mattresses, and, since it was still only half-past four, climbed back into bed, and vainly attempted to compose himself to sleep.

Already he was behindhand with work that should have been done yesterday morning, and when to-day, with the envelope containing the blade in his breast-pocket, he tried to make up for lost time, he only succeeded in losing more of it. There were other distractions as well, for owing to the spring cleaning in progress in the dining-room, he sat with Phœbe in the drawing-room, and she, quite recovered from her headache, and quite undisturbed by his presence, was reeling off sheet after sheet in her big, firm handwriting of the further trials that awaited Algernon. Sometimes she looked up at him with a bright, glad smile, born of the joy of creation; but for the most part her head was bent over her work, and but a short peal of silver-bell laughter from time to time denoted the ecstasy of invention. And falling more and more behind her, Philip lumbered in her wake, with three-quarters of his mind entirely absorbed in the awful problem regarding the contents of the envelope in his breast-pocket.

Suddenly, brighter than the noonday outside, an idea illuminated him, and he got up.

"I shall take ten minutes' stroll, my dear," he said. "Solvitur ambulando, you know, and you have given me a difficult chapter to write!"

She recalled herself with an effort to the real world.

"I think I won't come with you, darling," she said. "I am afraid of breaking the golden thread, as you once called it. Let me see ..." and she grabbed the golden thread again.

At the bottom of the garden ran a swift chalk-stream that had often figured in their joint works, and towards this Philip joyfully hurried. He picked up half a dozen pebbles from the gravel path, put them into the envelope which contained the instrument of death, tucked the flap in, and threw it into the stream. There was a slight splash, and he saw the white envelope shiningly sink through the water until it came to rest at the bottom. He returned to Phœbe with the sense that he had awoke from some strangling nightmare.

For a couple of days after that Philip enjoyed the ecstasy which succeeds the removal of some haunting terror. Basking in the sunshine of security, he could look down on the dark clouds through which he had passed, and feel with thankfulness how completely (though narrowly) he had escaped the misty fringe of some trouble of the brain, the claws and teeth and pincers of a fixed idea. The simple expedient of throwing the razor-blade into the stream had entirely dispersed those clouds, and till then he had never known the sweetness and sanity of the sun. Then, with tropical rapidity, the tempest closed in upon him again.

He and Phœbe had driven out in their motor-car one afternoon, and had dismissed it two miles from home in order to have the pleasure of walking back through the flowery lanes. Philip was something of a botanist, and since he was now engaged on the chronicling of the reunion of Eva and Algernon, which unexpectedly took place in a ruined temple near Rome, he wanted to refresh his memory by the sight of the glories of the early English summer, in order to deck the flowery fields in which the ruined temple lay with the utmost possible lavishness of floral tapestry.

"The ruin stands for the trial they have passed through, my dear," he explained to Phœbe, "and lo, all round Nature breaks into gladness!"

Phœbe gave a deep sigh.

"I think that's lovely," she said. "How you embellish my dry skeleton of a tale, darling, covering it with strong muscles and lovely supple skin. We are happy, aren't we? I wonder if Algernon and Eva were really as happy, even at that moment, as we always are!"

They had come near to the stream that flowed by the bottom of the garden, the bank of which was a tangle of flowers.

"Loosestrife, meadow-sweet, marsh-marigold, willow-herb," said Philip. "Delicious names, are they not?"

The sound of shrill juvenile voices was heard, and turning a bend in the lane, they came opposite the pool where Philip had thrown the razor-blade. There on the bank were half a dozen small boys in various degrees of nudity, and rosy from their bathing.

"Little darlings!" said Phœbe sympathetically. "What a jolly time they have been having in the water!"

"Willow-herb, marsh-marigold," murmured Philip mechanically, looking round for the traces of blood on the stream-bank....

He took a firm hold of himself, and managed to walk across the wooden bridge that led to the bottom of the garden with some show of steadiness. But he almost reeled and fell when, looking into the pool, he saw the razor-blade, its encompassing envelope having been destroyed by the water, shining on the pebbly bottom of the stream like tragic Rhinegold.

When they had had tea, he made some lame excuse of

studying flowers a little longer and slipped down again to the stream. The boys had gone, and taking off his shoes and socks, and rolling his trousers up to the knee, he waded out over the sharp pebbles to where his doom flickered in the sunshine. With the aid of his stick he propelled it into shallower waters and picked it up. Then, shivering from the brisk water, and tearing his socks as he pulled them over his wet feet, he returned with it to the house in a state of more miserable dejection than Algernon had ever been, even when he sat down on the ruins of the Roman temple, unaware that Eva was just about to come round the corner with April in her eyes.

For the next week Philip carried the razor-blade about with him in a stud-box that during the day never left his pocket, and at night reposed under his pillow. He made several attempts to get rid of it in a way that commended itself to his conscience, which seethed with scruples and imaginary terrors, burying it once in the garden, and at another time throwing it into the ash-bin. But the sight of his terrier digging in the potato patch for a suitable hiding place for his bone, caused him to disinter it from the first of these, and the second entailed a dismal midnight visit to the dust-bin, when, one evening, Phœbe casually alluded to the dustman's approaching visit.

On another occasion he was fired with the original notion of embedding it in the interstices of the rough bark of the ilex at the end of the garden, well out of reach of curious fingers, and with the stud-box in his pocket, climbed with infinite difficulty up into its lower branches. But while wedging it into a suitable crevice the bough on which his weight rested suddenly gave way, and he fell heavily to the ground, while the blade flashed through the air like Excalibur and plunged into a bramble-bush. It was, of course, necessary to get it out, and this prickly business, combined with a sprained ankle, brought him almost aground in the shoals of despair. He began contemplating enlisting as a private in the British army, though well over the military age and of obese figure. Perhaps he would find some opportunity in Flanders of throwing it, suitably weighted, into a German trench. Only the thought of Phœbe left alone and making up interminable plots, with no one to turn them into narrative for her, kept him from this desperate step.

Meantime his work halted and languished, for sleepless nights and nightmare days miserably affected his power of composition, his style and even such matters as punctuation and spelling. Phœbe grew anxious about him, and recommended a holiday, but he had the wisdom to know that the only thing that kept him on the safe side of the frontier between sanity and madness was determined application to work, however poor the output was. He felt that he might just as well pack his boxes and go straight to Bedlam instead of making a circuitous journey there via the Malvern Hills.

It was when his condition was at its worst that there gleamed a light through the tunnel of his despair. The editor of the Yorkshire Telegraph, who wanted another story by the Partingtons, with the shortest possible delay, wrote to him suggesting in the most delicate manner that life in New York would present an admirable setting for a tale, especially since the United States had come into the war, and offering to pay his passage to that salubrious city if he would favourably consider this proposal. And all at once Philip remembered having read in some book of physical geography, studied by him in happier boyish days, that the Atlantic in certain places was not less than seven miles deep....

He read this amiable epistle to his wife.

"Upon my word, it sounds a very good plan," he said brightly. "What do you say, Phœbe? It will give me the holiday of which you think I stand in need."

Phœbe shook her head.

"Do you propose that I should come with you?" she asked. "Why should a holiday among the submarines do you more good than the Malvern Hills?"

The thought of the deep holes in the Atlantic grew ever more rosy to Philip's mind. Even the hideous notion of being torpedoed failed to take the colour out of it.

"My dear, these are days in which a man must not mind taking risks," he said.

She smiled at him.

"I know your fearless nature, darling," she said; "but what is the point of running unnecessary risks?"

"Local colour. There is a great deal in Mr. Etherington's remarks."

"I don't agree. I should think with our experience we ought to be able to describe New York without going there. We didn't find it necessary to go to Athens, or Khartoum, or Mexico."

"True," said he; "but perhaps my descriptions might have gained in veracity if we had. That was a tiresome letter to the Yorkshire Telegraph about the spires on the Acropolis. If we had been there, we should have known that there weren't any."

He fingered the stud-box in his pocket for a moment, and his fingers itched to drop it over a ship's side.

"My part of our joint work might gain in true artistic feeling," he said, "if I described what I had actually seen. Art holds the mirror up to nature, you know."

"Yes, darling; but do you think Shakespeare meant that Art must hold the mirror up to New York?" asked she. "I fancy there is very little nature in New York."

He took a turn or two up and down the room, while the box positively burned his finger-tips.

"I can't help feeling as I do about it," he said. "And, Phœbe, one of our earliest vows to each other was that each of us should respect the other's literary conscience!"

She got up.

"You disarm me, dear," she said. "Apply for your passport, and if they give it you, go. I only ask you to respect my feminine weakness and not make me come with you among all those horrid submarines."

They sealed their compact with a kiss.

By the time Phœbe had interviewed her cook, her husband had already written his letter applying for his passport, on the grounds of artistic necessity in his profession. She read it through with high approval.

"Very dignified and proper," she said. "By the way, dear, there will be no work for us this morning. We are going over the factory for explosives with kind Captain Traill. You and I must observe the processes very carefully, as we want all the information we can get for 'The Hero of Ypres.'"

He jumped up with something of his old alacrity.

"Aha, there speaks your artistic conscience," he said. "And don't let me see too many soft glances between you and kind Captain Traill."

Phœbe looked hugely delighted and returned the compliment.

"And there are some very pretty girls working there," she observed slyly.

An hour afterwards they were padding in felt slippers round the room where bombs were packed with a fatal grey treacle, one spoonful of which was sufficient to blow them and the whole building into a million fragments. A new type of bomb was being made there, consisting of a cast-iron shell fitted with a hole through which the grey treacle was poured; an iron stopper was then screwed into the hole. There were hundreds of those empty shells, which slid along grooved ways to where the treacle was put into them, and they then were passed on to the girls, who fixed their stoppers. It was all soft, silent, deadly work, and Philip recorded a hundred impressions on his retentive memory.

Phœbe and Captain Traill were walking just ahead of him, when suddenly a great light broke, so vividly illuminating his brain that he almost thought some terrific explosion, seen and not heard, had occurred. Stealthily he drew from his pocket the stud-case, stealthily he opened it and took out the razor-blade. Then, bending over an empty bomb-case as if to examine it, he dropped the blade into it. It fell inside with a slight chink, which nobody noticed.

A couple of minutes afterwards the bomb-case had passed through the hands of the dispenser of treacle, and had its stopper screwed in.

"And where are all those little surprise packets going?" asked Philip airily.

"To aeroplanes on the west front," said kind Captain Traill. "We're sending off a lot to-night. Perhaps that one"—and he pointed to the identical bomb which Philip had had a hand in filling—"will make a mess in Mannheim next week."

"I hope so," said Philip fervently.

The only thing, now that Philip had disposed of the razor-blade, that clouded his complete content was the fear that his passport would be granted him, and that he would have to make a journey to America. Happily no such unnerving calamity occurred, for a week later he received a polite intimation from the passport office that the object for which he wanted to go there did not seem of sufficient importance to warrant the granting of a permit; so, wreathed in smiles, he passed this letter over to Phœbe.

"There's the end of that," he said.

"Philistines! Barbarians!" she said indignantly.

"I suppose they are acting to the best of their judgment," said he. "I dare say they have never heard of me."

"My dear, don't be so cynical," said Phœbe.

"Well, well! Certainly I am bitterly disappointed."

He took up the morning paper.

"Bitterly!" he said again. "Hallo! Our airmen bombed Mannheim two nights ago, and dropped three tons of high explosives. Well, that is very interesting. Captain Traill said that perhaps some of those bombs which we saw being filled would make a mess in Mannheim. I hope they were those actual ones."

"So do I," said Phœbe. "Was there much damage done?"

"The German account says that there was hardly any, but of course that is the German account. A few people were wounded and cut by fragments of the bombs. Cut!"

He got up and could hardly refrain from dancing round the table among the rushes.

"Some deep cuts, I shouldn't wonder," he said.

www.ingramcontent.com/pod-product-compliance
Lightning Source LLC
Chambersburg PA
CBHW011511170626
46810CB00009B/3316